More Acclaim for *Gallows View*

"An extremely well-fashion

Review

"The climax, choreographe

with the sound of pages turi

—*Toronto Star*

"This is a first novel that will knock you over with its maturity."

—Howard Engel

"Alan Banks shows promise of developing into the kind of avuncular copper that fans of Ruth Rendell's Inspector Wexford love."

—*The Globe and Mail*

"A fast-moving, gripping mystery story."

—*Winnipeg Free Press*

"This is [a] very impressive debut that weds psychological realism with good local colour, sound observation and solid suspense."

—*The London Free Press*

Acclaim for *A Necessary End*

"*A Necessary End* is proof that Robinson has his craft well in hand ... The perfect weekend escape."

—*The Globe and Mail*

"Well-written, and with a rich and varied cast of believable characters, *A Necessary End* is Robinson's best novel to date."

—*The London Free Press*

"A good mystery and a contemporary variation ... With the publishing of *A Necessary End*, I think we can now be assured that we have a series that is going to be with us for a long time to come."

—*The Vancouver Sun*

Acclaim for *A Dedicated Man*

"A perfect little portrait of a village in the Yorkshire dales ... First-rate stuff for the detective story buff."

—*The Province* (Vancouver)

"A first class story."

—*Toronto Star*

"*A Dedicated Man* is a satisfying sequel to Robinson's first published novel, *Gallows View*. The slow pace and delightful characterizations allow the narrator to expound on the lives and mores of rural Yorkshire without interrupting the flow of the story or the reader's absorption."

—*Quill & Quire*

Acclaim for *The Hanging Valley*

"A terrific book with a complex plot about murder and madness in the Yorkshire dales."

—*The Globe and Mail*

"[Peter Robinson] knows how to write an extremely good mystery and keep the reader hopping from page to page."

—*The Hamilton Spectator*

"Evocative ... Intriguing ... Emotionally rich."

—*New York Times Book Review*

PENGUIN CANADA

GALLOWS VIEW

PETER ROBINSON grew up in Leeds, Yorkshire. He
emigrated to Canada in 1974 and attended York
University and the University of Windsor, where
he was later writer-in-residence. His many awards
include five Arthur Ellis Awards, the Edgar Award for
best short story, The Crime Writers' Association's
Dagger in the Library Award, the Torgi talking book
of the year, France's Grand Prix de Littérature
Policière and Sweden's Martin Beck Award. His
books have been published internationally to great
acclaim and translated into fifteen languages. Peter
Robinson lives in Toronto.

Other Inspector Banks mysteries

A Dedicated Man

A Necessary End

The Hanging Valley

Past Reason Hated

Wednesday's Child

Final Account

Innocent Graves

Dead Right

In a Dry Season

Cold is the Grave

Aftermath

The Summer That Never Was

Playing with Fire

Strange Affair

Piece of My Heart

Inspector Banks collections

Meet Inspector Banks
(includes *Gallows View, A Dedicated Man* and *A Necessary End*)

Inspector Banks Investigates
(includes *The Hanging Valley, Past Reason Hated* and *Wednesday's Child*)

The Return of Inspector Banks
(includes *Innocent Graves, Final Account* and *Dead Right*)

Also by Peter Robinson

Caedmon's Song

No Cure for Love

Not Safe After Dark

GALLOWS VIEW

Peter Robinson

PENGUIN
CANADA

PENGUIN CANADA

Published by the Penguin Group

Penguin Group (Canada), 90 Eglinton Avenue East, Suite 700, Toronto, Ontario, Canada M4P 2Y3
(a division of Pearson Canada Inc.)

Penguin Group (USA) Inc., 375 Hudson Street, New York, New York 10014, U.S.A.
Penguin Books Ltd, 80 Strand, London WC2R 0RL, England
Penguin Ireland, 25 St Stephen's Green, Dublin 2, Ireland (a division of Penguin Books Ltd)
Penguin Group (Australia), 250 Camberwell Road, Camberwell, Victoria 3124, Australia
(a division of Pearson Australia Group Pty Ltd)
Penguin Books India Pvt Ltd, 11 Community Centre, Panchsheel Park, New Delhi – 110 017, India
Penguin Group (NZ), cnr Airborne and Rosedale Roads, Albany, Auckland 1310, New Zealand
(a division of Pearson New Zealand Ltd)
Penguin Books (South Africa) (Pty) Ltd, 24 Sturdee Avenue, Rosebank, Johannesburg 2196,
South Africa

Penguin Books Ltd, Registered Offices: 80 Strand, London WC2R 0RL, England

First published in a Viking Canada hardcover by Penguin Group (Canada),
a division of Pearson Canada Inc., 1987
Published in Penguin Canada paperback by Penguin Group (Canada),
a division of Pearson Canada Inc., 1988, 2002
Published in this edition, 2006

5 6 7 8 9 10 (WEB)

Copyright © Peter Robinson, 1987

LIBRARY AND ARCHIVES CANADA CATALOGUING IN PUBLICATION

Robinson, Peter, 1950–
Gallows view : an Inspector Banks mystery / Peter Robinson.

ISBN-13: 978-0-14-305100-8
ISBN-10: 0-14-305100-8

I. Title.

PS8585.O35176G34   2006   C813'.54   C2006-901656-9

Visit the Penguin Group (Canada) website at **www.penguin.ca**

Special and corporate bulk purchase rates available; please see
www.penguin.ca/corporatesales or call 1-800-399-6858, ext. 2477

For my father, Clifford Robinson,
and to the memory of my mother, Miriam Robinson,
1922–1985.

Now winter nights enlarge
    The number of their houres,
And clouds their stormes discharge
    Upon the ayrie towres;
Let now the chimneys blaze
    And cups o'erflow with wine,
Let well-tun'd words amaze
    With harmonie divine.
Now yellow waxen lights
    Shall waite on hunny Love,
While youthfull Revels, Masks, and Courtly sights,
    Sleepes leaden spels remove.

Thomas Campion
The Third Booke of Ayres

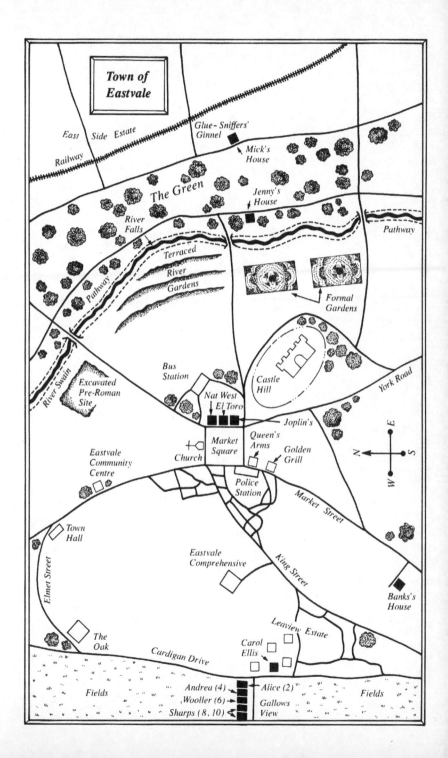

ONE

I

The woman stepped into the circle of light and began to undress. Above her black, calf-length skirt she wore a silver blouse with dozens of little pearl buttons up the front. She tugged it free of the waistband and started undoing the buttons from the bottom very slowly, gazing into space as if she were recalling a distant memory. With a shrug, she slid the blouse off, pulling at the left sleeve, which stuck to her wrist with static, then lowered her head and stretched her arms behind her back like wings to unclasp her bra, raising one shoulder and then the other as she slipped off the thin straps. Her breasts were large and heavy, with dark, upturned nipples.

She unzipped her skirt down the left side and let it slide to the floor. Stepping out of it and bending from the waist, she picked it up and laid it neatly over the back of a chair. Next she rolled her tights down over her hips, buttocks and thighs, then sat down on the edge of the bed to extricate herself from each leg, one at a time, careful not to make runs. As she bent over, the taut skin folded in a dark crease across her stomach and her breasts hung so that each nipple touched each knee in turn.

Standing again, she hooked her thumbs into the elastic of her black panties and bent forward as she eased them down. As she stepped out of them, she caught the waistband with her left foot and flicked them into the corner by the wardrobe.

At last, completely naked, she tossed back her wavy blonde hair and walked towards the dresser.

It was then that she looked towards the chink in the curtains. His whole body tingled as he watched the shock register in her eyes. He couldn't move. She gasped and instinctively tried to cover her breasts with her hands, and he thought how funny and vulnerable she looked with the triangle of hair between her legs exposed....

As she grabbed for her dressing-gown and dashed towards the window, he managed to drag himself away and run off, scraping his shin and almost falling as he jumped the low wall. He had disappeared into the night by the time she picked up the telephone.

II

"Where on earth did I put that sugar bowl?" Alice Matlock muttered to herself as she searched the cluttered room. It was a birthday present from Ethel Carstairs—a present for her eighty-seventh birthday three days ago. Now it had disappeared.

Alice was having trouble remembering little things like that these days. They said it happened when you got older. But why, then, should the past seem so vivid? Why, particularly, should that day in 1916, when Arnold marched off proudly to the trenches, seem so much clearer than yesterday. "What happened yesterday?" Alice asked herself, as a test, and she did remember little details like visiting the shop, polishing her silverware and listening to a play on the radio. But had she really done those things yesterday, the day before, or even last week? The memories were there, but the string of time that linked them like a pearl necklace was broken. All those years ago—that beautiful summer when the meadows were full of buttercups (none of those nasty new bungalows, then), the hedgerows bright with cow-parsley ("gypsy" she always called it, because her mother had told her that if she picked it the gypsies would take her) and her garden full of roses, chrysanthemums, clematis and lupins—Arnold had stood there, ready to go, his buttons reflecting the sunlight in dancing sparks on the whitewashed walls. He leaned against the doorway, that very same doorway, with his kitbag and that lopsided grin on his face—such a young face, one that had never even seen a razor—and off he marched, erect, graceful, to the station.

He never came back. Like so many others, he was destined to lie in a foreign grave. Alice knew this. She knew that he was dead. But hadn't she also been waiting for him all these years? Wasn't that why she had never married, even when that handsome shopkeeper Jack Wormald had proposed? Down on his knees, he was, by the falls at Rawley Force; got his knees wet, too, and that didn't half vex him. But she said no, kept the house on after her parents died, changed things as little as possible.

There had been another war, too, she vaguely remembered: ration books; urgent voices and martial anthems on the radio; faraway rumblings that could have been bombs. Arnold hadn't come back from that war either, though she could imagine him fighting in it like a Greek god, lithe and strong, with a stern face, a face that had never seen a razor.

Other wars followed, or so Alice had heard. Distant ones. Little wars. And he had fought in them all, an eternal soldier. She knew, deep down, that he would never come home, but she couldn't lose hope. Without hope, there would be nothing left.

"Where on earth did I put it?" she muttered to herself, down on her knees rummaging through the cupboard under the sink. "It must be somewhere. I'd forget my head if it was loose."

Then she heard someone running outside. Her eyes were not as good as they used to be, but she was proud of her hearing and often ticked off the shop-girls and bus conductors who assumed that they had to shout to make her hear them. After the sound of running came a gentle knock at her door. Puzzled, she stood up slowly, grasped the draining-board to keep her balance, and shuffled through to the living-room. There was always a chance. She had to hope. And so she opened the door.

III

"Perverts, the lot of them," Detective Chief Inspector Alan Banks said, adjusting the treble on the stereo.

"Including me?" asked Sandra.

"For all I know."

"Since when has making artistic representations of the naked human form been a mark of perversion?"

"Since half of them don't even have films in their cameras."

"But I always have film in my camera."

"Yes," Banks said enthusiastically, "I've seen the results. Where on earth do you find those girls?"

"They're mostly students from the art college."

"Anyway," Banks went on, returning to his scotch, "I'm damn sure Jack Tatum doesn't have a film in his camera. And Fred Barton wouldn't know a wide-angle lens from a putting iron. I wouldn't be at all surprised if they imagined you posing—a nice willowy blonde."

Sandra laughed. "Me? Nonsense. And stop playing the yahoo, Alan. It doesn't suit you. You don't have a leg to stand on, acting the idiot over photography while you're inflicting this bloody opera on me."

"For someone who appreciates artistic representations of the naked human form, you're a proper philistine when it comes to music, you know."

"Music I can take. It's all this screeching gives me a headache."

"Screeching! Good lord, woman, this is the sound of the human spirit soaring: '*Vissi d'arte, vissi d'amore.*'" Banks's soprano imitation made up in volume what it lacked in melody.

"Oh, put a sock in it," Sandra sighed, reaching for her drink.

It was always like this when he found a new interest. He would pursue it with a passion for anywhere between one and six months, then he would have a restless period, lose interest and move on to something else. Of course, the detritus would remain, and he would always profess to be still deeply interested—just too pushed for time. That was how the house had come to be so cluttered up with the novels of Charles Dickens, wine-making equipment, twenties jazz records, barely used jogging shoes, a collection of birds' eggs and books on almost every subject under the sun—from Tudor history to how to fix your own plumbing.

He had become interested in opera after seeing, quite by chance, a version of Mozart's *Magic Flute* on television. It was always like that. Something piqued his curiosity and he wanted to know more. There was no order to it, neither in his mind nor in his filing system. He would plunge into a subject with cavalier disregard for its chronological development. And so it was with the opera craze: *Orfeo* rubbed shoulders with *Lulu*; *Peter Grimes* was *Tosca's* strange bedfellow; and *Madama Butterfly* shared shelf-space with *The Rake's Progress*. Much as she loved music, opera was driving Sandra crazy. Already, complaints from Brian and Tracy had resulted in the removal of the television to the spare room upstairs. And Sandra was forever tripping over the book-sized cassette boxes, which Banks preferred to records, as he liked to walk to work and listen to Purcell or Monteverdi on his Walkman; in the car, it was generally Puccini or Guiseppe Verdi, good old Joe Green.

They were both alike in their thirst for knowledge, Sandra reflected. Neither was an academic or intellectual, but both pursued self-education with an urgency often found in bright working-class people who hadn't had culture thrust down their throats from the cradle onwards. If only, she wished, he would take up something quiet and peaceful, like beekeeping or stamp collecting.

The soprano reached a crescendo which sent involuntary shivers up Sandra's spine.

"You're surely not serious about some people in the Camera Club being perverts, are you?" she asked.

"I shouldn't be surprised if one or two of them got more than an artistic kick out of it, that's all."

"You could be right, you know," Sandra agreed. "They're not only women, the models. We had a very nice Rastafarian the other week. Lovely pector—"

The phone rang.

"Damn and blast it." Banks cursed and hurried over to pick up the offending instrument. Sandra took the opportunity to turn down the volume on *Tosca* surreptitiously.

"Seems that someone's been taking unasked-for peeks at the naked human form again," said Banks when he sat down again a few minutes later.

"Another of those Peeping Tom incidents?"

"Yes."

"You don't have to go in, do you?"

"No. It'll wait till morning. Nobody's been hurt. She's more angry than anything else. Young Richmond is taking her statement."

"What happened?"

"Woman by the name of Carol Ellis. Know her?"

"No."

"Seems she came back from a quiet evening at the pub, got undressed for bed and noticed someone watching her through a gap in the curtains. He took off as soon as he realized he'd been spotted. It was on that new estate, Leaview, those ugly bungalows down by the Gallows View cottages. Great places for voyeurs, bungalows. They don't even need to shin up the drainpipe." Banks paused and lit a Benson and Hedges Special Mild. "This one's taken a few risks in the past, though. Last time it was a second-floor maisonette."

"It makes my skin crawl," Sandra said, hugging herself. "The thought of someone watching when you think you're alone."

"I suppose it would," Banks agreed. "But what worries me now is that we'll have that bloody feminist group down on us again. They really seem to think we haven't bothered trying to catch him because we secretly approve. They believe all men are closet rapists. According to them, our secret hero is Jack the Ripper. They think we've got pin-ups on the station walls."

"You do. I've seen them. Not in your office, maybe, but down-stairs."

"I mean pin-ups of Jack the Ripper."

Sandra laughed. "That's going a bit far, I agree."

"Do you know how difficult it is to catch a peeper?" Banks asked. "All the bugger does is look and run away into the night. No finger-prints, no sightings, nothing. The best we can hope for is to catch him in the act, and we've had extra men and women walking the beat in the most likely areas for weeks now. Still nothing. Anyway," Banks said, reaching out for her, "all this talk about naked bodies is exciting me. Time for bed?"

"Sorry," answered Sandra, turning off the stereo. "Not tonight, dear, I've got a headache."

TWO

I

"And where the bloody hell do you think you were till all hours last night?" Graham Sharp roared at his son over the breakfast table.

Trevor glowered into his cornflakes. "Out."

"I know you were bloody out. Out with that good-for-nothing Mick Webster, I'll bet?"

"What if I was? It's my business who I hang out with."

"He's a bad 'un, Trevor. Like his brother and his father before him. A rotten apple."

"Mick's all right."

"I didn't raise you all these years with my own hands just so you could hang about with hooligans and get into trouble."

"Well, if you weren't such a bleeding little Hitler my mum might not have run off."

"Never mind that," Graham said quietly. "You don't know nothing about it, you was only a kid. I just want you to do well for yourself," he pleaded. "Look, I've not done much. Never had the opportunity. But you're a bright lad. If you work hard you can go to university, get yourself a good education."

"What's the point? There's no jobs anyway."

"It's not always going to be like this, Trevor. I know the country's going through a bad time right now. You don't need to tell me that. But look to the future, lad. It'll be five or six years by the time you've done your 'A' Levels and your degree. Things can change a lot in that time. All you need to do is stay in a bit more and do your homework. You never found it hard, you know you can do it."

"It's boring."

"Look what happened to Mick, then," Graham went on, his voice rising with anger again. "Left school a year ago and still on the bloody dole. Sharing a hovel with that layabout brother of his, father run off God knows where and his mother never home to take care of him."

"Lenny's not a layabout. He had a job in London. Just got made redundant, that's all. It wasn't his fault."

"I'm not going to argue with you, Trevor. I want you to stay in more and spend some time on your schoolwork. I might not have made much out of my life, but you can—and you're bloody well going to, even if it kills me."

Trevor stood up and reached for his satchel. "Better be off," he said. "Wouldn't want to be late for school, would I?"

After the door slammed, Graham Sharp put his head in his hands and sighed. He knew that Trevor was at a difficult age—he'd been a bit of a lad himself at fifteen—but if only he could persuade him that he had so much to lose. Life was hard enough these days without making it worse for yourself. Since Maureen had walked out ten years ago, Graham had devoted himself to their only child. He would have sent Trevor to a public school if he'd had enough money, but had to settle for the local comprehensive. Even there, despite all the drawbacks, the boy had always done well—top of the class, prizes every Speech Day—until last year, when he took up with Mick Webster.

Graham's hands shook as he picked up the breakfast dishes and carried them to the sink. Soon it would be opening time. At least since he'd stopped doing morning papers he got a bit of a lie-in. In the old days, when Maureen was around, he'd had to get up at six o'clock, and he'd kept it going as long as he could. Now he couldn't afford to employ a flock of paper-carriers, nor could he manage to pay the assistant he would need to deal with other business. As things were, he could just about handle it all himself—orders, accounts, stock checks, shelf arrangements—and usually still manage to come up with a smile and a hello for the customers.

His real worry was Trevor, and he didn't know if he was going about things the right way or not. He knew he had a bit of a temper and went on at the lad too much. Maybe it was better to leave him alone, wait till he passed through the phase himself. But perhaps then it would be too late.

Graham stacked the dishes in the drainer, checked his watch, and walked through to the shop. Five minutes late. He turned the sign to read OPEN and unlocked the door. Grouchy old Ted Croft was already counting out his pennies, shuffling his feet as he waited for his week's supply of baccy. Not a good start to the day.

II

Banks reluctantly snapped off his Walkman in the middle of Dido's lament and walked into the station, a Tudor-fronted building in the town centre, where Market Street ran into the cobbled square. He said "Good morning" to Sergeant Rowe at the desk and climbed upstairs to his office.

The whitewashed walls and black-painted beams of the building's exterior belied its modern, functional innards. Banks's office, for example, featured a venetian blind that was almost impossible to work and a grey metal desk with drawers that rattled. The only human touch was the calendar on the wall, with its series of local scenes. The illustration for October showed a stretch of the River Wharfe, near Grassington, with trees lining the waterside in full autumn colour. It was quite a contrast to the real October: nothing but grey skies, rain and cold winds so far.

On his desk was a message from Superintendent Gristhorpe: "Alan, Come see me in my office soon as you get in. G."

Remembering first to unhook the Walkman and put it in his desk drawer, Banks walked along the corridor and knocked on the superintendent's door.

"Come in," Gristhorpe called, and Banks entered.

Inside was luxury—teak desk, bookcases, shaded table lamps—most of which had been supplied by Gristhorpe himself over the years.

"Ah, good morning Alan," the superintendent greeted him, "I'd like you to meet Dr Fuller." He gestured towards the woman sitting opposite him, and she stood up to shake Banks's hand. She had a shock of curly red hair, bright green eyes with crinkly laugh-lines around the edges, and a luscious mouth. The turquoise top she was wearing looked like a cross between a straight-jacket and a dentist's smock. Below that she wore rust-coloured cords that tapered to a halt just above her shapely ankles. All in all, Banks thought, the doctor was a knock-out.

"Please, Inspector Banks," Dr Fuller said as she gently let go of his hand, "call me Jenny."

"Jenny it is, then," Banks smiled and dug for a cigarette. "I suppose that makes me Alan."

"Not if you don't want to be." Her sparkling eyes seemed to challenge him.

"Not at all, it's a pleasure," he said, meeting her gaze. Then he remembered Gristhorpe's recent ban against smoking in his office, and put the pack away.

"Dr Fuller is a professor at York University," Gristhorpe explained, "but she lives here in Eastvale. Psychology's her field, and I brought her in to help with the Peeping Tom case. Actually," he turned a charming smile in Jenny's direction, "Dr Fuller—Jenny—was recommended by an old and valued friend of mine in the department. We were hoping she might be able to work with us on a profile."

Banks nodded. "It would certainly give us more than we've got already. How can I help?"

"I'd just like to talk to you about the details of the incidents," Jenny said, looking up from a notepad that rested on her lap. "There's been three so far, is that right?"

"Four now, counting last night's. All blondes."

Jenny nodded and made the change in her notes.

"Perhaps the two of you can arrange to meet sometime," Gristhorpe suggested.

"Is now no good?" Banks asked.

"Afraid not," Jenny said. "This might take a bit of time, and I've got a class in just over an hour. Look, what about tonight, if it's not too much of an imposition on your time?"

Banks thought quickly. It was Tuesday; Sandra would be at the Camera Club, and the kids, now trusted in the house without a sitter, would be overjoyed to spend an opera-free evening. "All right," he agreed. "Make it seven in the Queen's Arms across the street, if that's okay with you."

When Jenny smiled, the lines around her eyes crinkled with pleasure and humour. "Why not? It's an informal kind of procedure anyway. I just want to build up a picture of the psychological type."

"I'll look forward to it, then," Banks said.

Jenny picked up her briefcase and he held the door open for her. Gristhorpe caught his eye and beckoned him to stay behind. When Jenny had gone, Banks settled back into his chair, and the superintendent rang for coffee.

"Good woman," Gristhorpe said, rubbing a hairy hand over his red, pock-marked face. "I asked Ted Simpson to recommend a bright lass for the job, and I think he did his homework all right, don't you?"

"It remains to be seen," replied Banks. "But I'll agree she bodes well. You said a woman. Why? Has Mrs Hawkins stopped cooking and cleaning for you?"

Gristhorpe laughed. "No, no. Still brings me fresh scones and keeps the place neat and tidy. No, I'm not after another wife. I just thought it would be politic, that's all."

Banks had a good idea what Gristhorpe meant, but he chose to carry on playing dumb. "Politic?"

"Aye, politic. Diplomatic. Tactful. You know what it means. It's the biggest part of my job. The biggest pain in the arse, too. We've got the local feminists on our backs, haven't we? Aren't they saying we're not doing our job because it's women who are involved? Well, if we can be seen to be working with an obviously capable, successful woman, then there's not a lot they can say, is there?"

Banks smiled to himself. "I see what you mean. But how are we going to be seen to be working with Jenny Fuller? It's hardly headline material."

Gristhorpe put a finger to the side of his hooked nose. "Jenny Fuller's attached to the local feminists. She'll report back everything that's going on."

"Is that right?" Banks grinned. "And I'm going to be working with her? I'd better be on my toes, then, hadn't I?"

"It shouldn't be any problem, should it?" Gristhorpe asked, his guileless blue eyes as disconcerting as a newborn baby's. "We've got nothing to hide, have we? We know we're doing our best on this one. I just want others to know, that's all. Besides, those profiles can be damn useful in a case like this. Help us predict patterns, know where to look. And she won't be hard on the eyes, will she? A right bobby-dazzler, don't you think?"

"She certainly is."

"Well, then." Gristhorpe smiled and slapped both his hands on the desk. "No problem, is there? Now, how's that break-in business going?"

"It's very odd, but we've had three of those in a month, too, all involving old women alone in their homes—one even got a broken arm—and we've got about as far with that as we have with the Tom business. The thing is, though, there are no pensioners' groups giving us a lot of stick, telling us we're not doing anything because only old people are getting hurt."

"It's the way of the times, Alan," Gristhorpe said. "And you have to admit that the feminists do have a point, even if it doesn't apply in this particular case."

"I know that. It just irritates me, being criticized publicly when I'm doing the best I can."

"Well, now's your chance to put that right. What about this fence in Leeds? Think it'll lead anywhere with the break-ins?"

Banks shrugged. "Might do. Depends on Mr Crutchley's power of recall. These things vary."

"According to the level of threat you convey? Yes, I know. I should imagine Joe Barnshaw's done some groundwork for you. He's a good man. Why bother yourself? Why not let him handle it?"

"It's our case. I'd rather talk to Crutchley myself—that way I can't blame anyone else if mistakes are made. What he says might ring a bell, too. I'll ask Inspector Barnshaw to show him the pictures later, get an artist in if the description's good enough."

Gristhorpe nodded. "Makes sense. Taking Sergeant Hatchley?"

"No, I'll handle this by myself. I'll put Hatchley on the peeper business till I get back."

"Do you think that's wise?"

"He can't do much damage in an afternoon, can he? Besides, if he does, it'll give the feminists a target worthy of their wrath."

Gristhorpe laughed. "Away with you, Alan. Throwing your sergeant to the wolves like that."

III

It was raining hard. Hatchley covered his head with a copy of *The Sun* as he ran with Banks across Market Street to the Golden Grill. It was a narrow street, but by the time they got there the page-three beauty was sodden. The two sat down at a window table and looked out at distorted shop-fronts through the runnels of rain, silent until their standing order of coffee and toasted teacakes was duly delivered by the perky, petite young waitress in her red checked dress.

The relationship between the inspector and his sergeant had changed slowly over the six months Banks had been in Eastvale. At first, Hatchley had resented an "incomer," especially one from the big city, being brought in to do the job he had expected to get. But as they worked together, the Dalesman had come to respect, albeit somewhat grudgingly (for a Yorkshireman's respect is often tempered with a sarcasm intended to deflate airs and graces), his inspector's sharp mind and the effort Banks had made to adapt to his new environment.

Hatchley had got plenty of laughs observing this latter process. At first, Banks had been hyperactive, running on adrenalin, chain-smoking Capstan Full Strength, exactly as he had in his London job. But all this had changed over the months as he got used to the slower pace in Yorkshire. Outwardly, he was now calm and relaxed—deceptively so, as Hatchley knew, for inside he was a dynamo, his energy contained and channelled, flashing in his bright dark eyes. He still had his tempers, and he retained a tendency to brood when frustrated. But these were good signs; they produced results. He had also switched to mild cigarettes, which he smoked sparingly.

Hatchley felt more comfortable with him now, even though they remained two distinctly different breeds, and he appreciated his boss's grasp of northern informality. A working-class Southerner didn't seem so different from a Northerner, after all. Now, when Hatchley called Banks "sir," it was plain by his tone that he was puzzled or annoyed, and Banks had learned to recognize the dry, Yorkshire irony that could sometimes be heard in his sergeant's voice.

For his part, Banks had learned to accept, but not to condone, the prejudices of his sergeant and to appreciate his doggedness and the sense of threat that he could, when called for, convey to a reticent suspect. Banks's menace was cerebral, but some people responded better to Hatchley's sheer size and gruff voice. Though he never actually used violence, Hatchley made criminals believe that perhaps the days of the rubber hosepipe weren't quite over. The two also worked well together in interrogation. Suspects would become particularly confused when the big, rough-and-tumble Dalesman turned avuncular and Banks, who didn't even look tall enough to be a policeman, raised his voice.

"Hell's bloody bells, I can't see why I have to spend so much time chasing a bloke who just likes to look at a nice pair of knockers," said Hatchley, as the two of them lit cigarettes and sipped coffee.

Banks sighed. Why was it, he wondered, that talking to Hatchley always made him, a moderate socialist, feel like a bleeding-heart liberal?

"Because the women don't want to be looked at," he answered tersely.

Hatchley grunted. "If you saw the way that Carol Ellis dressed on a Sat'day night at The Oak you wouldn't think that."

"Her choice, Sergeant. I assume she wears at least some clothes at The Oak? Otherwise you'd be derelict in your duty for not pulling her in on indecent exposure charges."

"Whatever it is, it ain't indecent." Hatchley winked.

"Everybody deserves privacy, and this peeper's violating it," Banks argued. "He's breaking the law, and we're paid to uphold it. Simple as that." He knew that it was far from simple, but had neither the patience nor the inclination to enter into an argument about the police in society with Sergeant Hatchley.

"But it's not as if he's dangerous."

"He is to his victims. Physical violence isn't the only dangerous crime. You mentioned The Oak just now. Does the woman often drink there?"

"I've seen her there a few times. It's my local."

"Do you think our man might have seen her there, too, and followed her home? If she dresses like you say, he might have got excited looking at her."

"Do myself," Hatchley admitted cheerfully. "But peeping's not my line. Yes, it's possible. Remember, it was a Monday, though."

"So?"

"Well, in my experience, sir, the women don't dress up quite so much on a Monday as a Sat'day. See, they have to go to work the next day so they can't spend all night—"

"All right," Banks said, holding up his hand. "Point taken. What about the others?"

"What about them?"

"Carol Ellis is the fourth. There were three others before her. Did any of them drink at The Oak?"

"Can't remember. I do recollect seeing Josie Campbell there a few times. She was one of them, wasn't she?"

"Yes, the second. Look, go over the statements and see if you can find out if any of the others were regulars at The Oak. Go talk to them. Jog their memories. Look for some kind of a pattern. They needn't have been there just prior to the incidents. If not, find out where they do drink, look up where they were before they were..."

"Peeped on?" Hatchley suggested.

Banks laughed uneasily. "Yes. There isn't really a proper word for it, is there?"

"Talking about peeping, I saw a smashing bit of stuff coming out of Gristhorpe's office. Is he turning into a dirty old man?"

"That was Dr Jenny Fuller," Banks told him. "She's a psychologist, and I'm going to be working with her on a profile of our peeper."

"Lucky you. Hope the missis doesn't find out."

"You've got a dirty mind, Sergeant. Get over to The Oak this lunchtime. Talk to the bar staff. Find out if anyone paid too much attention to Carol Ellis or if anyone seemed to be watching her. Anything odd. You know the routine. If the lunchtime staff's different, get back there tonight and talk to the ones who were in last night. And talk to Carol Ellis again, too, while it's fresh in her mind."

"This is work, sir?"

"Yes."

"At The Oak?"

"That's what I said."

Hatchley broke into a big grin, like a kid who'd lost a penny and found a pound. "I'll see what I can do, then," he said, and with that he was off like a shot. After all, Banks thought as he finished his coffee and watched a woman struggle in the doorway with a transparent umbrella, it was eleven o'clock. Opening time.

IV

It was a dull journey down the A1 to Leeds, and Banks cursed himself for not taking the quieter, more picturesque minor roads through Ripon and Harrogate, or even further west, via Grassington, Skipton and Ilkley. There always seemed to be hundreds of ways of getting from A to B in the Dales, none of them direct, but the A1 was usually the fastest route to Leeds, unless the farmer just north of Wetherby exercised his privilege and switched on the red light while he led his cows across the motorway.

As if the rain weren't bad enough, there was also the muddy spray from the juggernauts in front—transcontinentals, most of them, travelling from Newcastle or Edinburgh to Lille, Rotterdam, Milan or Barcelona. Still, it was cosy inside the car, and he had *Rigoletto* for company.

At the Wetherby roundabout, Banks turned onto the A58, leaving most of the lorries behind, and drove by Collingham, Bardsey and Scarcroft into Leeds itself. He carried on through Roundhay and Harehills, and arrived in Chapeltown halfway through "La Donna è Mobile."

It was a desolate area and looked even more so swept by dirty rain under the leaden sky. Amid the heaps of red-brick rubble, a few old houses clung on like obstinate teeth in an empty, rotten mouth; grim shadows in raincoats pushed prams and shopping-carts along the pavements as if they were looking for shops and homes they couldn't find. It was Chapeltown Road, "Ripper" territory, host of the '81 race riots.

Crutchley's shop had barred windows and stood next to a boarded-up grocers with a faded sign. The paintwork was peeling and a layer of dust covered the objects in the window: valves from old radios; a clarinet resting on the torn red velvet of its case; a guitar with four strings; a sheathed bayonet with a black swastika inlaid in its handle; chipped plates with views of Weymouth and Lyme Regis painted on them; a bicycle pump; a scattering of beads and cheap rings.

The door jerked open after initial resistance, and a bell pinged loudly as Banks walked in. The smell of the place—a mixture of mildew, furniture polish and rotten eggs—was overwhelming. Out of the back came around-shouldered, shifty-looking man wearing a threadbare sweater and woollen gloves with the fingers cut off. He eyed Banks suspiciously, and his "Can I help you?" sounded more like a "Must I help you?"

"Mr Crutchley?" Banks showed his identification and mentioned Inspector Barnshaw, who had first put him onto the lead. Crutchley was immediately transformed from Mr Krook into Uriah Heep.

"Anything I can do, sir, anything at all," he whined, rubbing his hands together. "I try to run an honest shop here, but," he shrugged, "you know, it's difficult. I can't check on everything people bring in, can I?"

"Of course not," Banks agreed amiably, brushing off a layer of dust and leaning carefully against the dirty counter. "Inspector Barnshaw told me he's thinking of letting it go by this time. He asked for my advice. We know how hard it is in a business like yours. He did say that you might be able to help me, though."

"Of course, sir. Anything at all."

"We think that the jewellery the constable saw in your window was stolen from an old lady in Eastvale. You could help us, and help yourself, if you can give me a description of the man who brought it in."

Crutchley screwed up his face in concentration—not a pretty sight, Banks thought, looking away at the stuffed birds, elephant-foot umbrella stands, sentimental Victorian prints and other junk. "My memory's not as good as it used to be, sir. I'm not getting any younger."

"Of course not. None of us are, are we?" Banks smiled. "Inspector Barnshaw said he thought it would be a crying shame if you had to do time for this, what with it not being your fault, and at your age."

Crutchley darted Banks a sharp, mean glance and continued to probe his ailing memory.

"He was quite young," he said after a few moments. "I remember that for sure."

"How young, would you say?" Banks asked, taking out his notebook. "Twenty, thirty?"

"Early twenties, I'd guess. Had a little moustache." He gestured to his upper lip, which was covered with about four days' stubble. "A thin one, just down to the edge of the mouth at each side. Like this," he added, tracing the outline with a grubby finger.

"Good," Banks said, encouraging him. "What about his hair? Black, red, brown, fair? Long, short?"

"Sort of medium. I mean, you wouldn't really call it brown, but it wasn't what I'd call fair, either. Know what I mean?"

Banks shook his head.

"P'raps you'd call it light brown. Very light brown."

"Was the moustache the same?"

He nodded. "Yes, very faint."

"And how long was his hair?"

"That I remember. It was short, and combed-back, like." He made a brushing gesture with his hand over his own sparse crop.

"Any scars, moles?"

Crutchley shook his head.

"Nothing unusual about his complexion?"

"A bit pasty-faced and spotty, that's all. But they all are, these days, Inspector. It's the food. No goodness in it, all—"

"How tall would you say he was?" Banks cut in.

"Bigger than me. Oh, about . . ." He put his hand about four inches above the top of his head. "Of course, I'm not so big myself."

"That would make him about five-foot-ten, then?"

"About that. Medium, yes."

"Fat or thin?"

"Skinny. Well, they all are these days, aren't they? Not properly fed, that's the problem."

"Clothes?"

"Ordinary."

"Can you be a bit more specific?"

"Eh?"

"Was he wearing a suit, jeans, leather jacket, T-shirt, pyjamas—what?"

"Oh. No, it wasn't leather. It was that other stuff, bit like it only not as smooth. Brown. Roughish. 'Orrible to touch—fair makes your fingers shiver."

"Suede?"

"That's it. Suede. A brown suede jacket and jeans. Just ordinary blue jeans."

"And his shirt?"

"Don't remember. I think he kept his jacket zipped up."

"Do you remember anything about his voice, any mannerisms?"

"Come again?"

"Where would you place his accent?"

"Local, like. Or maybe Lancashire. I can't tell the difference, though there are some as says they can."

"Nothing odd about it? High-pitched, deep, husky?"

"Sounded like he smoked too much, I can remember that. And he did smoke, too. Coughed every time he lit one up. Really stank up the shop."

Banks passed on that one. "So he had a smoker's cough and a rough voice with a local accent, that right?"

"That's right, sir." Crutchley was shifting from foot to foot, clearly looking forward to the moment when Banks would thank him and leave.

"Was his voice deep or high?"

"Kind of medium, if you know what I mean."

"Like mine?"

"Yes, like yours, sir. But not the accent. You speak proper, you do. He didn't."

"What do you mean he didn't speak properly? Did he have some kind of speech impediment?" Banks could see Crutchley mentally kicking himself for being so unwisely unctuous as to prolong the interview.

"No, nothing like that. I just meant like ordinary folks, sir, not like you. Like someone who hadn't been properly educated."

"He didn't stutter or lisp, did he?"

"No, sir."

"Fine. One last question: had you ever seen him before?"

"No, sir."

"Inspector Barnshaw will want you to look at some photos later today, and he's going to ask you to repeat your description to a police artist. So do your best, keep him in focus. And if you see him again or think of anything else, I'd appreciate your getting in touch with me." Banks wrote down his name and number on a card.

"I'll call you, sir, I'll do that, if I ever clap eyes on him again," Crutchley gushed, and Banks got the distinct impression that his own methods appealed more than Barnshaw's.

Banks heard the sigh of relief when he closed his notebook and thanked Crutchley, avoiding a handshake by moving off rather sharply. It wasn't a great description, and it didn't ring any bells, but it would do; it would take him closer to the two balaclava-wearing thugs who had robbed three old ladies in one month, scared them all half to death, vandalized their homes and broken the arm of one seventy-five-year-old woman.

THREE

I

The white Cortina skidded to a halt outside Eastvale Community Centre, splashing up a sheet of spray from the kerbside puddles. Sandra Banks jumped out, ten minutes late, pushed open the creaking door as gently as she could, and tiptoed in, aware of the talk already in progress. One or two of the regulars looked around and smiled as they saw her slip as unobtrusively as possible into the empty chair next to Harriet Slade.

"Sorry," she whispered, putting her hand to the side of her mouth. "Weather. Damn car wouldn't start."

Harriet nodded. "You've not missed much."

"However beautiful, majestic or overwhelming the landscape appears to your eyes," the speaker said, "remember, you have no guarantee that it will turn out well on film. In fact, most landscape photography—as I'm sure those of you who have tried it know—turns out to be extremely disappointing. The camera's eye differs from the human eye; it lacks all the other senses that feed into our experience. Remember that holiday in Majorca or Torremolinos? Remember how wonderful the hills and sea made you feel, with their magical qualities of light and colour? And remember when you got the holiday snaps developed—if they came out at all!—how bad they were, how they failed to capture the beauty you'd seen?"

"Who's this?" Sandra whispered to Harriet while the speaker paused to sip from the glass of water on the table in front of him.

"A man called Terry Whigham. He does a lot of pictures for the local tourist board—calendars, that kind of thing. What do you think?"

It wasn't anything new to Sandra, but she had more or less dragged poor Harriet into the Camera Club in the first place, and she felt that she owed it to her not to sound too smug.

"Interesting," she answered, covering her mouth like a schoolgirl talking in class. "He puts it very well."

"I think so, too," Harriet agreed. "I mean, it all seems so obvious, but you don't think about it till an expert points it out, do you?"

"So the next time you're faced with Pen-y-Ghent, Skiddaw or Helvellyn," Terry Whigham continued, "consider a few simple strategies. One obvious trick is to get something in the foreground to give a sense of scale. It's hard to achieve the feeling of immensity you get when you look at a mountain in a four-by-five colour print, but a human figure, an old barn or a particularly interesting tree in the foreground will add the perspective you need.

"You can also be a bit more adventurous and let textures draw the viewer in. A rising slope of scree or a field full of buttercups will lead the eye to the craggy fells beyond. And don't be slaves to the sun, either. Mist-shrouded peaks or cloud shadows on hillsides can produce some very interesting effects if you get your exposure right, and a few fluffy white clouds pep up a bright blue sky no end."

After this, the lights went down and Terry Whigham showed some of his favourite slides to illustrate the points he had made. They were good, Sandra recognized that, but they also lacked the spark, the personal signature, that she liked to get into her own photographs, even at the expense of well-proven rules.

Harriet was a newcomer to the art, but so far she had shown a sharp eye for a photograph, even if her technique still had a long way to go. Sandra had met her at a dreadful coffee morning organized by a neighbour, Selena Harcourt, and the two had hit it off instantly. In London, Sandra had never been short of lively company, but in the North the people had seemed cold and distant until Harriet came along, with her pixyish features, her slight frame and her deep sense of compassion. Sandra wasn't going to let her go.

When the slide show was over and Terry Whigham left the dais to a smattering of applause, the club secretary made announcements about the next meeting and the forthcoming excursion to Swaledale, then coffee and biscuits were served. As usual, Sandra, Harriet, Robin

Allott and Norman Chester, all preferring stronger refreshments, adjourned to The Mile Post across the road.

Sandra found herself sitting between Harriet and Robin, a young college teacher just getting over his divorce. Opposite sat Norman Chester, who always seemed more interested in the scientific process than the photographs themselves. Normally, such an oddly assorted group would never have come together, but they were united in the need for a real drink—especially after a longish lecture—and in their dislike for Fred Barton, the stiff, halitoxic club secretary, a strict Methodist who would no more set foot in a pub than he would brush the dandruff off the shoulders of his dark blue suit.

"What's it to be, then?" Norman asked, clapping his hands and beaming at everyone.

They ordered, and a few minutes later he returned with the drinks on a tray. After the usual round of commentary on the evening's offering—most of it, this time, favourable to Terry Whigham, who would no doubt by now be suffering through Barton's fawning proximity or Jack Tatum's condescending sycophancy—Robin and Norman began to argue about the use of colour balance filters, while Sandra and Harriet discussed local crime.

"I suppose you've heard from Alan about the latest incident?" Harriet said.

"Incident? What incident?"

"You know, the fellow who goes around climbing drainpipes and watching women get undressed."

Sandra laughed. "Yes, it's difficult to know what to call him, isn't it. 'Voyeur' sounds so romantic and 'Peeping Tom' sounds so *Daily Mirror*ish. Let's just call him the peeper, the one who peeps."

"So you have heard?"

"Yes, last night. But how do you know about it?"

"It was on the radio this afternoon. Local radio. They did an interview with Dorothy Wycombe—you know, the one who made all the fuss about hiring policies in local government."

"I know of her. What did she have to say?"

"Oh, just the usual. What you'd expect. Said it was tantamount to an act of rape and the police couldn't be bothered to make much of an effort because it only affected women."

"Christ," Sandra said, fumbling for a cigarette. "That woman makes me mad. She's not that stupid, surely? I've respected the way she's dealt with a lot of things so far, but this time..."

"Don't you think you're only getting upset because Alan's involved?" Harriet suggested. "I mean, that makes it personal, doesn't it?"

"In a way," Sandra admitted. "But it also puts me on the inside, and I know that he cares and that he's doing the best he can, just as much as he would for any other case."

"What about Jim Hatchley?"

Sandra snorted. "As far as I know they're keeping Hatchley as far away from the business as possible. Oh, Alan gets along with him well enough now they've both broken each other in, so to speak. But the man's a boor. They surely didn't let him talk to the press?"

"Oh no. At least not as far as I know. No names were mentioned. She just made it sound as if all the police were sexual deviants."

"Well that's a typical attitude, isn't it? Did she call them the 'pigs,' too?"

Harriet laughed. "Not exactly."

"What do you think of this business, anyway?"

"I don't really know. I've thought about what... what I would feel like if he watched me. It gives me the shivers. It's like someone going through your most private memories. You'd feel soiled, used."

"It gives me the creeps, too," said Sandra, suddenly aware that the others had finished their own conversations and were listening in with interest.

"But, you know," Harriet went on slowly, embarrassed by the larger audience, "I do feel sorry for him in a way. I mean, he'd have to be very unhappy to go around doing that, very frustrated. I do think it's a bit sad, don't you?"

Sandra laughed and put her hand on Harriet's arm. "Harriet Slade," she said, "I'm sure you feel sorry for Margaret Thatcher every time another thousand people lose their jobs."

"Have you never thought that we're most likely to find the culprit among ourselves?" Norman suggested. "That he's probably a member of the club? Everyone's a voyeur, you know," he announced, pushing back a lock of limp, dark hair from his pale forehead. "Especially us. Photographers."

"True enough," Sandra agreed, "but we don't spy on people, do we?"

"What about candids?" Norman replied. "I've done it often enough myself—shoot from the hip when you think they're not looking."

"Women undressing?"

"Good Lord, no! Tramps asleep on park benches, old men chatting on a bridge, courting couples sunbathing."

"It really is a kind of spying, though, isn't it?" Robin cut in.

"But it's not the same," Norman argued. "You're not invading some-one's privacy when they're in a public place like a park or a beach, are you? It's not as if they think they're alone in their own bedrooms. And anyway, you're doing it for an artistic purpose, not just for a sexual thrill."

"I'm not always sure there's much of a difference," Robin said. "Besides, it was you who suggested it."

"Suggested what?"

"That it might be a member of the club—that we're all voyeurs."

Norman coloured and reached for his drink. "I did, didn't I? Perhaps it wasn't a very funny remark."

"Oh, I don't know," Sandra said. "I could certainly see Jack Tatum staring through bedroom windows."

Harriet shivered. "Yes. Every time he looks at you, you feel like he can see right through your clothes."

"I'm sure the peeper's someone much more ordinary, though," Sandra said. "It always seems the case that people who do the most outlandish things live quite normal lives most of the time."

"I suppose a policeman's wife would know about things like that," Robin said.

"No more than anyone who can read a book. They're all over the place, aren't they, biographies of the Yorkshire Ripper, Dennis Nilsen, Brady and Hindley?"

"You're not suggesting the peeper's as dangerous as that, are you?" Norman asked.

"I don't know. All I can say is that it's a bloody weird thing to do, and I don't understand it."

"Do you think he understands it himself?" Robin asked.

"Probably not," replied Sandra. "That's why Harriet feels sorry for him, isn't it dear?"

"You're a beast," Harriet said and flicked a few drops of lager and lime in her direction.

Sandra bought the next round and the conversation shifted to the upcoming club trip to Swaledale and a recent exhibition at the National Museum of Photography in Bradford. When they had all said their goodbyes, Sandra dropped Harriet off and carried on home. Turning into the driveway, she was surprised to hear no opera coming from the front room, and even a little angry to find Brian and Tracy still up watching a risqué film on Channel 4. It was almost eleven o'clock and Alan wasn't back yet.

II

If you picture the Yorkshire Dales as a splayed hand pointing east, then you will find Eastvale close to the tip of the middle finger. The town stands at the eastern limit of Swainsdale, a long valley, which starts in the precipitous fells of the west and broadens into meandering river-meadows in the east. Dry-stone walls criss-cross the lower valley-sides like ancient runes until, in some places, the grassy slopes rise steeply into long sheer cliffs, known locally as "scars." At their summits, they flatten out to become wild, lonely moorlands covered in yellow gorse and pinkish ling, crossed only by unfenced minor roads where horned sheep wander and the wind always rages. The rock is mostly limestone, which juts through in grey-white scars and crags that change hue with the weather like pearls rolled under candlelight. Here and there, a more sinister outcrop of dark millstone grit thrusts out, or layers of shale and sandstone streak an old quarry.

Eastvale itself is a busy market-town of about fourteen thousand people. It slopes up from Swainsdale's eastern edge, where the River Swain turns south-east towards the Ouse, rises to a peak at Castle Hill, then drops gradually eastwards in a series of terraces past the river and the railway tracks.

The town is certainly picturesque; it has a cobbled market square, complete with ancient cross and Norman church, tree-shaded river-fulls, sombre castle ruins, and excavations going back to pre-Roman times. But it has some less salubrious areas that tourists never visit—among them the East Side Estate, a sprawl of council housing put up in the sixties and declining fast.

A visitor sitting in the flower gardens on the western bank of the River Swain would probably be surprised at some of the things that go on across the river. Beyond the poplars and the row of renovated Georgian houses stretch about fifty yards of grass and trees called The Green. And beyond that lies the East Side Estate.

Amid the graffiti-scarred walls, abandoned prams and tires, uncontrolled dogs and scruffy children, the inhabitants of the overcrowded estate try to survive the failure of the town's two main industries outside of tourism—a woollen mill on the river to the northwest, and a chocolate factory near the eastern boundary. Some are quiet, peace-loving families, who keep themselves to themselves and try to make ends meet on the dole. But others are violent and angry, a mixed bunch of deadbeats, alcoholics, wife-beaters, child-abusers and junkies. Drawing the "east side beat," as it is known in the police station, is a duty most young constables do their utmost to avoid.

Of course, there had been protests over the council's plan, but the sixties was an era of optimism and new ideas, so the houses went up. It was also a period of rank political corruption, so many councillors enjoyed holidays abroad at the expense of various contractors, and a great deal of tax-free money changed hands. Meanwhile, the tenants, crammed into their terrace blocks, towers and maisonettes, just had to put up with the flimsy walls, inadequate heating and faulty plumbing. Many thought themselves lucky; they were living in the country at last.

The railway track, raised high on its embankments, ran north to south and cut right through the estate, giving its passengers a fine view of the overgrown back gardens with their lines of washing, tiny greenhouses and rabbit hutches. Several low, narrow tunnels ran under the tracks to link one part of the estate to another, and it was in one of these that Trevor Sharp and Mick Webster stood smoking and discussing business.

The tunnel had been christened "Glue-Sniffers' Ginnel" by the estate's residents because of the great numbers of plastic bags that littered its pathway. It was a dark place, lit at one end by a jaundiced streetlamp, and it reeked of glue, dog piss and stale vomit. Locals avoided it.

Mick Webster, whatever one might call him, was not one of the glue-sniffers. Naturally, he had tried it, along with just about everything else, but he had decided it was for the birds; it dulled the brain and made you spotty, like Lenny. Not that Lenny sniffed glue, though—he just ate too much greasy fish and chips. Mick preferred those little red pills that Lenny seemed to possess in abundance: the ones that made his heart race and made him feel like Superman. He was a squat, loutish sixteen-year-old with a pug nose, a skinhead crop and a permanent sneer. People crossed the street when they saw him coming.

Trevor, on the other hand, was not the kind of boy that the average townsperson would take for a bad sort. He was quite handsome, like his father, and was a slave to fashion in neither clothing nor haircut. Because he was regarded as an exceptionally hard case, nobody ever ragged him about his neat, conservative appearance.

The 10:10 from Harrogate rattled overhead and Trevor lit another cigarette.

"Lenny says it's time we stopped it with the old dears and got onto something a bit more profitable," Mick announced, kicking at some shards of broken glass.

"Like what?"

"Like doing houses. Proper houses where rich folk live. When they're out, like. Lenny says he can let us know where and when. All we got to do is get in, pick up the gear and get out."

"What about burglar alarms?"

"They ain't got burglar alarms," Mick said scornfully. "Peaceful little place this is, never have any crime."

Trevor thought it over. "When do we start?"

"When Lenny gives us a tip."

"Lenny's been taking too much of a cut, Mick. It hardly makes it worth our while. You'd better ask him to give us a bigger percentage if we're gonna get onto this lark."

"Yeah, yeah, all right." It wasn't a new subject, and Mick was getting tired of Trevor's constant harping. Besides, he was too scared of Lenny to mention anything about it.

"How are we going to break in?" Trevor asked.

"I don't fucking know. Window. Back door. Lenny'll give us what we need. It'll be people on holidays or away for the weekend. That kind of thing. Dead easy. He keeps his ear to the ground."

"Got the money for that last lot?"

"Oh, nearly forgot." Mick grinned and pulled out a wad of bills from his hip pocket. "He said he only got fifty for the gear. That's ten quid for you and ten for me."

Trevor shook his head. "It's not right, Mick. That's sixty percent he's taking. And how do we know he only got fifty quid for it? Looked like it was worth nearer a hundred to me."

"We believe him 'cos he's my fucking brother, that's why," Mick said, getting nettled. "And without him we wouldn't be able to get rid of any of the stuff. We wouldn't get nothing, man. So forty percent of what he does is better than a hundred percent of fuck all, right?"

"We could fence it ourselves. It can't be that difficult."

"How many times do I have to tell you? You need the contacts. Lenny's got contacts. You can't just walk into one of those wanky antique shops on Market Street and ask the geezer if he wants to buy a pile of stolen jewellery or a fancy camera, can you?"

"I just don't think it can be all that difficult, that's all."

"Look, we've got a nice little racket going here, let's leave it the way it is. I'll try and get us up to fifty percent, all right?"

Trevor shrugged. "Okay."

"Did I tell you Lenny's got a shooter?" Mick went on excitedly.

"No. Where'd he get it from?"

"Down The Smoke. This bloke what owns a club in Soho. Big fucker it is too, just like on telly."

"Does it work?"

"Of course it works. What good's a shooter that don't work?"

"Have you tried it? Do you know it works?"

"Of course I haven't fucking tried it. What do you expect me to do, walk downtown on market day and start fucking target practice?"

"So you don't know for sure if it works?"

Mick sighed and explained as if to a small child. "These blokes down The Smoke, they don't give you dud shooters, do they? Wouldn't be in their interest."

"What kind is it?"

"I don't fucking know. A big one, like the ones on telly. Like that one Clint Eastwood carries in those Dirty Harry flicks."

"A Magnum?"

"That's right. One of those."

"Powerful shooter," Trevor said. "'Seeing as this is a forty-four Magnum, the most powerful handgun in the world, and can blow your head clean off, you gotta ask yourself, punk, do I feel lucky today? Well, do ya, punk?'"

The Dirty Harry impersonation went down very well, and the two traded shooting noises until the 10:25 to Ripon clattered overhead and drowned them out.

III

"Look, before we start," Jenny Fuller said, "I'd like to tell you that I know why I was chosen to help on this case."

"Oh," said Banks. "What do you mean?"

"You know damn well what I mean. Don't think I didn't notice that eye contact between you and Gristhorpe this morning. There are at least two male professors in the area better qualified to deal with this kind of thing—both experts on deviant psychology. You wanted a woman because it looks good in the public eye, and you wanted me because I've had connections with Dorothy Wycombe."

They were lounging comfortably in armchairs by the crackling fire, Banks cradling a pint of bitter, Jenny a half.

"It's not that I mind," she went on. "I just want you to know. I don't like being taken for a fool."

"Point taken."

"And another thing. You needn't imagine I'm going to go reporting to Dorothy Wycombe on everything that goes on. I'm a professional, not a snooper. I've been asked to help, and I intend to do my best."

"Good. So now we know where we stand. I'm glad you said that, because I didn't feel too happy about working with a spy, whatever the circumstances."

Jenny smiled and her whole face lit up. She really was an extraordinarily beautiful woman, Banks thought, feeling rather distressing tugs of desire as he watched her shift her body in the chair. She was wearing tight jeans and a simple white T-shirt under a loose lemon jacket. Her dark red hair spilled over her shoulders.

Banks himself had paid more attention than usual to his appearance that evening: at least, as much more attention as he could without giving Sandra cause for suspicion. Over a hasty supper, he had told her he would be spending the evening with Dr Fuller discussing the psychological angle of the peeper case. Getting ready, he had resisted the temptation to apply some of the unopened cologne a distant relative had bought him several Christmases ago, and settled instead for a close shave and a liberal application of Right Guard. He had also taken care to smooth down his short, black hair, even though it was always cut so close to the skull that it never got a chance to stand on end.

He had arrived at the Queen's Arms at least ten minutes before Jenny was due—not simply because he didn't believe in keeping a woman waiting, but because he didn't like the idea of her waiting alone in a pub, even a place as congenial as the Queen's Arms. When she walked in five minutes late, all the heads at the bar turned in her direction.

"So where do we start?" he asked, lighting a cigarette and opening his notebook.

"Oh, put that thing away," Jenny protested. "Let's keep this informal while we build up some kind of a picture. I'll give you a full report when I've got things worked out."

Thus admonished, Banks put away his notebook.

"What are your own ideas?" she asked. "I know I'm supposed to be the expert, but I'd like to know what you think." There was a slightly taunting tone in her voice, and he wondered if she was trying to draw him out, make a fool of him. It was probably just her seminar manner, he decided. Like doctors have bedside manners, teachers have classroom manners.

"I'm afraid I wouldn't know where to begin."

"Let me help. Do you think the women ask for it, by the way they dress?"

It was a loaded question, exactly the one he had expected.

"They might well be inviting someone to try and pick them up in a normal, civilized way," he answered, "but of course they're not inviting voyeurs or rapists, no."

He could tell that she approved by the way she looked at him. "On the other hand," he went on, just to provoke her, "if they walk in dark alleys after ten o'clock at night dressed in high-heels, mini-skirts and low-cut blouses, then I'd say they were at least being foolish, if not asking for something."

"So you do think they ask for it?" she accused him, green eyes flashing.

"Not at all. I just think that people, especially women, ought to be more careful these days. We all know what the cities are like, and there's no longer any reason to think a place like Eastvale is immune from sex offenders."

"But why shouldn't we be able to go where we want, when we want and dressed how we want?"

"You should. In a perfect world. This isn't a perfect world."

"Well, thank you for pointing that out to me. Bit of a philosopher, aren't you?"

"I do my best. Look, is this what you want, some kind of sparring match over women's issues? I thought you were playing straight with me. All right, so I'm a man, guilty, and I can never in a million years fully understand what it's like to be a woman. But I'm not a narrow-minded hypocrite, at least I don't think I am, so don't treat me like one."

"Okay. I'm sorry. I'm not really a shrill virago, either. I'm just interested in men's attitudes, that's all. It's my field—male and female, masculine and feminine psychology, similarities, differences. That's why they thought I was the next best thing to a brilliant, ideally qualified man for this job."

She laughed at herself and Banks laughed with her. Then she held out her hands as if holding up a clapper-board, snapped them together and said, "Banks and Fuller: *Co-operation*, Take Two. More drinks first, though. No, I'll get them this time."

Enjoying the slow, feline grace of her movements, Banks watched her walk to the bar and lean on it as the barman drew the beer. When she got back, she smiled and put the drinks on the table.

"Right," she said. "Down to business. What do you want to know?"

"A great deal."

"Well, that'll take a long time."

"I'm sure it'll be time well spent."

Jenny smiled in agreement. "Yes," she said, "I do believe you're right."

To cut through the silence that followed, Banks put his first question: "Is there any chance of this peeper moving on to more violent sex acts?"

"Mmmm," Jenny said. "I'm afraid I'm going to seem as noncommittal as any scientist on some of these matters. According to most of the evidence, voyeurism in itself isn't regarded as a very serious disorder, and it's unlikely to spiral into other forms."

"But?"

"But it's only 'unlikely' according to existing evidence. All that means is that we don't have many documented cases of voyeurs becoming rapists—peeping is usually about as far as they can go. It doesn't mean there are no cases, though, and it doesn't mean that your man might not be one of them. Something could snap. If just looking ceases to give him what he needs, he could either break down or turn to other, more aggravated forms of sexual violence. I'll see if I can look up some case histories for you."

"You call it violence, but he hasn't physically hurt anyone."

"I call it violence purposely, because that's what it is. Look at it this way. We all like to watch the opposite sex. Men more than women— and I think I can safely say that your peeper's definitely not a woman. So why do men do this? There's always the sense, in childhood, of not being permitted to look at a woman's body, so it becomes mysterious and desirable. You don't need a degree in psychology to figure out why men like breasts, for example—they're one of the first sources of love and nourishment we ever experience. Okay so far?"

Banks nodded.

"So we all like to look. You look at women in the street. They seem to dress just to make you look at them. And why not? It makes the world go round, keeps the race going. But at what point does looking, the kind we all do—and women these days now and then glance at a man's bum or the bulge in his pants—become voyeurism?

In the streets, in pubs, in all public places, it's fine, there's an implicit permission to look. We even have special places such as strip-clubs which legitimize the voyeuristic impulse—all quite legal. But when a woman is in her bedroom getting undressed for bed, unless she's doing it for her husband or lover, she doesn't want anyone to watch. Often enough, she doesn't even want her husband to watch. The permission is no longer there, and to look then is an act of sexual violence because it's an intrusion, a violation, a penetration into her world. It degrades her by turning her into an object. Am I making myself clear?"

"Very," Banks said. "What does the voyeur get out of it, then? Why does he do it?"

"They're both very difficult questions to answer. For one thing, he's getting power over her, a certain triumph in dehumanizing her, and perhaps he's also getting revenge for some past wrong that he imagines women have done him. At the same time, he's re-enacting a primal sexual scene, whatever it was that first excited him. He just keeps on repeating himself because it's the only way he can achieve sexual pleasure. You see how complicated it is? When the voyeur penetrates his victim's privacy, then he dominates her, and the element of risk, of 'sin' involved only endows that act with a special intensity for him. Does your man masturbate while he's watching?"

"I don't know. We haven't found any traces of semen."

"Have you looked?"

"The lab boys have been brought in on every incident. I'm sure if it was there they'd find it."

"Okay. It doesn't really matter. I suppose his pants would act as a prophylactic—either that or he stores the image and masturbates later."

"What kind of person are we talking about?"

"His personality?"

"Yes."

"Again, I'm going to have to be a bit vague. He could be an introvert or an extrovert, tall or short, thin or fat..."

"That's certainly vague."

Jenny laughed. "Yes, it is. Sorry, but there's no one type. In a way, it's much easier to describe the true psychopath—a sex murderer, for example. A voyeur—the scientific term is scopophiliac, by the way—is not simply a grubby loner in a dirty mac. Our man's actions are caused by frustration, basically. Intense frustration with life in general and with relationships in particular. It might be that the most meaningful early sexual experience he had was voyeuristic—he saw something he shouldn't have seen, like his parents making love—and since then everything's been a let-down, especially sex. He'd certainly have difficulty handling the real thing.

"What makes voyeurism, or 'scopophilia,' what we call 'abnormal' is simply that the scopophiliac gets all his gratification from looking. Nobody would deny that looking is an integral part of the sex act. Lots of men like to watch their partners undress; it excites them. Plenty of men like to go to strip-clubs too, and whatever the women's movement thinks of that, nobody would seriously consider such men to be clinically abnormal. The scopophiliac, though, gets stuck at the pre-genital stage—his development gets short-circuited. Whatever relationship he's living in—alone, with a wife or a dominating mother or father—it's essentially a frustrating one, and he probably feels great pressure, an intense desire to break through.

"It's unlikely that he's married, but if he is, there are serious problems. In all probability, though, he's living alone. His sexuality wouldn't be mature enough to deal with the demands of a real, flesh-and-blood woman, unless she's a particularly unusual person herself."

"I see," said Banks, lighting a cigarette. "It doesn't look like it's going to be easy, does it?"

"No. It never is when it comes to people. We're all such incredibly complex beings."

"Oh? I always thought of myself as simple and straightforward."

"You're probably one of the most complex of the lot, Alan Banks. First off, what's a nice man like you doing in the police force?"

"Earning a living and trying to uphold the law. See? Simple."

"Would you uphold a law you didn't believe in?"

"I don't know."

"What if the law said that anyone caught stealing a loaf of bread should lose his or her hand? Would you actively go looking for people stealing bread?"

"I think that, in that kind of society, I wouldn't be a policeman."

"Oh, what an evasive answer!"

Banks shrugged. "What can I say? At least it's an honest one."

"All right, what about the drug laws? What about students smoking pot?"

"What are you asking me?"

"Do you pester them? Do you think people should be prosecuted for smoking pot?"

"As long as it's against the law, yes. If you want to know whether I agree with every law in the country, the answer's no. There's a certain amount of discretion allowed in the enforcement, you know. We don't tend to bother students smoking pot so much these days, but we are interested in people bringing heroin up from London or the Midlands."

"Why shouldn't a person take heroin if he or she wants to? It doesn't hurt anyone else."

"I could well ask why shouldn't a man go around watching women get undressed. That doesn't hurt anyone, either."

"It's not the same thing and you know it. Besides, the woman is hurt. She's shocked, degraded."

"Only the ones who know."

"What?"

"Think of it this way. So far, four incidents have been reported. How many do you think have gone unnoticed? How many times has he got away with it?"

"I never really thought of that," Jenny admitted. "And by the way, I'm not going to forget our discussion of a few moments ago, before you so cleverly sidetracked me back to work." She smiled sharply at him as he went off to buy two more drinks.

"I suppose," she said when Banks returned, "that he could actually do it every night, though I doubt it."

"Why?"

"Most sexual activities, normal or perverted, require a kind of gestation period between acts. It varies. The pressure builds again and there's only one way to relieve it."

"I see. Would once or twice a week be too much?"

"For who? You or me?"

"Don't distract me. For our man."

"No. I'd say once a week might do him fine, two at the most." She broke into a fit of laughter and covered her mouth with her hand. "Sorry. I get a bit gigglish sometimes. I think you must make me nervous."

"It comes with the job. Though I sometimes wonder which came first. A chicken or egg thing. Do I make people nervous because I've learned to do it unconsciously through dealing with so many criminals, or was I like that in the first place? Is that why the job suited me?"

"Well?"

"I didn't say I knew the answer, only that I wonder sometimes. Don't worry, when you get to know me better it won't bother you."

"A promise?"

"Let's get back to business."

"All right." Jenny wiped her eyes, full of tears of laughter, sat up straight and once again broke into a laughing fit. Banks watched her, smiling, and soon the others in the pub were looking. Jenny was turning as red as her hair, which was shaking like the fire in the grate. "Oh, I'm sorry, I really am," she said. "Whenever I get like this it's so hard to stop. You must think I'm a real idiot."

"Not at all," Banks said drily. "I appreciate a person with a sense of humour."

"I think it's better now," she said, sipping cautiously at her half of bitter. "It's just all those *double entendres*. Oops," she said, putting her hand to her chest. "Now I've got hiccups!"

"Drink a glass of water in an inverted position," Banks told her. "Best cure for hiccups I've ever known."

Jenny frowned at him. "Standing on my head?"

"No, not like that." Banks was just about to demonstrate to her, using his pint glass, when he sensed a shadow over the table and heard a polite cough. It was Fred Rowe, the station desk-sergeant.

"Pardon me for bothering you, sir," Rowe said quietly, pulling up a chair, "but there's been some trouble."

"Go on," Banks said, putting down his glass.

"It's an old woman, sir, she's been found dead."

"Cause?"

"We can't say yet, sir, but it looks suspicious. The friend who reported it said the place had been robbed."

"All right. Thanks, Fred. I'll get right over. Address?"

"Number two, Gallows View. That's down by—"

"Yes, I know it. Look, get onto Sergeant Hatchley. He'll be in The Oak. And get Dr Glendenning and the photographer out there, and as many of the Scene-of-Crime boys as you can rustle up. Better get DC Richmond along too. Does the super know?"

"Yes, sir."

"Fine. Tell him I'm on my way, then."

Sergeant Rowe returned to the station and Banks stood up to leave, making his apologies to Jenny. Then he remembered that Sandra had taken the Cortina.

"Dammit," he cursed, "I'll have to go over and sign out a car."

"Can't I drive you?" Jenny offered. "I know where Gallows View is."

"Would you?"

"Of course. You're probably over the limit, anyway. I've only been drinking halves."

"You'll have to keep out of the way, stay in the car."

"I understand."

"Right, then, let's go."

"Yes, sir," Jenny said, saluting him.

FOUR

I

It had stopped raining only an hour earlier, and the air was still damp and chilly. Trevor held his jacket collar tight around his neck as he set off across The Green thinking over what Mick had said. Past the Georgian semis, he crossed the fourteenth-century bridge and spat in the water that cascaded over the terraced falls. Then he strode through the riverside gardens, and took the road that curved around Castle Hill to the market square.

Sometimes Mick scared him. Not his physical presence, but his stupidity. There would be no increased percentage from Lenny, Trevor was certain, because Mick wouldn't even dare ask him. Trevor would. He wasn't frightened of Lenny, gun or no gun. The gun didn't really interest him at all; it seemed more like a silly toy for Mick to show off about.

It was the pills, most likely. Them and natural stupidity. Trevor was sick of seeing Mick sweating and ranting on, hopping from one foot to the other as if he wanted to piss all the time. It was pathetic. He hadn't tried them himself, though he thought he might do one day. After all, he wasn't Mick; they wouldn't affect him the same way.

He hadn't tried sex either. Mick kept boasting about having it off with some scrubber up against an alley wall, but Trevor was unimpressed. Even if it was true, it wasn't the kind of fun he was interested in. He would do it all: drugs, sex, whatever. All in his own sweet time. And he would know when the time was right.

As for the new idea, it made sense. Old people seemed to have nothing worth much these days. Probably had to pawn all their old keepsakes just to keep them in pabulum. Trevor laughed at the image. The first time it had been fun, a change from dipping, or mugging the odd tourist—"Just doing my bit for the Tourist Board, your honour, trying to make the New Yorkers feel at home"—it was exciting being able to do whatever you wanted in somebody else's house, break stuff, and them too feeble to do a thing about it. Not that Trevor was a bully; he would never touch the old women (more out of disgust than kindness, though). That was Mick's specialty—Mick *was* a bully.

This would be something different. The old folks' houses all smelled of the past: lavender water, Vicks chest rub, commodes, old dead skin. This time they would be in the classy homes, places with VCRs, fancy music centres, dishwashers, freezers full of whole cows. They could take their time, enjoy it, maybe even do some real damage. After all, they wouldn't be able to carry everything away. Best stick to the portables: cash, jewellery, silver, gold. He could just imagine Mick and Lenny being stupid enough to try and sell stolen colour tellys and videos at Eastvale market. These days everyone wrote their bloody names and postcodes on everything from microwaves to washing-machines with those ultraviolet pens, and the cops could read them under special lights. He hoped Mick was right about burglar alarms, too. It seemed that people were becoming very security-conscious these days.

He crossed the south side of the deserted market square and walked through the complex of narrow, twisted streets to King Street. Then he cut through Leaview Estate towards Gallows View. The terrace of old cottages stood like a wizened finger pointing west to the Dales.

As he passed the bungalows and crossed Cardigan Drive to the dirt track in front of the cottages, Trevor noticed some activity outside the first house, number two. That was where the old bag, Matlock, lived. He walked by slowly and saw a crowd of people through the open door. There was that hotshot copper from London, Banks, who'd got his picture in the local paper when he'd got the job a few months back; that well-known local thug, Hatchley, who looked a bit unsteady on his pins; and the woman standing in the doorway. What on earth was she doing there? He was sure it was her, the one who lived in the fancy Georgian semis across The Green from the East Side Estate, the one Mick was always saying he'd like to fuck. Maybe she was a cop, too. You never could tell. He walked into number eight to confront his father once again over homework not done.

II

Jenny, who had disobeyed Banks's orders and stood unobserved in the doorway, had never seen a corpse before, and this one looked particularly bad. Its wrinkled bluish-grey face was frozen in a grimace of anger and pain, and pools of dark blood had coagulated under the head on the stone flags of the room. Alice Matlock lay on her back at the foot of a table, on the corner of which, it appeared, she had fractured her skull while falling backwards. These were only appearances, though, Jenny realized, and the battery of experts arriving in dribs and drabs would soon piece together what had really happened.

Despite the horror of the scene, Jenny felt outside it all, taking in the little details as an objective observer. Perhaps, she thought, that was one of the qualities that made her a good psychologist: the ability to stand outside the flux of human emotions and pay careful attention. Outside looking in. Perhaps it also made her not so acceptable as a woman—at least one or two of her lovers had complained that however enjoyable she was in bed and however much fun she was to be with, they felt that they couldn't really get close to her and were always aware of themselves being studied like subjects in a mysterious experiment. Jenny brushed aside the self-criticism; if she didn't conform to men's ideas of what a woman should be—fainting, crying, subjective, irrational, intuitive, sentimental—then bugger them.

The house was oppressive. Not just because of the all-pervading presence of death, but because it was absolutely cluttered with the past. The walls seemed unusually honeycombed with little alcoves, nooks and crannies where painted Easter eggs and silver teaspoons from Rhyll or Morecambe nestled alongside old snuff boxes, delicate china figurines, a ship in a bottle, yellowed birthday cards and miniatures. The mantelpiece was littered with sepia photographs: family groups, stiff and formal before the camera, four women in nurses' uniforms standing in front of an old-fashioned army ambulance; and the remaining wall space seemed taken up by framed samplers, and watercolours of wildflowers, birds and butterflies. Jenny shuddered. Her own house, though structurally old, was sparse and modern inside. It would drive her crazy to live in a mausoleum like this.

She watched Banks at work. As she had expected, he was professional and efficient, but he often seemed distracted, and sometimes a look of pain and sadness crossed his features when he leaned against the wall and gazed at the old woman's body. The photographer popped his flash from every angle. He looked far too young, Jenny thought, to be so matter-of-fact about death. The doctor, one of those older, cigarette-smoking types who pay house calls when you have flu or tonsillitis, busied himself with thermometers, charts and other tools of his trade. Out of decency, Jenny turned away and tried to name the wildflowers depicted on the walls. She felt invisible, standing by the doorway, arms folded across her breasts. Everyone seemed to think she had come with Banks. Nobody even paid her the slightest bit of attention; no one, that is, except the slightly squiffed detective she had seen earlier on her visit to the station, who occasionally cast lecherous glances in her direction. Jenny ignored him and watched the men at work.

Also in the midst of this routine, robotic activity sat Ethel Carstairs, who had discovered the body. Though trembling and white with shock as she sipped the brandy a police constable had brought her from Alice's medicinal bottle in the kitchen, she had regained enough control to talk to Banks.

"Alice was supposed to call on me this evening," said Ethel in a weak, shaky voice. "She always comes on Sundays and Tuesdays. We play rummy. She's not on the phone, so when she didn't come there wasn't much I could do. As time went on I got worried, then I decided to walk over and see if she was all right. She was eighty-seven just last week, Inspector. I bought her that sugar bowl broken on the floor there."

It looked as if someone had pulled all the drawers out of the old oak sideboard, and a pretty, rose-patterned sugar bowl lay in several places on the flags.

"She always did have a sweet tooth, despite what the doctor told her," Ethel went on, pausing to wipe her eyes with a lace-edged handkerchief.

"Is this exactly how you found her?" Banks asked gently.

"Yes. I didn't touch a thing. I watch a lot of telly, Inspector. I know about fingerprints and all that. I just stood in the doorway there, saw her and all the mess and went to the box on the corner of Cardigan Drive and phoned the police."

Banks nodded. "Good, you did exactly the right thing. What about the door?"

"What?"

"The door. You must have touched it to get in."

"Oh yes, silly of me. I'm sorry but I did have to open the door. I must have smudged all the prints."

Banks smiled over at Vic Manson, who was busy dusting the furniture with aluminium powder. "Don't worry, Mrs Carstairs," Manson assured her. "Whoever it was probably wore gloves. The criminals watch a lot of telly these days, too. We have to look, though, just in case."

"The door," Banks went on. "Was it ajar, open, locked?"

"It was just open. I knocked first, then when I got no answer, I tried the handle and it just opened."

"There's no sign of forced entry, sir," added Detective Constable Richmond, who had been examining the doorframe beside Jenny. "Whoever it was, she must have let them in."

Hatchley came down from his search of the upper rooms. He wasn't irredeemably drunk, only about two sheets to the wind, and like most professionals, he could snap back into gear in a crisis. "It's been gone over pretty thoroughly," he said to Banks. "Wardrobe, drawers, laundry chest, the lot."

"Do you know if Mrs Matlock owned anything of value, Mrs Carstairs?" Banks asked.

"It's Miss Matlock, Inspector. Alice was a spinster. She never married."

"So she has no immediate family?"

"Nobody. She outlived them all."

"Did she own anything valuable?"

"Not really what you'd call valuable, Inspector. Not to anyone else, that is. There was some silverware—she kept that in the sideboard cupboard, bottom shelf." The cupboard door gaped open and there was no sign of cutlery among the bric-à-brac scattered on the flags. "But her most valuable possessions were these." Ethel gestured towards the knick-knacks and photographs that filled the room. "Her memories."

"What about money? Did she keep much cash in the house?"

"She used to keep a bit around, just for emergencies. She usually kept it in the bottom drawer of her dressing table."

"How much did she have there, as a rule?"

"Oh, not much. About fifty pounds or so."

Banks glanced at Hatchley, who shook his head. "It's a mess up there," he said. "If there was any money, it's gone now."

"Do you think our man, or men, knew where to look?"

"Not by the looks of it," Hatchley answered. "They searched everywhere. Same pattern as the other break-ins."

"Yes," Banks said quietly, almost to himself. "The victims always let them in. You'd think older people would be more careful these days."

"Prosopagnosia," announced Jenny, who had been listening carefully to all this.

"Pardon?" Banks said, seeming as surprised to see her there as she was by the sound of her own voice. The others looked around, too. With an angry glance, Banks introduced her: "Dr Fuller. She's helping us with a case." Everyone smiled or nodded and went back to work. "Can you explain it, then?" Banks asked.

"Prosopagnosia? It's the inability to recognize faces. People sometimes get it after brain damage, but it's most common in senility."

"I don't quite see the connection."

"Alice wasn't senile, young lady," Ethel Carstairs cut in, "but it's true that she was beginning to forget little, day-to-day things, and the past was much closer to her."

Jenny nodded. "I didn't mean to be insulting, Mrs Carstairs. I just meant it's part of the aging process. It happens to us all, sooner or later." She turned back to Banks. "Most of us, when we see a face, compare it with our files of known faces. We either recognize it or we don't, all in about a split second. With prosopagnosia, the observer can see all the components of the face but can't assemble the whole to check against memory files. It makes elderly people vulnerable to strangers, that's why I mentioned it."

"You mean she might have thought she recognized whoever it was?" Banks asked.

"Or thought she *should* have and not wanted to be rude. That's the most common problem. If you're a kind, polite person, you'll want to avoid giving offence, so you'll pretend you know who it is. It's like when you forget the name of an acquaintance and find ways of avoiding having to say it, only this must be much worse."

Dr Glendenning packed up his battered brown bag, lit a cigarette—strictly forbidden at the scene of a crime, but generally overlooked in his case—and shambled over to Banks and Jenny. "Dead about twenty-four hours," he said out of the corner of his mouth in a nicotine-ravaged voice with a strong trace of Edinburgh in it. "Cause of death, fractured skull, most likely inflicted by that table edge there."

"Can you tell if she was pushed?"

"Looks like it. One or two bruises on the upper arms and shoulders. That's just preliminary, though. Can't tell you more till after the autopsy. But unless the old dear was poisoned, too, I shouldn't imagine there'll be much more to tell. You can get her to the morgue now. There'll be a coroner's inquest, of course," he said, and walked out.

Everybody had finished. Manson had plenty of fingerprints to play with, most of them probably Alice Matlock's, and the other two Scene-of-Crime boys had envelopes filled with hairs, fragments of clothing and blood scrapings.

"You can go now, Mrs Carstairs," Banks said. "I'd appreciate it if you'd drop by the station in the morning and give a formal statement." He called Detective Constable Richmond to drive Ethel home and instructed him also to pick her up in the morning and take her statement.

"Right, then. I'm off home, too," Banks said in a tired voice. "It's up to you now, Sergeant. See there's someone posted here all night. Deal with the ambulance. And you might as well start talking to the neighbours. They'll still be up. Curiosity's a great cause of insomnia. Do Gallows View and the six end bungalows over the street here. The rest can wait till tomorrow. Remember, the doctor puts the time of death at about twenty-four hours ago—let's say between ten o'clock and midnight last night. Find out if anyone saw or heard anything. Okay?"

Hatchley nodded glumly. Then his expression brightened when he saw Richmond leading Ethel Carstairs outside. "Don't be long, lad," he said, baring his yellow teeth in what passed for a smile. "I've got work for you to do."

Banks and Jenny left. She was surprised that he didn't vent his anger at her disobedience, but they broke the silence in the car only to arrange another meeting to work on the profile later in the week, then she dropped him off and drove home, unable to get the image of Alice Matlock's body out of her mind.

III

Detective Constable Philip Richmond was almost as pleased with his recent promotion to the CID as he was with his new moustache: the latter made him look older, more distinguished, and the former, more important, successful. He had worn the uniform, driven the Panda cars and walked the beat in Eastvale for as long as he cared to, and he had an intimate knowledge of every alley, snicket and back-street in the town: every lover's lane, every villain's hangout and every pub where visiting squaddies from Catterick camp were likely to cut up a bit rough at closing time.

He also knew Gallows View, the cottages at the far western edge of the town. Developers had petitioned for their demolition, especially when Leaview Estate was under construction, but the council, under pressure from the Parks and Monuments Commission, had reluctantly decided that they could stay. There were, after all, only five cottages, and two of those, at the western end of the street, had been knocked together into a shop and living quarters. Richmond had often bought gob-stoppers, Tizer and lucky-bags there as a lad, later graduating to cigarettes, which the owner would often trade him for his mother's coupons giving threepence off Tide or Stardrops.

Richmond stood in the street, drawing his raincoat tighter to keep out the chill, and cursed that damned slave driver Hatchley to himself. The bastard was probably guzzling the dead woman's medicinal brandy while his junior paid the house calls in the rain. Well, blow him, Richmond thought. Damned if he's going to get credit for anything I come up with.

Resigned, he knocked on the door of number four, which was opened almost immediately by an attractive young woman holding the lapels of her dressing-gown close around her throat. Richmond showed his identification proudly, stroked his moustache and followed her indoors. The place might be an old cottage, he thought, but by heck they'd done a good job on the inside: double-glazing, central heating, stucco walls, nice framed paintings, a bit abstract for his taste, but none of your Woolworth's tat, and one of those glass-topped coffee tables between two tube-and-cushion armchairs.

He accepted her offer of coffee—it would help keep him awake—but was surprised at how long she took to make it and at the odd, whirring noises he heard coming from the kitchen. When he finally got to taste the coffee, he knew; it was made from fresh-ground beans, filter-dripped, and it tasted delicious. She put a coaster on the low table in front of him—a wild flower, wood sorrel, he guessed, pressed between two circles of glass, the circumference bound in bamboo—then, at last, he was able to get down to business.

First he took her name, Andrea Rigby, and discovered that she lived there with her husband, a systems analyst, who was often away during the week working on projects in London or Bristol. They had lived in Gallows View for three years, ever since he had landed the well-paying job and been able to fulfill his dream of country living. The woman had an Italian or Spanish look about her, Richmond couldn't decide which, but her maiden name was Smith and she came originally from Leominster.

"What's happened?" Andrea asked. "Is it Miss Matlock next door?"

"Yes," Richmond answered, unwilling to give away too much. "Did you know her?"

"I wouldn't say I *knew* her. Not well, at any rate. We said hello to each other and I went to the shops a few times for her when she was ill last year."

"We're interested to know if you heard anything odd last night between ten and midnight, Mrs Rigby."

"Last night? Let me see. That was Monday, wasn't it. Ronnie had gone back down to London...I just sat around reading and watching television. I *do* remember hearing someone running in the street, over in Cardigan Drive. It must have been about eleven because the news had finished and I'd been watching an old film for about half an hour. Then I turned it off because it was boring."

"Someone running? That's all?"

"Yes."

"You didn't go to the window and look out?"

"No. Why should I? It was probably just kids."

Richmond jotted in his notebook. "Anything else? Did you hear any sounds from next door?"

"I thought I heard someone knocking at a door after the running, but I can't be sure. It sounded muffled, distant. I'm sorry, I really wasn't paying attention."

"How long after the running?"

"Right after. The one stopped, then I heard the other."

"Did the running fade into the distance or stop abruptly?"

Andrea thought for a moment. "More abruptly, really. As soon as people or cars or anything pass the corner of our street you can't hear them anymore, so it doesn't mean much."

"Did you hear any sounds at all from Miss Matlock's, next door?"

"No, nothing. But then I never do, not even when her friend comes to see her. I can hear knocking at the door, but nothing from inside. The way these old places were built the walls are very thick and we both have our staircases back to back, so there's quite a gap, really, between her living-room and mine. I sometimes hear the stairs creak when she's going up to bed, but that's all."

Richmond nodded, closing his notebook. "You haven't noticed anyone hanging around here lately, have you? Kids, a stranger?"

Andrea shook her head. Richmond couldn't think of any more questions, and it was getting late—he still had others to talk to. He thanked Andrea Rigby for her excellent coffee, then went to knock at number six.

The door opened a crack and a man wearing thick glasses peered out. Once Richmond had gained entry, he recognized Henry Wooller, the branch librarian, a bit of an oddball, loner, dry stick. Wooller's house was a tip. Scraps of newspaper, dirty plates, worn socks and half-full cups of tea with clumps of mould floating in them were strewn all over the room; and the place stank: an acrid, animal smell. Richmond noticed the corner of a pornographic magazine sticking out from under the *Sunday Times* Review section, where it had probably been hastily hidden. It was one he recognized, imported from Denmark, and the *UNCY* of its name, *BIG'N'BOUNCY*, was clearly visible. Wooller made a pretence of tidying things up a bit and was careful to hide the magazine completely.

Richmond asked the same questions he'd put to Andrea Rigby, but Wooller insisted that he had heard nothing at all. It was true that he was one cottage further from Cardigan Drive, which ran at right angles to the easternmost end of Gallows View, along the western edge of Leaview Estate, but Richmond didn't think the distance was a factor. He felt not only that Wooller didn't want to get involved, a common enough reaction to police enquiries, but also that he was hiding something. The expression behind the distorting glasses, however, remained fixed and deadpan; Wooller was giving nothing away. Richmond thanked him cursorily and left, making a note of his dissatisfaction.

The entrance to the living quarters of the shop was what used to be the door to number eight. Hearing voices raised, Richmond paused outside, hoping to learn something of value. He could only catch the odd word—the door must have been thick, or perhaps they were in the back—but it didn't take long to work out that a young lad was being told off for staying out too late and for not spending enough time on his schoolwork. Richmond smiled, feeling an immediate sympathy for the boy. How many times had he heard the same sermon himself?

When he knocked, the voices stopped immediately and the door was opened abruptly. Graham Sharp looked worried when he found out that a policeman wanted to see him. Everybody did, Richmond reflected, and it usually meant nothing more than an outstanding parking ticket.

"No, I didn't know her well," he said. "She came in here to do some of her shopping. It was convenient for her, I suppose. But she kept herself to herself. What happened to her?"

"Did you hear anything around eleven o'clock last night?" Richmond asked.

"No, nothing," Sharp answered. "I was watching telly in the room upstairs. We've converted one of the old bedrooms into a kind of sitting-room. It's right at the western end, as far as you can get in Eastvale without being in a field, so I wouldn't be able to hear anything from Cardigan Drive way."

"Noticed anything odd lately? Any strangers, kids hanging about?"

"No."

"No newcomers in the shop? Nobody asking questions?"

"Only you." Sharp smiled tightly, clearly relieved to see Richmond pocketing his notebook.

"Could I speak to your son for a moment, sir?" Richmond asked before leaving.

"My son?" Sharp echoed, sounding nervous again. "What for? He's just a young lad, only fifteen."

"He might be able to help."

"Very well." Sharp called Trevor from upstairs and the boy slouched down moodily.

"Where were you at about eleven o'clock last night?" Richmond asked.

"He was here with me," Sharp butted in. "Didn't I already tell you? We were upstairs watching telly."

Richmond flipped back through his notebook—mostly for effect, because his memory was good. "You told me that *you* were upstairs watching television, sir. You didn't say anything about your son."

"Well, that's what I meant. I just took it for granted. I mean, where else would he be at that time?" He put his arm around Trevor's shoulder. The boy winced visibly.

"Well?" Richmond addressed Trevor.

"It's like he says, we were watching telly. Not much else to do around here, is there?"

Richmond thanked them both and left, again jotting down his reservations in his book, and also noting that he thought he recognized Trevor Sharp from somewhere. All in all, it wasn't turning out to be a bad evening's haul. Already he was enjoying the responsibility of interrogation and feeling less vitriolic towards Sergeant Hatchley.

Nobody was at home in the first two houses on Cardigan Drive. Residents of two of the others had been out late at a club fundraiser the previous evening, and the remaining two had heard somebody running past at about eleven, but neither had looked out of their windows nor heard anyone knocking on Alice Matlock's door.

Richmond, who had thought to show some keenness by doing more than the first six houses, was beginning to tire a little by then, and as he'd done his duty, he decided to report back to Hatchley.

He found the sergeant sitting in Alice Matlock's armchair, his feet up on the stool, snoring loudly. The body was gone and all that remained were the chalk outline on the worn flags and the pools of dried blood. The place was still dusty with Manson's aluminium powder. The level in the brandy bottle had dropped considerably.

Richmond coughed and Hatchley opened a bloodshot eye. "Ah, back already, lad? Just thinking about the case, taking in the atmosphere. Done all the houses?"

Richmond nodded.

"Good lad. I think we'd better be off now. You'll need your beauty sleep for all the report writing you've got to do in the morning."

"Inspector Banks said to leave someone on duty here, sir."

"Did he? Yes, of course. One of the uniformed blokes. Look, you hang on here and I'll call the station on my way. Someone should be down in about fifteen minutes. All right, lad?"

Weary, cold and wet, Richmond mumbled, "Yes, sir," and settled down to comfort himself with thoughts of the beautiful Andrea Rigby not more than about seven or eight feet away from him through the wall. Taking out his notebook, he thought he might as well draft the outline of his report, and he began to look over his small, neat handwriting to see how it all added up.

FIVE

I

Wednesday was a difficult morning for Banks. His desk was littered with reports, and he couldn't get Jenny Fuller out of his mind. There was nothing wrong with his marriage—Sandra was all, if not more than, he had ever expected in a partner—so there was no reason, Banks told himself, why he should find himself interested in another woman.

It was Paul Newman, he remembered, who had said, "Why go out for hamburger if you can get steak at home?" But Banks couldn't remember the name of the subversive wit who had countered, "What if you want pizza?"

At thirty-six, he surely couldn't have hit middle-age crisis point, but there was no doubt that he was strongly attracted to the bright, red-headed Doctor of Philosophy. The sensation had been immediate, like a mild electric shock, and he was certain that she had felt it, too. Their two meetings had been charged with a strong undercurrent, and Banks didn't know what to do about it. The sensible thing would be to walk away and avoid seeing her anymore, but his job made that impractical.

He slugged back some hot, bitter station coffee and told himself not to take the matter so seriously. There was nothing to feel guilty about in fancying an attractive woman. He was, after all, a normal, heterosexual male. Another mouthful of black coffee tightened him back into the job at hand: reports.

He read over Richmond's interview statements and thought about the young detective's reservations for a while before deciding that they should be pursued. He also remembered Trevor Sharp, who had been a suspect in a tourist mugging shortly after Banks had arrived in Eastvale. The boy hadn't been charged because his father had given him a solid alibi, and the victim, an "innocent abroad" from Oskaloosa, Iowa, wasn't able to give a positive identification when the case relied solely on his word.

Hatchley had wasted his time at The Oak. He had talked to the bar staff and to the regular customers (and would no doubt be putting in a lengthy expenses claim), but nobody remembered anything special about Carol Ellis that night. It had been a quiet evening, as Mondays usually were, and she had sat at a corner table all evening talking to her friend, Molly Torbeck. Both had left before closing time and had, presumably, gone their separate ways. Nobody had tried to pick either of them up, and nobody had spent the evening giving them the eye.

The sergeant had also talked to Carol, Molly and the three other victims. When it was all added up, two of the four, Josie Campbell and Carol Ellis, had been in The Oak on the nights in question, and the other two in pubs at opposite ends of Eastvale. It wasn't the kind of pattern Banks had been hoping to find, but it was a pattern: pubs. Jenny Fuller might have something to say about that.

Skipping his morning break at the Golden Grill, Banks tidied up his own report on the interview with Crutchley and left the file in his pending tray to await the artist's impression.

He missed his lunch, too, looking over the preliminary post mortem report on Alice Matlock, which offered no new information but confirmed Glendenning's earlier opinions about time and cause. The bruises on her wrists and arms indicated that there had been a struggle in which the woman had been pushed backwards, catching the back of her head on the table corner.

Glendenning was nothing if not thorough, and he had a reputation as one of the best pathologists in the country. He had looked for evidence of a blow by a blunt instrument prior to the fall, which might then have been engineered to cover up the true cause, but had discovered only a typical *contre-coup* head injury. Though the skull had splintered into the brain tissue at the point of impact, the occipital region, there was also damage to the frontal lobes, and that only occurs when the body is falling. The effect, Glendenning had noted, is similar to that of a passenger bumping his head on the windscreen when a car brakes abruptly. If, however, the blow is delivered while the victim's head is stationary, then the wound is restricted to the area of impact. The blow that killed Alice Matlock was the kind of blow that could have killed anyone—and she was old, her bones were brittle—but it wasn't necessarily murder; it could have been accidental; it could have been manslaughter.

A red-eyed Richmond brought in Ethel Carstairs' statement. Again, there was nothing new, but she had given an itemized description of the missing silverware. Manson had found only two different sets of fingerprints in the house: one belonged to the dead woman herself and the other to Ethel, who had been good enough to offer hers for comparison.

At about two-fifteen, Superintendent Gristhorpe stuck his head round the door. "Still at it, Alan?"

Banks nodded, gesturing to the papers that covered his desk.

Gristhorpe looked at his watch. "Go get a pie and a pint over the road. I think we'd better have a conference about three o'clock and I don't want your stomach rumbling all through it."

"A conference?"

"Aye. A lot's been happening. The peeper, the break-ins, now this Alice Matlock business. I don't like it. It's time we threw a few ideas around. Just me, you, Hatchley and Richmond. Have you read the young lad's reports, by the way?"

"Yes, I've just finished."

"Good, aren't they? Detailed, no split infinitives or dangling modifiers. He'll go far, that lad. See you at three in the boardroom."

II

The "boardroom" was so called because it was the most spacious room in the station. At its centre was a large, shiny, oval table, around which stood ten matching, stiff-backed chairs. The set-up looked impressive, but the conference was informal; a coffee pot sat on its warmer in the middle, surrounded by files, pencils and notepads.

There were no ashtrays, though; unless he was in a pub or a coffee shop, where it was unavoidable, Gristhorpe didn't approve of people smoking in his presence.

"Right," the superintendent announced when they had all arranged their papers and helped themselves to coffee. "We've got four break-ins—all at old people's houses—involving one assault and one death. We've also got a Peeping Tom running around town looking in any window he damn well pleases, and we've got hardly a thing to go on in either case. I reckon it's about time we pooled what brainpower we've got and let's see if we can't come up with some ideas. Alan?"

Banks coughed. He needed a cigarette but had to content himself by fiddling with a paper clip while he spoke. "I think Detective Constable Richmond should speak first, sir. He conducted interviews with the dead woman's neighbours last night."

Gristhorpe looked at Richmond, inviting him to begin.

"Well, sir, you've all seen copies of the report. I don't really have anything to add. We had a uniformed man on duty all night, and another made inquiries all the way down Cardigan Drive. A couple of people heard someone running, but that was all."

"We know who that someone was, don't we?" Gristhorpe asked.

"Well, not his identity, sir. But, yes, it was that chap who's been looking in on women getting undressed."

"Right," Gristhorpe said, turning over a page of the report in front of him. "Now, Andrea Rigby says that she heard running, then a knock at a door. Never mind the alternative explanations for the moment. Could there be any possibility that it was the peeper, not a burglar, who killed Alice Matlock? Maybe she knew him, maybe he came for help or protection, or to confess—she threatened to report him, they struggled and he pushed her? Manslaughter."

"The place had been gone over just like the others, sir," Sergeant Hatchley pointed out.

"And no prints."

"No prints, sir."

"Couldn't it have been made to look like it was a burglary?"

"How would the peeper know to do that?" Banks asked.

"Surely he must read the papers?" Gristhorpe suggested.

"It doesn't fit, though. It's all too deliberate. If it happened as you say, then it was probably an accident. He probably just panicked and ran."

"People have been known to cover their tracks after crimes of passion, Alan."

"I know, sir. It just doesn't seem to fit the profile we have so far."

"Go on."

"Dr Fuller"—there it was again, so formal. Why couldn't he call her Jenny in front of others?—"Dr Fuller said we're dealing with a very frustrated man who's probably going about as far as he dares in peeping through windows. No one can be certain, but she said it's unlikely that a voyeur would progress to more serious sex crimes. On the other hand, as the pressure builds in him, he might feel the need to break out. It's a trap he's in, a treadmill, and there's no predicting what he'd do to escape it."

"But this wasn't a sex crime, Alan. Alice Matlock, thank the Lord, hadn't been interfered with in any way."

"I know, sir, but it still doesn't fit. The peeper does what he does when pressure or tension builds up and he can only find one way of releasing it, watching women undress. It wouldn't even really work for him in a strip-club—the women would have to be unaware of him, he would have to get that feeling of power, of dominance. When he's done it, though, the pressure's released. A personality like that is hardly likely to go running to an old woman and confess, let alone murder her just after he's satisfied himself."

"I see your point, Alan," Gristhorpe agreed. His bushy eyebrows joined in the middle and drew a thick grey line over his child-like blue eyes. "Perhaps the best thing to do would be to rule it out by checking into who Alice Matlock knew."

"She seemed to be a bit of a loner, sir," Richmond chipped in. "Most of the neighbours didn't know much about her, not much more than to say hello if they met in the street."

"I knew Alice Matlock," Gristhorpe told them. "She was a friend of my mother's. Used to come to the farm for fresh eggs when I was a kid. She always brought me some boiled sweets. But you're right, lad, she was a bit of a recluse. More so as she got older. Lost her young man in the first war, as I recall. Never did marry. Anyway, look into it. See if she's been at all friendly with a likely young peeper."

"There is one other thing."

"Yes, Alan?"

"Even if it wasn't the same person, if it was the usual lot did the break-in and the peeper just looked and ran, they might have seen each other."

"You mean, if we get one we might get a lead on the other?"

"Yes."

"But right now we've very little on either?"

"That's right."

"Where do you think our best chance lies?"

"The break-ins," Banks answered without hesitation. "I'll be getting an artist's impression of the man who fenced the stuff in Leeds any time now. I've already got a fairly good description but it doesn't check with any of the local villains I know. Sergeant Hatchley and Constable Richmond don't recognize him either."

"So maybe he's not local. New in town?"

"Or been away," Richmond suggested. "Only here every now and then."

"Possible. Know anyone who fits that profile?"

Richmond shook his head. "Only Andrea Rigby's husband. He's a computer whizz and he spends a lot of time away. But I saw a photo of him on the mantelpiece and he doesn't fit the description. He wouldn't be the type, anyway. From what I could see, he gets plenty of money from fiddling about with computers."

"Ask around, then," Gristhorpe advised. "See if you can come up with anything. You mentioned Wooller in your report, Richmond. He seemed suspicious. Anything in particular?"

"Well, no, sir." Richmond felt flustered, caught out on a hunch. "There was the dirty magazine, sir, that's in the report."

"Yes," Gristhorpe said dismissively, "but most of us have looked at pictures of naked women now and then, haven't we?"

"It's not just naked women, sir," Richmond pressed on, realizing only when it was too late that he had walked right into it. "Some of them are tied up, sir..." His voice faltered. "...and they do it with animals."

"Well," Gristhorpe said, beaming at him, "I can see you've been doing your homework, lad. But even if the stuff is illegally imported there's not a lot we can do. What exactly are you getting at?"

"Just that he seemed suspicious, sir. Completely uncommunicative, shifty, acted as if he was hiding something."

"Think he might be our peeper, do you?"

"Could be, sir."

"Alan?"

Banks shrugged. "I've not had the pleasure of meeting him, but I've been told that our man could take any size, shape or form. Certainly if he lives a frustrated existence and gets his kicks from bondage and bestiality magazines, then there's a chance."

"All right," Gristhorpe said, making a note. "Keep an eye on him. Drop by for a chat. Nothing heavy, though." He glanced sternly at Hatchley, who looked down at his notes and straightened his tie.

"The kid, sir. Trevor Sharp," Richmond said.

"Yes?"

"There was something funny about that, too. I heard them arguing about him being late all the time and neglecting his homework, and when I asked about the night before, his father only mentioned himself at first, sir. Said he was watching telly, right at the far end of the block. Then, later, when I asked, he said the kid was with him, too."

"Think he was lying?"

"Could be."

"We had the kid on suspicion of mugging four months ago," Banks added. "No case."

"Well," Gristhorpe said, "seeing as the only information we've got on the burglars so far is that they're young, we might as well follow up. Maybe you could talk to them, Alan? Father and son together. See if you get the same impression as Richmond here."

"All right," Banks agreed. "I'll drop by after school today."

"Might be a good idea to have a word with the head, too. You never know, some of 'em keep tabs on the kids. What school is it?"

"Eastvale Comprehensive, sir," Richmond answered. "Same place I went to."

"That'll be old Buxton, right?"

"Yes, sir. 'Boxer' Buxton we used to call him. He must be close to retiring age now."

"He's been at that school going on for forty years. Been head for twenty or more, since back when it was Eastvale Grammar School.

He's a bit of a dodderer now, lost in his own world, but have a word with him about young Trevor anyway, see if he's been acting strangely, playing truant, associating with a bad crowd. Is there anything else?" Gristhorpe turned to Sergeant Hatchley. "Anything for us, Sergeant?"

"I can't seem to find a pattern to the peeper's operation, sir," Hatchley said. "Except that he always picks blondes."

"What do you mean?"

"How he chooses his victims, sir, how he latches onto them, knows who to follow."

"The women weren't all single, were they?" Gristhorpe asked.

"Bloody hell, no, sir," Hatchley said. "One of 'em had her husband right there in bed dozing off while our chap was doing his bit through the curtains."

"He must do some reconnaissance first," Banks added. "He knows which window to look through, knows the layout of the house. Even picks the best time to be there."

"So he chooses his victims well in advance?"

"Must do."

"They'd all been in pubs the nights they were peeped on," Hatchley said. "But I couldn't find any evidence that they were being watched."

"That would explain it, though, wouldn't it?" Banks said. "If he already knew who he was going to spy on, he'd know something about their habits. If he'd watched the houses, he'd know when a woman comes home from the pub and how soon the bedroom light goes on. He'd know if the husband stayed downstairs or took a bath while she undressed. He must do his groundwork."

"Fair enough, Alan," Gristhorpe said, "but it doesn't help us much, does it?"

"We could warn people to make sure they're not being followed, to keep an eye out for strangers hanging about the street."

"I suppose we could." Gristhorpe sighed and ran his hand through his hair. "Anything's better than nothing. You talked to the victims again, Sergeant Hatchley?"

"Yes, sir. But I didn't find out anything new, just that all the incidents had occurred after a night out."

"Maybe it makes him feel that they're sinners or something," Banks guessed. "It's possible that he needs to feel like that about them. A lot of men don't like the idea of women smoking or going to pubs. They think it cheapens them. Maybe it's like that with him; perhaps he needs to feel that they're impure in the first place."

Gristhorpe scratched his neck and frowned. "I think you've been talking to Dr Fuller too much, Alan," he said. "But maybe you've got a point. Follow it up with her. When are you meeting again?"

"Tomorrow."

"Evening?"

Banks felt himself begin to flush. "We're both too busy during the day, sir."

Hatchley suppressed a guffaw by covering the lower half of his face with a huge dirty handkerchief and blowing hard. Richmond shifted uneasily in his seat. Banks could sense their reactions, and he felt angry. He wanted to say something, to tell them it was just bloody work, that's all. But he knew that if he did, they would think he was protesting too much, so he kept quiet and seethed inside.

"Put it to her, then," Gristhorpe said, ignoring the others. "Ask her if there could be any connection between the peeper and Alice Matlock's death, and find out if it's likely our man has a thing about women in pubs."

"She'll probably laugh at me," Banks said. "We all seem to fancy ourselves as amateur psychologists at one time or another."

"Not surprising, though, is it, Alan? We'd be a pretty bloody incurious race if we didn't think about our nature and behaviour once in a while, wouldn't we? Especially us coppers. Is that all?" he asked, rising to end the meeting.

Everyone kept silent. "Fine, then, that's it. Follow up Wooller and the Sharp kid, get that drawing circulated soon as it comes in, and check with Ethel Carstairs about any other friends Alice Matlock may have had."

"Should we say anything to the press?" Banks asked. "A warning to women about keeping their eyes open for strangers?"

"It can't do any harm, can it? I'll take care of that. Off you go, then. Meeting adjourned."

III

Graham Sharp rolled off Andrea Rigby and sighed with pleasure: "Ah, Wednesdays. Thank God for half-day closing."

Andrea giggled and snuggled in the crook of his arm. He could feel the weight of her breasts against his rib cage, the nipples still hard, and the sharp, milky scent of sex made them both warm and sleepy. Andrea traced a line from his throat to his pubic hair. "That was wonderful, Gray," she said dreamily. "It's always wonderful with you. See how much better you feel now."

"I was just a bit preoccupied, that's all."

"You were all tense," Andrea said, massaging his shoulders. Then she laughed. "Whatever it was, it certainly made you wild, though."

"When are you going to tell him?"

"Oh, Gray!" She snuggled closer, her breasts crushed against his chest. "Don't spoil it, don't make me think about bad things."

Graham smiled and caressed her hair. "Sorry, love. It's the secrecy. It gets me down sometimes. I just want us to be together all the time."

"We will be, we will," Andrea murmured, rubbing against him slowly as she felt him begin to stiffen again. "Oh God, Gray." She breathed hard as he took hold of her breast and squeezed the nipple between thumb and forefinger. "Yes...yes..."

Graham knew, in his more rational moments, that they would never be together all the time. Whatever Andrea thought about her husband, he wasn't such a bad sort really. He didn't beat her, and as far as Graham knew, he didn't cheat on her either. They got on well enough when he was around, which wasn't often, and, perhaps more important than Andrea would have cared to admit to herself—especially now, as she was nearing orgasm—he made a lot of money. Soon, in fact, she had told Graham sadly, they would be moving from their first country home into something a bit more authentic: an isolated Dales cottage, or perhaps somewhere in the Cotswolds, where the climate was milder. Why he wanted to live in the country, Andrea said she had no idea—he was hardly ever there anyway—but she had found Eastvale a great deal more interesting than she had expected.

Graham also knew deep down that Trevor would never accept

another mother, especially one who lived two doors away and was, at twenty-four, closer to the age of an older sister. There was the money, too. Graham could hardly make ends meet, and if he really thought about it (which he tried not to) he couldn't see Andrea as a shop-keeper's wife: not her, with her Paris fashions, original art works, and holidays in New York or Bangkok. No, just as he knew that Trevor would never accept her, he also knew she would never give up her way of life.

But they were both romantics at heart. At first, Andrea had come to the shop more and more often, just for little things like a packet of Jacob's Cream Crackers, some fresh Baps or perhaps a bottle of tar-ragon vinegar, and if there had been no other customers around she had lingered a little longer to talk each time. Over a week or two, Graham had come to know quite a lot about her, especially about how her husband was away so much and how bored she got.

Then, one evening, one of her fuses blew and she had no idea how to fix it. She went to Graham for help, and he came along with torch and fuse wire and did it in a jiffy. Coffee followed, and after that an exciting session of kissing and groping on the sofa, which, being one of those modern things made up of blocks you can rearrange any way you want, was soon transformed into an adequate approximation of a bed.

Since then, for about two months, Graham and Andrea had been meeting quite regularly. Theirs was a circumscribed life, however: they couldn't go out together (though they did once spend a nervous evening in York having dinner, looking over their shoulders the whole time), and they had to be very careful about being seen in each other's company at all. Always Graham would visit Andrea, using the back way, where the high walls of the back yards kept him from view and muffled the sound of his passing. Sometimes they had candlelight din-ners first; other times they threw themselves straight into lovemaking. Andrea was more passionate and abandoned in bed than anyone Graham had ever known, and she had led him to new heights of joy.

It was easier at first. Trevor spent three weeks in France on a school trip, so Graham was a free agent. On the boy's return, though, there were difficulties, which was why half-day closing was such a joy. Weekends were out, of course. That was when Andrea's husband was around, so the most they could manage was the occasional evening when Trevor was allowed to go out to the pictures with his mates, to the youth club or a local dance. Lately, though, with Trevor being out so often and taking so little notice, Graham had spent much more time with Andrea.

When they had finished, they lay back and lit cigarettes. Andrea blew the smoke out of her nose like an actress in a forties movie.

"Did they talk to you last night?" she asked.

"The police?"

"Yes."

"What do you think happened?"

"The old woman, Alice Matlock. She's dead."

Andrea frowned. "Was it murder?"

"They must think so or they wouldn't waste their time asking everyone what they were doing and where they were."

He sounded irritated. Andrea stroked his chest. "Don't worry about it, darling. It's nothing to do with us, is it?"

"No, 'course not," he said, turning and running his palm over her damp stomach. He loved Andrea's body; it was so different from Maureen's. She had had smooth skin, smooth as marble and some-times as cold. He had hardly dared touch it, fearing it would be some kind of violation. But Andrea's skin had grain to it, a certain friction you could feel when you ran your hand over her buttocks or shoul-ders, even when they were moist as they were now.

"What did they want to know?" he asked her.

"Just if I heard anything the night before last."

"And did you?"

"After you'd gone, yes. I heard someone running along Cardigan Drive, then someone knocking at a door."

"The same person?"

"Could have been."

"There was a woman peeped on in Cardigan Drive Monday evening," Graham told her. "I read about it in the paper."

"Another of those Peeping Tom things?"

"Yes."

Andrea shivered and nestled closer. "So they think it might be the same person?"

"I guess they must," Graham said.

"What did they ask you?"

"Same thing. If I heard anything. And they asked Trevor where he was."

"They're always picking on kids, Gray, you know that. It doesn't mean anything. Since all that unemployment they automatically think kids are delinquents these days."

"True enough."

"What did you tell them?"

"That he was home with me, of course."

"Oh, Gray, should you have? I mean what if someone saw him somewhere else? It could make things really bad."

"He didn't do it, Andrea, he's not that kind of a lad, and I'm damned if I'm going to let the police get their hooks into him. Once they latch on they never let go. It was bad enough last time; it's not going to happen again."

"If you think it's best, Gray."

Graham frowned at her. "I know you don't think he's worth it," he said, "but he's a good lad, he'll turn out well in the end, you'll see."

Andrea put her arms around him. "I don't think ill of him, really I don't. It's just that you seem to dote on him so much. He can't do any wrong in your eyes."

"I'm his father, aren't I? I'm all he's got." He smiled and kissed her. "I know what I'm doing, love. Don't worry." He looked at his watch on the bedside table. "Bloody hell, I'd better be going. Trevor'll be home from school any minute."

Andrea moved away from him sadly. "You know I hate it when you leave, Gray," she said. "It's so lonely and boring being here all by myself in the evenings."

Graham kissed her lightly on the lips. "I know. I'll try and get back later if I can. I don't know what Trevor's got planned for tonight."

Graham slipped into his trousers, as Andrea watched from the bed.

"I'm getting a bit worried about Wooller, Gray," she said, just before he left.

"What about him?"

"I don't know if I'm being paranoid or feeling guilty or what, but it's just the way he looks at me, as if he *knows*. And worse, it's as if he's thinking about what to do with what he knows. Do you know what I mean? I feel like he's seen all of me, all of us."

"Don't worry about it," Graham said, sitting down on the edge of the bed and taking her hand. "You're probably overreacting. We've been discreet. The walls are very thick—I'm sure he wouldn't be able to hear a thing. And I'm always careful when I call. Really, love, don't worry about it. Must rush." He patted her hand and kissed her on the forehead. Andrea yawned and stretched, then turned over and lay in the impression his body had made. The bed still smelled of his Old Spice. She pulled the sheets around her shoulders and waved good-bye lazily as he slipped out through the door.

IV

It was six o'clock when Banks pulled up outside number eight Gallows View. He had decided to take on the Sharps himself and leave Wooller to Hatchley.

"Good evening," he said politely, introducing himself, as Graham Sharp opened the door, a forkful of sausage in his hand.

"We're just having dinner, can't it wait?"

"Won't take long," Banks said, already inside. "Just carry on eating."

The room wasn't exactly a living-room, it was more of a storage place full of boxes of tinned goods and crisps that could be easily carried into the shop. At the back, though, was a fairly modern kitchen, complete with a microwave oven, and Banks guessed that the real living quarters must be upstairs, spread out over the two adjoined cottages.

Graham and Trevor sat at the formica-topped table finishing what looked like bangers and mash with baked beans. Big white mugs of tea steamed in front of them.

"What is it, then?" Graham asked, polite enough not to talk with his mouth full. "We talked to one of your chaps last night. Told him all we knew."

"Yes," Banks said. "That's why I'm here. I just want to clear up a few things in the statement. Detective Constable Richmond is new to the job, if you know what I mean. We have to keep a close eye on new chaps, see that they get it right, go by the book."

"You mean you're here because you're doing some kind of job performance check on the young bloke?" Sharp asked incredulously.

It wasn't in the least bit true, but Banks thought it might put the Sharps at ease for as long as he wanted them to let their guards down. After that, of course, there were ways of putting them on the defensive again, a position which often turned out to be much more illuminating.

"Well, I never!" Sharp went on. "You know, I never really thought about the police force as a job like any other. I suppose you get wages as well and complain about pay-rises and poor canteen food?"

Banks laughed. "We don't have a canteen, but, yes, we complain a lot about pay-rises, or the lack of them." Innocently, he took out his notebook. "Detective Constable Richmond tells me that you heard nothing at around eleven o'clock on Monday night. Is that correct?"

"It is."

"Where were you?"

"Watching television in the sitting-room." He pointed towards the upstairs. "Far end of the house. Have a look if you want."

"Oh, I don't think that will be necessary, thanks all the same. You said you were watching television all evening?"

"Well, from about eight o'clock to midnight, anyway."

"Good," Banks said, peering into his notebook. "It looks like our man did a good job. You wouldn't, of course, hear anything from as far away as Cardigan Drive, or even number two Gallows View, if you were in the sitting-room with the television on, would you?"

"Nothing. You can try it if you want."

Banks waved aside his offer, then turned sharply to Trevor. "And where were you?"

Trevor, taken by surprise halfway through a mouthful of sausage and beans, spoke through the mush of semi-masticated food. "With him," he mumbled, pointing his fork at his father.

"Mr Sharp," Banks said, returning to Graham and frowning, "DC Richmond says that when you first told him you were watching television you made no mention of your son whatsoever. It was all in the first person, as if Trevor wasn't even home."

"What are you getting at?" Sharp said belligerently, putting down his knife and fork.

"Just checking up on the constable's statement, sir. Want to see if he got it right. He was a bit curious about this one point. He put a question mark by it."

Sharp glared at Banks for a few moments while Trevor went on chewing his food. "If you're insinuating that my Trevor had anything to do with this, you're barking up the wrong tree. He's straight as a die, always has been. Ask anyone."

"I'm not insinuating anything, Mr Sharp. I'd just like to know why the constable should mention this."

"It was a way of speaking, I suppose," Sharp said. "You don't always think you're going to have to account for the person who was with you, do you? I mean if someone asked you what you did last night and you stayed home watching telly, you probably wouldn't say 'My wife and I . . . blah-blah-blah . . .' would you?"

"You've got a point there, Mr Sharp. I probably wouldn't. So let me get this straight. You and Trevor spent the whole evening, from about eight till midnight, watching television, and you neither heard nor saw anything unusual. Am I right?"

"That's right. Only Trevor went to bed about eleven. Needs his sleep for school."

"Of course. What did you watch, Trevor?" Banks asked casually, turning to the boy.

"We watched—"

"I'm asking Trevor, Mr Sharp. What did you watch, son?"

"Don't really remember," Trevor said. "There was one of them American cop shows. You know, all car chases and shoot-outs." He shrugged. "Half the time I was reading my book and not paying attention."

"What book was that?"

"Now, look here," Graham burst out, the vein on his temple pulsating with anger. "You can't just come in here and interrogate my son like this, accuse us of lying to you. I told you, Trevor was with me all evening until he went to bed at about eleven o'clock."

"What was he reading?"

"Eh?"

"The book. What was he reading?"

"It was *The Shining*," Trevor answered, "Stephen King. Do you know it?"

"No," Banks said, smiling at Trevor. "Any good?"

"Yeah. Better than the film."

Banks nodded and packed away his notebook. "Well, I think I've got all I need. I'll let you finish your meal in peace. No, don't bother," he said, putting out his arm to stop Graham from standing up. "I can see myself out."

And with that he was gone. The Sharps ate the rest of their dinner slowly, in silence.

SIX

I

Thursday morning hit like a cold shower in the dumpy form of Ms Dorothy Wycombe. She was in Gristhorpe's office when Banks arrived at the station, and the superintendent called him in the moment he snapped off his Walkman. Gristhorpe clearly had no idea how to deal with her. For all his learning and compassion, he was a country gentleman and was not used to dealing with crusaders like Ms Wycombe. He looked lost.

Some people are susceptible to environment, but Dorothy Wycombe was not. Gristhorpe's office was a cosy, lived-in room with a studious air about it, but she might just as well have been standing on a platform at Leeds City Station waiting with her arms crossed for the 5:45 to King's Cross, glaring at everything within her field of vision. The dominant expression on her face during the meeting that followed was one of distaste, as if she had just eaten a particularly sour gooseberry.

"Er...Miss...er...Ms Wycombe, meet Detective Chief Inspector Banks," Gristhorpe muttered by way of introduction.

"Pleased to meet you," Banks said apprehensively.

No reply.

Through his job, Banks had come to realize that it was unwise to expect stereotypes; to do so only led to misunderstandings. On the other hand, he had also been forced to admit the existence of stereotypes, having met more than once, among others, the lisping, mincing homosexual, the tweedy retired colonel with handlebar moustache and shooting-stick, and the whore with the heart of gold.

So when Dorothy Wycombe stood before him looking like every-man's parody of a women's libber, he could hardly claim surprise. Disappointment, perhaps, but not surprise.

"Seems there's been a complaint, Alan," Gristhorpe began slowly. "It's about Sergeant Hatchley, but I thought you ought to hear it first." Banks nodded and looked at Dorothy Wycombe, whose chins jutted out in challenge.

That she was unattractive was obvious; what was not clear was how much of this was due to nature itself and how much to her own efforts. She had fizzed all the life out of her colourless hair, and the bulky sack that passed for a dress bulged in the most unlikely places. Above her double-chin was a tight, mean mouth, lined around the edges from constant clenching, and a dull, suet complexion. Behind the National Health glasses shone eyes whose intelligence, which Banks had no doubt she possessed, was glazed over with revolutionary zeal. Her speech was jagged with italics.

"I have been informed," she began, consulting a small black note-book for dramatic effect, "that while questioning the victims of your *Peeping Tom*, your sergeant's attitude was flippant, and, furthermore, that he expressed the desire to commit a similar act of violence against one interviewee in particular."

"Those are serious charges," Banks said, wishing he could smoke a cigarette. "Who made them?"

"I did."

"I don't remember you ever being a victim of the scopophiliac."

"Pardon?"

"I said I don't recall that you ever reported any invasion of your privacy."

"That's not the point. You're simply trying to obscure the issue."

"What issue?"

"Your sergeant's *lewd* and *lascivious* suggestions—an attitude, might I add, that reflects on the entire investigation of this whole scandalous affair."

"Who made the charges?" Banks repeated.

"I told you, *I'm* bringing them to your attention."

"On whose authority?"

"I represent the local women."

"Who says so?"

"Inspector Banks, this is infuriating! Will you or will you not listen to the charges?"

"I'll listen to them when I know who made them and what gives you the authority to pass them on."

Dorothy Wycombe moved further away from Banks and puffed herself up to her full size. "I am the chairperson of WEEF."

"Weef?"

"W.E.E.F., Inspector Banks. The Women of Eastvale for Emancipation and Freedom. WEEF."

Banks had often thought it was amusing how groups twisted the language so that acronyms of organizations would sound like snappy words. It had started with NATO, SEATO, UNO and other important groups, progressed through such local manifestations as SPIT, SHOT and SPEAR, and now there was WEEF. It didn't seem to matter at all that "Women of Eastvale" sounded vaguely mediaeval or that "Freedom" and "Emancipation" meant more or less the same thing. They simply existed to give birth to WEEF, which sounded to Banks like an impoverished "woof," or the kind of squeak a frightened mouse might utter.

"Very well," Banks conceded, making a note. "And who brought the complaint to your attention?"

"I'm not under any obligation to divulge my source," Dorothy Wycombe snapped back, quick as a reporter in the dock.

"Yesterday," Banks sighed, "Sergeant Hatchley spoke to Carol Ellis, Mandy Selkirk, Josie Campbell and Ellen Parry about their experiences. He also spoke to Molly Torbeck, who had been with Carol Ellis in The Oak on the night of the incident. Would you like me to interview each in turn and find out for myself? I can do that, you know."

"Do what you want. I'm not going to tell you."

"Right," Banks said, standing up to leave. "Then I've no intention of taking your complaint seriously. You must realize that we get a lot of unfounded allegations made against us, usually by overzealous members of the public. So many that we've got quite an elaborate system of screening them. I'm sure that, as a defender of freedom and emancipation, you wouldn't want anyone's career to suffer from injustice brought about by smear campaigns, would you?"

Banks thought Dorothy Wycombe was about to explode, so red did her face become. Her chins trembled and her knuckles whitened as she grasped the edge of Gristhorpe's desk.

"This is outrageous!" she shouted. "I'll not have my movement dictated to by a fascist police force."

"I'm sorry," Banks said, heading for the door. "We just can't deal with unidentified complainants."

"Carol Ellis!" The name burst from Dorothy Wycombe's tight mouth like a huge build-up of steam from a stuck valve. "*Now* will you sit down and listen to me?"

"Yes, ma'am," Banks said, taking out his notebook again.

"It's *Ms* Wycombe," she told him, "and I expect you to treat this matter seriously."

"It's a serious charge," Banks agreed, "as I said earlier. That's why I want it fully documented. What exactly did Carol Ellis say?"

"She said that Sergeant Hatchley seemed to treat the whole Peeping Tom business as a *bit of a lark*, that he seemed either *bored* or *amused* whilst interviewing her, and that he made certain *suggestions* about her body."

"Bored or amused, Ms Wycombe? Which? They're very different, you know."

"Both, at different times."

"Certain suggestions about her body? What kind of suggestions? Lewd, offensive?"

"What other kind are there, Inspector? He hinted that the Peeping Tom must have had *quite a treat*."

"Is that all?"

"Isn't it enough? What kind of—"

"I mean are there any other allegations?"

"No. That's all I wanted to say. I hope I can trust you, Inspector, to see that *something* is done about this."

"Don't worry, Ms Wycombe, I'll get to the bottom of it. If there's any truth in the charges, Sergeant Hatchley will be disciplined, you can be sure of that."

Dorothy Wycombe smiled grimly and suspiciously, then swished out of the office.

Gristhorpe took a deep breath. "Alan," he said, "when I made that joke about throwing your sergeant to the wolves the other day, I didn't mean it bloody literally. Whatever we might think about Ms Wycombe and her manner, we've got to concede that she's got a point. Don't you agree?"

"If what she says is true, yes."

"You think it might not be?"

"We both know how the truth gets twisted in emotional situations, sir. Let me get Hatchley's version before we go any further."

"Very well. But let me know, Alan. Are you getting any further?"

"No, but I'm seeing Jenny Fuller again today. Perhaps she'll have a bit more light to shed on things. If we can narrow the field down a bit, we might at least be able to start checking around."

"What about Alice Matlock?"

"Nothing yet."

"Get a move on, Alan. Too many things are piling up for my liking."

II

Back in his office, Banks found a note from Inspector Barnshaw accompanying a police artist's drawing of the man that the Leeds junk dealer, Crutchley, had described. He had recognized none of the file photographs, but the sketch was a good realization of the description Banks had taken.

He lit a cigarette, tidied the files on his desk, and sent for Sergeant Hatchley, who arrived about five minutes later.

"Sit down," Banks said, his abrupt tone foreshadowing the bollocking the sergeant was in for.

Banks decided not to beat about the bush. Instead, he told Hatchley exactly what Dorothy Wycombe had said and asked him for his version of what had happened during the Carol Ellis interview.

Hatchley blushed and scratched his chin, avoiding Banks's glance.

"Is it true?" Banks pressed. "That's all I want to know."

"Well, yes and no," Hatchley admitted.

"Meaning?"

"Look, sir, I know Carol Ellis. I'm a bachelor and she's not married either, and I'm not denying I've had my eye on her for some time—long before this business ever started."

"Go on."

"When I talked to her yesterday, she'd got over what happened. After all, it was just a bit of a shock. Nobody got hurt. And she was even joking about it a bit, wishing she'd worn her best underwear, given a better show, that kind of thing. 'Appen she was saying it to cover up her nerves, or maybe she was embarrassed. I don't know. But, like I told you, I know her and I quite fancy her myself, so I might have joked along, you know, made things a bit more personal."

"'Might have'?"

"All right, I did."

"Were you bored?"

"With Carol Ellis around? You must be joking, sir. A bit casual, maybe. It's not like interrogating someone you don't know, or a villain."

"Did you suggest that the peeper must have had quite a treat?"

"I don't rightly recollect. I might have joked along with her, like. When she said about wearing her best undies, I probably said she'd look fine to me in any underwear. You know, just like a compliment. A bit cheeky, but..."

Banks sighed. It was clear to him what had happened, but it was equally clear that it shouldn't have. The worst he could accuse Hatchley of was tactlessness and allowing personal affairs to come before police work. Whatever Carol Ellis had said to Dorothy Wycombe had probably been said in a spirit of fun, and was no doubt grossly distorted.

"I don't need to tell you that it was a bloody stupid thing to do, do I?" he said to Hatchley, who didn't reply. "Because of your actions, we're in for a lot more bad publicity, and we've got to spend time placating Dorothy bloody Wycombe. I do wish you'd learn to keep your urges to yourself. It's one thing to chat the woman up in a pub, but quite another to do it while you're interviewing her about a crime. Am I making myself clear?"

Hatchley pressed his lips together and nodded.

"Are you sure that Carol Ellis took your remarks in the spirit they were intended?"

Here, Hatchley beamed. "She's going out with me on Saturday night, sir, if that's of any account."

Banks couldn't help but smile. "Something must have got twisted in the communication network, then," he muttered. "I'll talk to her myself and straighten it out. But be bloody careful in future. I don't need the aggro, and the superintendent certainly doesn't. You'd better stay out of the peeper case in future. And you'd better stay out of the old man's way for a day or two, as well."

"What do you want me to do?"

"Concentrate on the break-ins and the Alice Matlock killing." He passed Hatchley the drawing. "Get copies done of this and spread them around. Help Richmond find out if Alice Matlock had any younger friends, any lame ducks, lonely hearts, that kind of thing. Did you see Wooller, by the way?"

"Yes, last night."

"Anything?"

Hatchley shook his head. "Nah. He's an odd one all right, but I'm pretty damn sure he didn't see or hear anything."

"Did you get the impression he was holding something back?"

"Lots of things. He's a dark horse, sure enough. But nothing about the Matlock case, no. I still reckon he's worth keeping an eye on for the other business, though. You definitely get a kind of dirty feeling, talking to him."

"Okay," Banks said. "But you're off that. And if the press get hold of Dorothy Wycombe's story, which I'm sure they will, I want no comments from you. None at all. That understood?"

"Yes, sir. Bit of an Amazon, eh, that Dorothy Wycombe?"

"Off you go, Sergeant."

Hatchley left and Banks relaxed, glad it was over. He didn't mind yelling at the sergeant in the course of duty, but he hated the formality of the official reprimand. It was easy to see why Gristhorpe had passed the buck to him in the first place; the superintendent was diplomatic enough, all right, but he was also too soft-hearted when it came to his men. He looked at his watch. It was just after eleven. He decided to take his coffee and toasted teacake alone this morning, and leave Hatchley to lick his wounded pride for a while.

III

Eastvale Comprehensive used to be called Eastvale Grammar School. In the old days it was a respectable institution attended by promising children from miles around, many of whom gained scholarships to Oxford or Cambridge, or went on to the northern red-brick universities closer to home.

The building itself was Victorian, attractive in a Gothic way from the outside, with turrets, a clock and a bell tower, and full of high gloomy corridors within. A number of "temporary" classrooms, trailers propped up on bricks, for the most part, had been added to the original building in the early seventies, and they looked as if they were definitely there to stay.

Things changed for the school when the comprehensive system was turned loose on the country. Now teachers struggled with overcrowded classes of such mixed abilities that it was impossible to nurture the bright and do justice to the slow. Often the children had to suffer inept teaching by fools who knew more about athletics and rugby than Caesar's conquest, Shakespeare, or the square roots of negative numbers.

Banks knew the place, though he had never set foot inside the main building before. Both Brian and Tracy went there, and the tales they told did a lot to undermine Banks's faith in the comprehensive system.

As a working-class boy in Peterborough, he had always felt a strong aversion to any kind of elitism, yet as a moderately well-educated man with a taste for knowledge, he had to admit that no amount of special treatment and mollycoddling could turn a lazy, hostile slob into a star pupil; far from it, too many mediocre minds could do nothing but discourage exceptional students from doing their best. At school, he remembered, kids want to belong; they do not want to be ostracized by their peers, which happens if they excel at anything other than sports.

As far as natural abilities went, he had no real opinion. Perhaps some were born with better brains than others. But that wasn't, to him, the issue—the point was that everybody should be given the chance to find out, and the idealistic basis of the comprehensive system seemed to grant just that possibility. In practice, it didn't seem to be turning out that way.

In his own education, he had been very lucky indeed. After failing his "eleven-plus" exam, he had been condemned to the local secondary modern school, there to be moulded into an ideal electrician, brick-layer or road sweeper. He had nothing against manual occupations—his own father had been a sheet-metal worker until angina forced an early retirement—except that he wasn't interested in any of them.

Fortunately, because he did well at his studies, he got a shot at the "fourteen-plus." He worked long and hard, passed, and found himself a new boy, an outsider at the grammar school. It seemed that all the relationships had been formed already during the three years he had spent in exile, and for the first two terms he despaired of making any friends. It was only typical schoolboy stand-offishness, though. As soon as the others found out that he was a terror in a scrap, owned the toughest conker in the school, and made perhaps the finest rugger scrum-half the team had ever seen, he had no problem gaining acceptance.

It had been a cruel process, though, he reflected. The first exam split his groups of friends in the most divisive way: grammar school kids rarely talked to secondary modern boys, no matter how many games of commandos or cricket they had played together in their childhood; and his next exam accomplished much the same thing in reverse. This time, however, the friends that Banks had made at the secondary modern school never spoke to him again because they thought he had betrayed them. Entering the gates of Eastvale Comprehensive somehow brought back the good and the bad of his own schooldays.

When Banks walked through the yard it was lunchtime; the children played hand-tennis or cricket against stumps chalked on the wall in the yard, or smoked behind the cycle sheds, and the teachers lounged in the smoky staff room reading the *Guardian* or grappling with the *Sun* crossword. The head, however, was in his sanctuary, and it was into this haven that Banks was ushered by a slim, pretty secretary, who looked hardly older than school-leaving age herself.

The institutional-green corridors were half glass, so that anyone passing by could look into the classrooms. Now, the desks
stood empty, and the blackboards were still partly covered in
indecipherable scrawl. Many of the desks, Banks noticed, were
just as desecrated with the carved initials of girlfriends and the
names of famous cricketers, footballers and rock-and-roll bands as
they had been in his own schooldays. Only the names had
changed. And the place smelled pleasantly of bubble gum, chalk
dust and satchel leather.

The head was sipping tea in his panelled office, a well-thumbed
copy of Cicero on the desk in front of him. He greeted Banks and
turned sadly to the book. "Latin, Inspector. Such an elegant, noble
language, quite easily capable of sustaining lengthy flights of poetry.
Nobody, it seems, has any use for it these days. Anyway," he sighed,
standing up, "you've not come to hear about my problems, have you?"

The head, like his book, looked as though he had seen better
days. His face was haggard, his hair grey, and he had a pronounced
stoop. His most noticeable feature, however, was a big red nose, and
it didn't take much imagination to guess what nicknames the kids
had for him. Though he wore a bat-like cape, there was no mortar-
board in sight. The study looked so much like Banks's old headmaster's lair that he felt the same quiver of adrenalin as he had all those
years ago while waiting for the cane.

"No, sir," Banks smiled, slipping easily into the language of
respect. "I came to ask a few questions about one of your boys."

"Oh, dear. Not been getting himself into trouble, has he? I'm
afraid, these days, it's very difficult to keep track of them, and there
are several bad elements in the school. Do sit down."

"Thank you, sir. It's nothing definite," Banks went on. "We're just
faced with one or two discrepancies in a statement and we'd like to
know if you can tell us anything about Trevor Sharp."

There was no flash of recognition in Buxton's expression.
Obviously he had long since given up trying to keep track of all his
pupils. He got up and walked towards his filing cabinet, from which,
after much muttering and tut-tutting, he pulled out a sheaf of papers.

"Reports," he said, tapping the papers with a bony finger. "These
should tell us what you want to know. I'd appreciate it, though,

Inspector, if this got no further than you and me. These are supposed to be confidential...."

"Of course. In return, I'd be pleased if you didn't mention my visit, especially to the boy himself or to anyone who might tell him."

The head nodded and started turning the pages. "Let me see... 1983...no...winter...summer...1984...excellent...ninety percent...very good..." and he went on in this fashion for some time before returning to Banks. "A bright boy, young Master Sharp. The name suits him. Look at this." And he passed Banks the reports for the previous year. They were full of "excellents" and high marks in all subjects except Geography. About that, his teacher had said: "Does not seem interested. Obviously capable, but unwilling to work hard enough."

As it turned out, that lone failure foreshadowed the more recent reports, which were scattered with remarks such as "Could do better," "Does not try hard enough" and "Takes negative attitude towards subject." There were also several complaints from the teachers about his absences: "If Trevor were in class more often he would attain a better grasp of the subject," wrote Mr Fox, his English teacher, and "Failure to hand in homework and to appear in class have contributed greatly towards Trevor's disappointing performance in History this term," commented Mr Rhodes.

"What this adds up to, then," Banks said, "is a promising pupil who seems to have lost his way."

"Yes," Mr Buxton agreed sadly. "It happens so often these days. There seem to be so many distractions for the boys. Of course, in most cases it's a phase they have to go through. Rebellion. Have to get it out of their systems, you know."

Banks knew, but the transformation from star pupil with a great career ahead into truant and slacker was certainly open to other interpretations.

"Who are his friends?" Banks asked. "Who does he hang around with?"

"I'm afraid I wouldn't know, Inspector. It's so hard to keep track.... His form master, Mr Price, might be able to tell you." He picked up his phone, handling it as if it were a severed limb. "I'll ask Sonia to bring him in."

When Mr Price arrived, he looked both annoyed at having been disturbed on his dinner break and apprehensive about the purpose of the call. The head soon put him at ease, and curiosity then gained the better edge, turning him into a garrulous pedant. After trying to impress both Banks and the head for several minutes with his modern approach to language teaching and his theories on classroom management, he finally had to be brought around to the point of his visit.

"I've come to inquire about one of your students, Mr Price— Trevor Sharp."

"Ah, Sharp, yes. Odd fellow, really. Doesn't have much of anything to do with the other lads. Rather sullen and hostile. One simply tends to stay away from him."

"Is that what the other boys do?"

"Seems so. Nobody's actively against him or anything like that, but he goes his way and they go theirs."

"So he has no close friends here?"

"None."

"Is he a bully?"

"Not at all, though he could be if he wanted. Tough kid. Very good at games. He always dresses conservatively, while the others are trying to get away with whatever they can—purple hair, mohawk cuts, spiky bracelets, studded leather jackets, you name it. Not Sharp, though."

"The others don't make fun of him?"

"No. He's the biggest in the class. Nobody bothers him."

"I understand from his school reports that he's been absent a lot lately. Have you talked to him about this?"

"Yes, certainly. In fact, last parents' day I had a long chat with his father, who seemed very concerned. Doesn't seem to have done much good, though; Sharp still comes and goes as he pleases. Personally, I think he's just bored. He's bright and he's bored."

There was nothing more to say, especially as Banks had no concrete grounds on which to investigate Trevor. He thanked both the headmaster and Mr Price, repeated his request for discretion, and left.

IV

As Banks was shuffling through the reports in the headmaster's office, Trevor himself was about a mile away. He had gone out of bounds to meet Mick at a pub where the question of drinking age was rarely broached, especially if the coins kept passing over the counter. They sat over the last quarters of their pints, smoking and listening to the songs that Mick had chosen on the jukebox.

Trevor kept sucking and probing at his front teeth, pulling a face.

"What's the matter with you," Mick asked. "It's driving me bleeding barmy, all that fucking around with your gob."

"Don't know," Trevor answered. "Hurts a bit, feels rough. I think I've lost a filling."

"Let's take a look."

Trevor bared his teeth in an evil grin, like a horse with the bit in its mouth, while Mick looked and pronounced his verdict. "Yeah, one of 'em's getting a bit black round the edges—that little one next to the big yellow one. I'd see a fucking dentist if I was you."

"I don't like dentists."

"Fucking coward!" Mick jeered.

Trevor shrugged. "Maybe so, but I don't like them. Anyway, you said we'd got two jobs on?" he asked when the music had finished.

"That's right. One tonight, one next Monday."

"Why tonight? It seems pretty short notice to me."

"Coming back from 'oliday tomorrow, aren't they? And Lenny says the pickings'll be good."

"What about next Monday?"

"Bird always goes to her country club Mondays. Lenny's heard she always keeps quite a bit of jewellery around the place. Rich divorcée, like."

"Has Lenny given you any idea about how we get in?"

"Better." Mick grinned pimplishly. "He's given me this." And he opened his parka to show Trevor the tip of what looked like a crowbar. "Easy," he went on. "Just stick it between the door and the post and you're home free."

"What if someone sees us?"

"Nobody will. These are big 'ouses, detached like. And we'll go in the back way. All quiet, nobody around. Better wear the balas to be on the safe side, though."

Trevor nodded. The thought of breaking into a big, empty, dark house was frightening and exciting. "We'll need torches," he said. "Little ones, those pen-lights."

"Got 'em," Mick said proudly. "Lenny gave us a couple before he split for The Smoke."

"Fine, then," Trevor smiled. "We're on."

"We're on," Mick echoed. And they drank to it.

SEVEN

I

Jenny laughed at Banks's theory about the peeper spying on female pub *habitutées*: "Only been working for me three days and already coming up with ideas of your own, eh?"

"But is it any good?"

"Might be, yes. It could be part of his pattern, like his fixation on blondes. On the other hand it was perhaps just the most convenient time. A time when nobody would miss him or see him. Or a time when he could depend on his victims going to bed after a few drinks. He wouldn't have to hang around too long to get what he came for."

"Now you're doing my job."

Jenny smiled. They sat in deep, comfortable chairs by the crackling fire and looked as if they should have been drinking brandy and smoking cigars. But both preferred Theakston's bitter, and only Banks puffed sparingly at his Benson and Hedges Special Milds.

"How many pubs are there in Eastvale?" Jenny asked.

"Fifty-seven. I checked."

Jenny whistled through her teeth. "Alcoholic's paradise. But still, you must know which areas he operates in?"

"Random so far. He's spread himself around except for picking two from the same pub, so that doesn't help us much, but we do have some evidence that indicates a possible link between our peeper and the Alice Matlock killing. Could it be the same person?"

"Do you expect a yes-or-no answer?"

"All I want is your opinion. Is it likely that the peeper, after watching Carol Ellis get undressed, ran down the street, knocked on Alice

Matlock's door and, for some reason, killed her either intentionally or accidentally?"

"You want an answer based purely on psychological considerations?"

"Yes."

"I'd say no, then. It's very unlikely. In the first place, he would have no reason to run to Alice Matlock's house. If he'd been spotted, his impulse would be to get as far away as possible, as quickly as possible."

"You're still doing my job."

"Well, dammit," Jenny said, "they're so close. What do you want me to say?"

"I don't know. Something about a peeper not being the murdering kind."

Jenny laughed. "Primary-school psychology? You won't get that from me. I've told you it's unlikely and I've given you one good reason. If he got the release he needed from watching Carol Ellis, I doubt that he'd be emotionally capable of murder immediately afterwards."

"That's what I said to the superintendent."

"Well, why the bloody hell...." Jenny started, and then began to laugh. "We really are doing each other's jobs, aren't we? But seriously, Alan, I say it's unlikely but it's not impossible."

"Would he go to her to confess, perhaps?"

Jenny shook her head. "I don't think so. Not to an old woman. Doesn't fit at all. Offhand, I'd say you're looking for a bald, short-sighted, middle-aged man wearing a plastic mac, bicycle-clips and galoshes."

"If only."

"Stereotypes do exist, you know."

"Oh, I know. Believe me, I do."

"What do you mean?"

"Dorothy Wycombe."

"Ah," Jenny said. "Had a visit, have you?"

"This morning."

"Ah, yes. Dorothy's quite a formidable opponent, don't you think? I find her a bit hard to take, myself."

"I thought you two were friends."

"Acquaintances. We've worked together on one or two projects,

that's all. We don't really have a lot in common, but Dorothy is ener-
getic and very good at her job."

"WEEF?"

"Yes, WEEF. Pretty pathetic, isn't it?"

Banks nodded.

"Anyway," Jenny went on, "Dorothy is an intelligent woman, but
she lets her dogma get in the way of her thinking. What was it all
about, if it's not private?"

"It is a bit delicate," Banks told her, then gave an abbreviated
account, not mentioning any names, and they both had another
laugh.

"The poor man," Jenny sympathized. "He was just trying to chat
her up."

"Not so much of the 'poor man,' if you please. He should have
known better."

"But why did she report him to Dorothy?"

"She didn't. I popped round to see her on my way here, and she
was very annoyed by what had happened. Apparently Ms Wycombe
had been visiting the victims—rather like some Victorian lady visiting the poor, I should imagine—and trying to gather some ammuni-
tion against us. The woman chatted in quite a friendly way to Ms
Wycombe and joked about my man's visit. She'd actually been quite
flattered as she'd had her eye on him for a while and wondered when,
if ever, he was going to make his move. Anyway, Dorothy Wycombe
twisted the information to suit her purposes and marched in demand-
ing blood."

"What a job you do."

"I know. It's a dirty job—"

"—but somebody's got to do it. Talking of dirty jobs," Jenny went
on, "I've dug out a couple of case histories for you."

"I'm listening."

"Ever heard of Charles Floyd or Patrick Byrne?"

Banks shook his head. "I'm afraid my history of crime's not what it
should be. Tell me."

"Patrick Byrne murdered a girl in the Birmingham YWCA in 1959.
He was a labourer on a building site near the hostel, and one
afternoon he got sent back to the yard by his foreman for returning

to work drunk after lunch. He'd often peeped on the girls undressing in the hostel, but this time he went in and strangled a girl. After that, he undressed her, raped her, then cut off her head with a table knife. He also made an attempt to eat one of her breasts with sugar."

"That's not a very encouraging tale, is it?"

"No. Apparently Byrne had had sadistic fantasies, including cutting women in half with a circular saw, since he was about seventeen. He said he wanted to get his own back on women for causing him nervous tension through sex. Before that, he'd been content with simply watching girls undress, but because he was drunk and upset by being told off by his foreman, he went beyond everything he'd ever done before. He also left a note that read, 'This was what I thought would never happen.'"

"Is the other case just as heartening?"

"Yes. About the only consolation is that it happened in Texas in the forties. Charles Floyd started by watching women get undressed. Then he waited till they went to sleep, killed them and raped them, in that order. There was one woman who never closed her curtains, and he watched her for several nights before he finally climbed in after she fell asleep. He battered her to death, then wrapped her head in a sheet and raped her. After that, he spent the rest of the night in bed with her. He killed other women, too, and when he got caught he admitted he'd been a Peeping Tom who turned to murder and rape when the sexual excitement got too much for him."

"The woman didn't close her curtains?" Banks commented. "Surely that was asking for it in a way?"

Jenny shot him a cold glance. "We've already been through that."

"And I did say that women should be careful not to appear to be inviting men to sex."

"And I said that we should be able to dress how we like and go where we damn well please."

"So we agree to differ."

"It looks like it. But please understand, I'm not condoning the woman leaving her curtains open. It was probably a very stupid thing to do. All I'm saying is that what Floyd did was an act of violence more than of sex, and that such things will happen anyway, whatever we do, until more men start to see women as people, not as sex objects."

"I don't believe the solution is as simple as that, admirable as it sounds," Banks said. "Yes, they are acts of violence, but it's violence that is highly sexual in nature. I think it's true that at least one of the reasons for the rise in sex crimes is the increase in stimulation—and that includes fashions, pornography, advertising, films, TV, the lot."

"And who determines women's fashions?"

"Mostly men, I should imagine."

"That's right. You dress us the way you want us, you create us in the image you desire, and then you have the gall to accuse us of asking for it!"

"Okay, calm down," Banks said, concerned at seeing Jenny so hurt and angry. He put his hand on her shoulder and she didn't brush it off. "I understand what you're saying. It's a very complex subject and it's hard to portion out blame. I'm willing to take my share. How about you?"

Jenny nodded and they shook hands.

"What conclusions have you drawn from those cases?" Banks asked.

"None, really. Only the most obvious ones."

"I must be thick, nothing's obvious to me."

"Until we know our man's motivation, we can't know whether some kind of trigger might exist for him, or how close he is to reaching it."

"Look," Banks said, glancing at his watch, "it's almost ten o'clock. Can I get you another drink?"

"Yes, please."

"Right you are. And while I'm at the bar, think about this. Is there any indication at all, from what little we know already, that our man might cross the same borders as Floyd and Byrne did?"

II

The area around the lock splintered easily when Mick pushed on the crowbar, and the two of them broke into the dark, silent house in no time. The light from their small torches criss-crossed the kitchen, picking out the gleaming appliances: fridge, washing machine, microwave, dishwasher, oven. Quickly, they moved on; only the poor kept their money in jam jars in the kitchen.

Down a short hallway was the split-level living-room, and Mick cursed as he tripped over the divide. It was a big room, sparsely furnished as far as they could make out. Their torches picked out a three-piece suite, TV and video on a stand, and a music centre. By the door stood a tall cabinet full of china and crystal glasses. Mick opened the lower doors and found it full of booze—scotch, gin, vodka, brandy, rum, everything under the sun—and he grabbed a bottle of Rémy Martin by the neck. He slugged it back greedily and began to cough and splutter. Trevor told him to keep quiet.

Trevor was awed just to be in the place. Already he'd forgotten what they came for and was trembling with the excitement of violation. This was someone's home, someone's "castle," and he wasn't supposed to be in it. It felt like a vast cave full of possibilities, one of those boat rides through dark tunnels he used to take as a child at Blackpool Pleasure Beach—a ghost train, even, because he did feel fear, and each tiny detail his light picked out was a surprise: a wall-lamp curving upwards like a bent arm holding a torch; an ornate standard lamp with carved snakes winding around its column; an antique pipe on the mantelpiece. And his light caught occasional images from the big framed paintings on the walls: a giant bird terrorizing a man; some naked tart standing on a seashell. He could hear his heartbeat, his breathing, and every movement he made was a further violation of somebody else's silence.

Mick finished with the cognac and dropped the bottle on the floor. Wiping his lips with the back of his hand, he tapped Trevor on the shoulder and suggested that they look around upstairs. In the master bedroom, their eyes, now accustomed to the dark, picked out the outlines of bed, wardrobe and dresser. The gleam of a streetlamp through the net curtains helped visibility, too, and they turned off their pen-lights.

Trevor began searching through the drawers, using his light again to illuminate the contents. He found dark, silky underwear: bras, panties, tights, slips, camisoles. They were soft and slippery in his hands, charging him with static, and he rubbed them against his face, smelling the fresh, lemony scent of the woman. He also found an old cigar box in a drawer full of the man's socks, string vests and under-pants; inside it were a set of keys and about a hundred and fifty pounds in cash.

Mick found what looked like a jewellery box on the dresser. When he opened it up, a ballet dancer began spinning to tinkling music. He dropped the box and spilled the jewels on the floor; then, cursing, he bent and scooped them up.

Trevor looked around for any locked cabinets that the keys might fit, but he found nothing. The two of them went back downstairs, feet sinking luxuriously into the deep pile carpeting, and, shining their torches again, had another look around the living-room. There, in a corner, set into the wall, was what looked like a safe. Trevor tried his keys but none fit. Mick tried the crowbar but it bent. Eventually, they gave up.

"Let's take the VCR," Mick whispered.

"No. It's too heavy, too easy to trace."

"Lenny'll get rid of it in London."

"No, Mick. We're not taking big stuff like that. It'll slow us down. You've got the jewels and I've got a hundred quid. It's enough."

"Enough!" Mick snorted. "These people are fucking rolling in it. We've not got much more than we get from the old bags."

"Yes, we have. And people are more careful these days—we're bloody lucky to have got so much."

Reluctantly Mick gave up the idea and agreed to leave. Trevor was still enjoying just being there, though, still tingling, and he wanted to do something. Finally, he unzipped his fly and started to urinate over the TV, VCR and music centre, spraying lavishly on the carpet, paintings and mantelpiece, too. It seemed to go on forever, a powerful, translucent stream glittering in the pen-light's beam, and with it, he felt himself relax, felt a delicious warmth infuse his bones.

Not to be outdone, Mick lowered his pants and dropped a steaming pile on the sheepskin rug in front of the fireplace, giggling softly to himself as he did it.

When they'd both finished, they left the way they came, pausing only briefly to check the kitchen drawers and cupboards, just in case.

III

"There's no evidence that we've got a Byrne or a Floyd on our hands," Jenny said, sipping her half of bitter. "I think that if we had, something would have happened before now. The trouble with psychology is that it works best when you know all the facts. It's hard to make guesses in the dark. It's also unscientific."

"Police work's the same," Banks added. "There's nothing like facts, but I've always found that occasional guesses, or some kind of hunch based on limited knowledge, can often work well. It gives you a bit of room for the intuition, imagination."

"That's surprising, coming from you," Jenny said, looking at him as if all her earlier theories had been wrong.

"Why?"

"It just is. I suppose I've been used to you asking for facts, looking for evidence."

"It's important, I'm not denying it. But more often than not forensic evidence is only useful in getting a conviction. First you have to catch the criminal, and he's as cunning and imaginative as can be. Some aren't, of course, some are plain stupid. But they're the easy ones."

"I should think your peeper is probably quite intelligent. Again, this is mostly guesswork, but he has avoided capture so far, and he's got his system worked out quite well. It remains to be seen how adaptable he is. He's certainly not a fool."

"Back to my original question," Banks said. "You don't think he'll escalate?"

"I said I didn't think we had a serious sex criminal on our hands. I don't think he's likely to move on to necrophilia or eating breasts, with or without sugar, but I wouldn't be too sure that merely peeping will keep him happy for much longer. It might be getting too easy for him, especially if he's intelligent. If he stops getting his thrills that way...then..." She shrugged. "At best he might turn to exhibitionism, at worst some kind of attack, molestation."

"Rape?"

"Ultimately. Although it might not be rape in the legal sense.

There may be no penetration; he might simply force women to strip. I don't know, I'm just trying to project the pattern. He might feel the need for greater danger, more risk; he might need to see and absorb the fear of his victims. Yes, it could happen. Especially the closer he gets to his original impulse."

"What do you mean?"

"If he finds someone who reminds him of his mother, or whoever he was first struck by, then the stimulus might be too much; it might cause him to push through to another level."

"What can we do with what we've got so far, then?" Banks asked.

"You want me to tell you your job?"

"Why not? You've not done so badly at it so far."

"All right. What I'd do is this: find out how many men between the ages of about twenty and thirty-five are either living alone or with a single parent, most likely a mother."

"Why?"

"It's just what the statistics show. Not completely reliable of course, but better than a slap in the face with a wet fish, wouldn't you say?"

"I would. I was just wondering about the single-parent business."

"I think there's generally more stability with both parents around, unless the marriage is in a really bad way. It's what the stats show, anyway. Shall I go on?"

"Yes."

"There shouldn't be all that many in Eastvale, I don't think. Most people move away or get married. Next I'd 'stake out' selected pubs, as they say on the telly."

"I've told you how many pubs there are in Eastvale. We don't have anything like the manpower."

"Use what you have. He's tried the same pub twice. Why not a third time? There's one you can cover. And you must have some pretty policewomen around who'd be happy to work overtime to help get rid of this particular criminal, surely?"

Banks nodded. "Go on."

"As far as the other two pubs are concerned, you can cover them, too. If he struck lucky once he might try for a second time."

"So you suggest that we cover the pubs he's already operated in?"

"Yes."

"Good. We're already doing that."

"Bastard!" Jenny laughed and slapped his arm playfully. "You've got to admit, though, I was on the right track, wasn't I?"

"Definitely. Any time you need a job. Is there anything else?"

"You might check around the pornographic bookshops—if there are any in Eastvale—and the strip-clubs. I don't mean that you should pester everyone who enjoys seeing a bit of tit and ass now and then, but make your presence felt. Maybe if you put the wind up him he'll make a mistake."

"You think he's likely to hang around such places?"

"It's possible. After all, it's looking, isn't it? Even if it's not as thrilling as the other kind. By the way, are there places like that in Eastvale?"

"One or two. We keep an eye on them, but I'll do as you recommend, push a bit harder."

Jenny nodded. "Excuse me for asking," she said, "but how did you get that scar?" And she leaned forward and touched the small scar by Banks's right eye.

"Accident," he said tersely. "Years ago."

"How disappointing. And I thought you must have got it in some heroic struggle with a knife-wielding maniac, or perhaps from a gun that went off as you grappled to save someone's life."

"You've got quite a romantic imagination for a psychologist."

"And you've got none! Come on, where did you get it?"

"I told you, an accident."

"What kind of accident?"

"I fell off my tricycle."

"Liar. You're only doing this because you think it makes you mysterious, aren't you?"

"And you're only teasing me because you've had too much to drink."

"Ooh, I haven't."

Banks laughed. "Perhaps not. But if you drink any more you will have, and then I'll have to book you for drunken driving."

"I haven't got my car. I walked up to town before we met and spent an hour or so in the library."

"I've got mine today—and I haven't had too much to drink. Come on, I'll give you a lift."

It was raining fast again, and Banks drove carefully around the base of Castle Hill, down the narrow, winding streets, crossed the river, and pulled up outside Jenny's house by The Green about five minutes later.

"Coming in for a coffee?" she asked.

"Just a quick one."

IV

Trevor and Mick sat in the front room sharing out the money. Trevor had already palmed about fifty pounds, and he then managed to persuade Mick to tell Lenny that they'd only found fifty. He knew that Lenny would make up his profit by selling the jewellery, anyway.

Mick was restless. He'd taken some uppers before going out and some downers when they got back, just to take the edge off. Now the drugs were clashing and fighting it out in his body. He couldn't settle and listen to music or watch telly, and Trevor, bored with him, was getting ready to go. They looked out of the window at the rain. Across The Green, they saw a car pull up outside one of the old houses.

"It's that bird," Mick said. "The redhead with the long legs. Ooh, I'd like to feel them wrapped around my waist. Who's she with? Some fucking wanker for sure."

"I think it's that copper," Trevor said, recognizing Banks. "Funny, that, I saw him with her the other night at the old bag's house."

"Maybe she's a cop, then. Waste of a good screw, if you ask me. Nice pair of tits she's got, though."

"Maybe he's just knocking her off," Trevor said. "He's going in, anyway."

"Lucky bastard."

"It's funny, though, seeing them twice like that."

"What's so funny? I see her all the time. She only lives across The Green, you know."

"I mean seeing them together like that."

"He's probably poking her. Fucking hell, wouldn't I just like those long legs wrapped around my waist."

But Mick was fast slipping into the arms of Morpheus. The amphetamine, already mostly burned up, was losing to the barbiturate, and he felt as if his brain was slowly turning to cotton-wool and his senses were closing like valves. The light around the edges of his eyes dimmed, and he could hear a gentle whooshing, like the ocean, in his ears; his tongue felt too tired and too heavy to speak.

Trevor recognized the signs, put on his coat and left. It had been a good night, one of the best in years, and he felt, as he walked home through the quiet town reliving the excitement, that he could hardly wait for next Monday.

EIGHT

I

The sudden creaking of rusty hinges broke the silence in the cool church. Sandra and Harriet looked around and saw Robin Allott coming in, followed closely by Norman Chester.

"So this is where you're hiding," Norman said, as he shut the heavy door behind them. "We were wondering where the lovely ladies had got to." His voice echoed from the stone walls.

"What are you doing?" Robin asked.

"Waiting for the sun," Sandra replied. "I want to get a good shot of the stained-glass window here."

"It shouldn't be long," Robin said, walking down the aisle towards them. "The clouds seem to be breaking up and the wind's pushing them along nicely. It is quite beautiful, isn't it?"

Sandra nodded, glancing up again at the east window. They stood in the Parish Church of St Mary, Muker, one of the places the Camera Club was visiting on its trip to Swaledale. Most club members were out walking along Ivelet Side putting Terry Whigham's ideas on landscape photography into practice with shots of the spectacular view of Oxnop, Muker Side and the dark mass of Great Shunner Fell. Harriet and Sandra, however, had stuck to the village itself, photographing the craft centre, village store and old Literary Institute, before approaching St Mary's.

"It's supposed to depict the landscape outside," Robin went on, pointing to the window. "You can see Christ the Good Shepherd there, leading his flock and carrying a lamb—real horned Swaledale sheep. The hill is Kisdon, that big one out there, and you can see the River Swale to the right and Muker Beck to the left."

"You seem to know a bit about it," Sandra said. "Have you been here before?"

"Once or twice."

Norman's footsteps echoed as he wandered around examining the font and chalice.

"It is a wonderful church, though," Robin said. "And the cemetery's interesting, too. It's the kind of place I wouldn't mind being buried in."

"How morbid."

"Not at all. They used to have to carry people in wicker coffins ten or fifteen miles away to Grinton church before this place was built. They took the old Corpse Way along Ivelet Side. People wanted to be buried on consecrated ground. I'd hope for a long and healthy life first, though, like poor Alice Matlock."

"Alice Matlock?"

"Yes. The old lady they found dead in her cottage the other day. Surely your husband must have mentioned her?"

"Yes, of course," Sandra said. "I was just surprised to hear you talk about her, that's all."

Robin looked up at the dim stained glass. "I knew her, that's all. I was a bit shaken to hear that someone who'd lived through so much should have died so violently. Does your husband have any clues?"

"None that he's told me about. How did you come to know her?"

"I suppose I'm exaggerating a bit. I haven't seen her for a few years. You know how it is; we lose touch with the old so easily. She was a friend of my grandmother's, my father's mother. They were about the same age and both of them worked as nurses at Eastvale Infirmary for years. My gran used to take me over to visit Alice when I was a kid."

"Haven't you thought that you might be able to help?" Sandra asked.

"Me?" said Robin, startled. "How? I said I hadn't seen her for years."

"Alan says it's frustrating not to know much about her background. Most of her friends are dead. Anything you could tell him might be a help."

"I don't see how."

"When you've lived with a policeman for as long as I have," Sandra said, "you don't ask how. Would you be willing to see him?"

"I don't know...I...I can't see how it could help."

"Come on. Alan won't eat you. You said you were upset about her death. Surely it's not too much to ask?"

"No, no, I don't suppose it is. If you think it'll help, of course..."

"It might."

"Very well."

"Good. I'll tell him, then. If I see him. He's not home much these days. Still, we are supposed to be going out tonight, if he hasn't forgotten. When's a good time? I'm sure he won't want to inconvenience you."

"I don't know. This weekend sometime? I should be home."

"Fine." Sandra took Robin's address and turned her attention back to the stained-glass window. "Come on, come on," she urged the sun.

They stood there a full minute or more until, slowly, the glass brightened and the red of Christ's robe, the blue of the rivers at his feet and the purple, orange and green of the hills behind began to glow. Sandra selected a wide aperture and let the built-in exposure-meter set the shutter speed.

"It's strange," Robin said, watching, "but it sometimes seems to me as if we're looking outside through a clear window at some idealized image."

"Yes, it does," Harriet agreed. "Like a vision. Ooh, look how the colours are shining on us!"

"Vision indeed," Norman sneered, walking over from the north-west window. "A right lot of romantics, you are." And he joined them as they took it in turns to capture the stained glass on film.

II

Friday brought a lull in affairs at the Eastvale station. Nothing had come of the previous evening's pub surveillance, and Richmond said that he'd shown the artist's impression of their one suspect in the robberies to some of the lads on the beat, but nobody had recognized him. After sending the detective constable to the Town Hall to check on the statistics of young men living alone or with single parents, Banks found himself with little to do. No Dorothy Wycombe marched in to liven up the day; no Jenny Fuller; nothing.

He had plenty of time to think, though, and spent the rest of the morning puzzling over the three cases, whose outlines had become blurred in his mind. There was a Peeping Tom in Eastvale, that was clear enough. Also, two young thugs had robbed defenceless old women. But had any of them killed Alice Matlock?

On the evidence so far, it looked like it: she had been old and alone, her home had been left in a shambles, and money and silverware had been stolen. It was certainly possible that she had tried to struggle with them and had fallen or been pushed backwards, catching the back of her head on the sharp corner of the table.

There was still room for doubt, though, and Banks found himself wondering if it could have happened some other way for some other reason. He had ruled out the peeper after what Jenny had said, so the next step was to try and discover if anyone had a motive for getting rid of Alice Matlock, or at least for engaging in such a violent confrontation with her.

According to Sergeant Hatchley, Ethel Carstairs had said that Alice had kept herself to herself over the past few years, and that she had not been the type to take in strays or befriend strangers. If the two young tearaways were not responsible for her death, then who was, and why?

Unfortunately, the slow afternoon allowed Banks more time than he would have liked to reflect on the events of the previous evening. Sandra had been asleep when he got home, so he was spared a telling off, but she had been very frosty in the morning, reminding him that they had arranged to go out that evening with Harriet Slade and her husband, who had already booked a sitter, and that he'd promised to take the kids up to Castle Hill on Saturday morning. It was her way of hinting that he wasn't spending enough time with his nearest and dearest, whatever else he might be up to.

Though he certainly felt pangs of guilt, he hadn't really been up to anything much at all.

His first move, after Jenny had led him into her front room, had been to remark on the expensive stereo system and the lack of a television.

"I used to have one," she said, heading for the kitchen, "but I gave it to a colleague. Without it I get much more done—reading, listening to music, going out, seeing films. When I had it I was terribly lazy; I always take the line of least resistance."

"It doesn't look much like a professor's living-room," Banks shouted through. There were only a couple of recent psychology journals and a folder of notes on the table.

"The study's upstairs," she yelled back. "I *do* work hard, honestly, Inspector. Milk and sugar?"

"No, thanks."

Banks squinted at the framed print on the wall. It showed an enormous dark mountain, more steep than broad, completely dominating a small village in the foreground.

"Who did this?" he asked Jenny when she came into the room carrying two mugs of coffee.

"That? It's an Emily Carr."

"I've never heard of her," said Banks, who had gained a basic knowledge of art through Sandra.

"That's not surprising; she's a Canadian. I spent three years doing postgraduate work in Vancouver. She's a West Coast artist, did a lot of totem poles and forest scenes. Oddly enough, I saw that painting in a gallery at Kleinburg, near Toronto. I fell in love with it right away. Everything looks alive, don't you think?"

"Yes, in a dark, creepy kind of way. But I'm not sure it would pass my simple test for paintings."

"Don't tell me!" she said, imitating a Yorkshire accent. "'Ah don't know much about art bu'rah knows whar'ah likes.' Not bad for a Leicester girl, eh?"

Banks laughed. "Better than I could do. Anyway, that's not my test. I just ask myself if I could live with it on my living-room wall."

"And you couldn't?"

"No. Not that."

"What could you live with? It sounds like a very hard test."

Banks thought back over some of the paintings Sandra had introduced him to. "Modigliani's *Reclining Nude*, maybe Chagall's *I and the Village*. Monet's *Waterlilies*."

"Good lord, you'd need an entire room for that one."

"Yes, but it would be worth it."

With the coffees, Jenny also poured out generous measures of cognac, giving Banks no time to refuse, then she put some music on the cassette deck and sat down beside him.

"This is good music," he said. "What is it?"

"Bruch's violin concerto."

"Mmm, I've never heard it before. Are you a classical music buff?"

"Oh, no. I mean, I enjoy classical, but I like a bit of everything, really. I like jazz—Miles Davis and Monk. I still love some of the old sixties stuff—Beatles, Dylan, Stones—but my old copies are a bit scratched up by now."

"For a psychology teacher you seem to know a lot about the arts."

"English was my second subject, and my father was a bit of an amateur artist. Even now I seem to spend more time with the arts faculty than the sciences. Most psychologists are so boring."

"Do you like opera?"

"That's one thing I don't know very well. My sister took me to an Opera North performance of *La Traviata* once, years ago, but I'm afraid I don't remember much about it."

"Try some. I'll lend you a couple of tapes. *Tosca*, that's a good one."

"What's it about?"

"An evil chief of police who tries to coerce a singer into sleeping with him by threatening to have her lover killed."

"That sounds cheerful," Jenny said; then she shivered. "Someone just walked over my grave."

"The music's good. Some fine arias."

"All right. Here's to opera," said Jenny, smiling and clinking glasses. "Do you think we did a good evening's work?"

"Yes, I think so. We didn't expect miracles. That's not why we brought you in."

"Charming! I know why you brought me in."

"I mean why we brought a psychologist in."

"Yes. I know that, too."

"Why?"

"You were all afraid that this was going to spiral into a rash of rapes and sex-murders, and you wanted to check on the evidence."

"Partly true. And given that, we also wanted to make damn sure we had a better chance of stopping him before he went too far."

"Are you any closer?"

"That remains to be seen."

As they sat in silence, Banks could feel his heart beating faster and his throat constricting. He knew he shouldn't be there, knew there could only be one interpretation of his accepting the offer of coffee, and he was nervous about what to do. The music flowed around them and the tension grew so strong it made the muscles in his jaw ache. Jenny stirred and her scent wafted towards him. It was too subtle to be called a perfume; it was the kind of fresh and happy smell that took him back to carefree childhood trips to the country.

"Look," Banks finally blurted out, putting down his coffee and facing Jenny, "I'm sorry if I've given you the impression that . . . the wrong impression . . . but I'm married." Then, having confessed in what he felt to be as graceless a manner as possible, he started to apologize and rephrase, but Jenny cut in.

"I know that, you fool. You think a psychologist can't spot a married man a mile off?"

"You know? Then . . ."

Jenny shrugged. "I'm not trying to seduce you, if that's what you mean. Yes, I like you, I'm attracted to you. I get the impression that you feel the same way. Dammit, then, maybe I am trying to seduce you. I don't know." She reached out and touched his face. "No strings, Alan. Why must you always be so serious?"

Immediately, he felt himself freeze, and it shocked her so much that she jumped away and turned her face to the wall.

"All right," she said, "I've made an idiot of myself. Now go. Go on, go!"

"Listen, Jenny," Banks said. "You're not wrong about anything. I'm sorry, I shouldn't have come."

"Why did you, then?" Jenny asked, softening a little but still not facing him.

Banks shrugged and lit a cigarette. "If I went to bed with you once," he said, "I wouldn't want it to stop there."

"You don't know till you try it," she said, turning and managing a thin smile.

"Yes, I do."

"I might be lousy in bed."

"That's not the point."

"I knew you wouldn't do it, anyway."

"You did?"

"I'm a psychologist, remember? I've spent enough time with you to know you're not frivolous and that you're probably a very monogamous person."

"Am I so transparent?"

"Not at all. I'm an expert. Maybe you were testing yourself, taking a risk."

"Well, they do say there's no better test of virtue than temptation."

"And how do you feel now?"

"Intolerably virtuous."

Jenny laughed and kissed him swiftly on the lips. It was a friendly sort of kiss, and instead of increasing Banks's desire it seemed to diffuse it and put things back on a simpler, more relaxed level.

"Don't go just yet," Jenny said. "If you do I'll think it's because of all this and it'll keep me awake all night."

"All right. But only if I get another black coffee—and no more cognac."

"Coming up, sir."

"By the way," Banks asked as Jenny headed for the kitchen, "what about you? Divorced, single?"

"Single." Jenny leaned against the doorpost. "Marriage never happened to me."

"Not even almost?"

"Oh, yes, almost. But you can't be almost married, can you? That would be like being a little bit pregnant." And she turned to go and make the coffee, leaving a smile behind her which faded slowly like the Cheshire cat's.

Banks snapped out of his reverie feeling half-remorseful for having gone so far and half-regretful that he hadn't seized the moment and abandoned himself to Eros. He put on his headphones, rewound *Dido and Aeneas* to the lament, "When I am laid in earth," and left the building. Abandoned by her lover, Queen Dido sang "Remember me, remember me . . ." It sent shivers up and down Banks's spine.

III

The evening out with Harriet and David went well. They drove along the Dale on the road by the River Swain, which was coursing high and fast after the recent rains. Beyond the sloping commons, dark valley sides rose steeply on both sides like sleeping whales. At Fortford, David took an unfenced minor road over the hills and down into the village of Axeby. The Greyhound, an old low-ceilinged pub with walls three feet thick, held a folk night there every Friday that was so well respected it even drew people from as far afield as Leeds, Bradford and Manchester.

They were early enough to find a table for four near the back, which provided a relatively unobstructed view of the small stage. David brought the first round and they drank to a good evening. Though Banks thought David, an assistant bank manager, a bit of a bore, he made an effort to like him for Sandra's sake, and the two of them got on well enough. But Banks still found himself wondering what such a lively and interesting woman as Harriet saw in her husband.

The music was good; there were none of the modern, whining protest songs that got up Banks's nose. You could usually depend on The Greyhound for solid, traditional folk music—"Sir Patrick Spens," "The Wife of Usher's Well," "Marie Hamilton," "The Unquiet Grave" and the like—and that night there was nothing to spoil Banks's joy in the old ballads, which he loved almost as much as opera. The "high" and "low" or "culture" and "folk" distinctions didn't concern him at all—it was the sense of a story, of drama and tension in the music, that enthralled him.

Because it was David's turn to drive that night, Banks was allowed more than his usual two pints, and as the beer at The Greyhound— brewed on the premises—was famous for its quality, he indulged himself freely. He could take his drink, though, for a small man, and the only signs that he'd had one or two too many were that he smoked and talked more than usual. Sandra stuck to gin and tonic, and drank slowly.

The day, which had been heavy with disturbing feelings for Banks, seemed to be ending well. This evening out with Sandra and the Slades, good music and good beer, was driving Jenny from his mind. Looking back from a distance of four or five pints, what he had done didn't seem so bad. Many men would have done much worse. True, he had sounded terribly moral and sanctimonious—but how else can you sound, he asked himself, if you have to say no to a beautiful, intelligent woman?

As he reached for a cigarette, Sandra glanced over from her conversation and they smiled at each other.

IV

It was a good position on the sloping roof because, lying down, he seemed to melt into the slates, but it was very uncomfortable and he was getting tired of waiting.

He'd done his reconnaissance well enough—not hanging around the front, especially as the street was a cul-de-sac, but just passing by occasionally, watching from the unlit alley at the back, nothing more than a narrow dirt track between fenced back gardens. Ideal. He'd slipped through the fence, climbed the pipe up the side of the wall—it was an addition to the house, a kind of storeroom or workshop attached to the back—and found himself just on a level with the bedroom window. He knew it was the right one because he'd seen the children's wallpaper in the front rooms as he'd passed by one day. He also knew that she tended to go to bed first. The husband would often stay up in the front room and listen to music or read for a while.

What was keeping her? They'd been home half an hour and still no sign. Finally the bedroom light came on and he took his position by the chink at the bottom of the curtains. The woman tied back her straight blonde hair and reached behind her back for her zipper. Slowly, she pulled it down and slipped the black, silky dress from her pale shoulders, letting it fall all the way to the carpet, then picked it up and hung it carefully in the wardrobe.

There she stood, the dark V of cleavage clear at the front of her bra, the inviting curve in at the waist and out again, softly, at the hips.

Her figure was slight; there was nothing out of proportion, nothing in excess. It was what he had been waiting for, what had first stirred his feelings and had eluded him ever since. He felt himself getting more and more excited as she sat at the dressing table and removed her makeup before undressing any more. He could see her reflection, her concentration as she applied the tufts of cotton wool. It was just like he remembered. Almost unconsciously he rubbed himself as he watched, not wanting her to finish, willing it to go on for ever.

Finally she stood up again and pulled her nightdress out from under the pillow. Facing him, she unclipped her bra and he watched her small breasts fall slightly as it loosened. He was rubbing himself all the time, faster and faster, and then it happened. What he'd been waiting for. She saw him.

It all happened in slow motion. One moment she was taking off the bra, the next a look of shock spread across her face slowly, like spilled milk on a table, as she caught his eye. At the same moment he climaxed, and the spasms shook his body with pleasure. He slid off the roof, dropped to the garden and shot out through the fence before she could even open the curtains.

V

Sandra couldn't say exactly how or at what moment she knew she was being watched. It was sudden, a feeling of not being alone. And when she looked she saw an eye. It seemed disembodied, just hanging there in the gap in the curtains, but as she ran forward, yelling for Alan at the same time, she caught a glimpse of a figure in a dark raincoat slipping through the gap in the fence and making off down the back alley.

Banks came running up and then left Sandra to calm down the children, who had heard her cry out, while he gave chase. There was nobody in the alley, and it was too dark to see clearly anyway. First, Banks ran up to the main road end, but there was nobody in sight. Then he walked slowly and quietly in the other direction, wishing he'd had the foresight to bring a torch, but he saw nothing move in the shadows, and however still he stood, he couldn't hear breathing or rustling—nothing. All he managed to do was disturb a cat, which darted across his path and almost gave him a heart attack.

He walked as far down as the narrow gap at the far end that led to the park, but it was pitch black. There was no point in going any further. Whoever it was had melted back into the darkness, another victory. Banks cursed and kicked the rickety fence hard before storming back indoors.

NINE

I

On Saturday morning, as promised, Banks stood high on the castle battlements and looked out over his "patch," or "manor," as he would have called it in London. It was a sharp, fresh day and all the clouds had gone. The sky was not the deep, warm cerulean of summer, but a lighter, more piercing blue, as if the cold of the coming winter had already wormed its way into the air.

Banks looked down over the cobbled market square. The ancient cross and square-towered church were almost lost among the makeshift wooden stalls and the riot of colour that blossomed every market day. The bus station to the east was full of red single-decker buses, and in the adjacent car park, green and white coaches dwarfed the cars. Small parties of tourists ambled around, bright yellow and orange anoraks zipped up against the surprising nip in the air. Banks wore his donkey-jacket buttoned right up to the collar and the children wore kagoules over their woollen sweaters.

To Tracy, Eastvale Castle represented a living slice of history, an Elizabethan palace where, it was rumoured, Mary Queen of Scots had been imprisoned for a while and a Richard or a Henry had briefly held court. Ladies-in-waiting whispered royal secrets to one another in echoing galleries, while barons and earls danced galliards and pavanes with their elegant wives at banquets.

To Brian, the place evoked a more barbarous era of history; it was a stronghold from which ancient Britons poured down boiling oil on Roman invaders, a citadel riddled with dank dungeons where thumbscrews, rack and Iron Maiden awaited unfortunate prisoners.

Neither was entirely correct. The castle was, in fact, built by the Normans at about the same time as Richmond, and, like its more famous contemporary, it was built of stone and had an unusually massive keep.

While the children explored the ruins, Banks looked over the roofs below, chequer-board patterns of red pantile, stone and Welsh slate, and let his eyes follow the contours of the hills where they rose to peaks and fells in the west and flattened into a gently undulating plain to the east. In all directions the trees were tinged with autumn's rust, just like the picture on his calendar.

Banks could make out the town's limits: beyond the river, the East Side Estate, with its two ugly tower blocks, sprawled until it petered out into fields, and in the west, Gallows View pointed its dark, shrivelled finger towards Swainsdale. To the north, the town seemed to spread out between the fork of two diverging roads—one leading to the northern Dales and the Lakes, the other to Tyneside and the east coast. Beyond these older residential areas, there were only a few scattered farmhouses and outlying hamlets.

Though he saw the view, Banks could hardly take it in, still troubled as he was by the events of the previous evening. He hadn't reported the incident, and that nagged at his sense of integrity. On the other hand, as he and Sandra had decided, it would probably have been a lot more embarrassing and galling all round to have reported it. It was easy to imagine the headlines, the sniggers. And even as he worried about his own decision, Banks also wondered how many others had not seen fit to tell the police of similar incidents. If women were still reluctant to report rape, for example, would many of them not also balk at reporting a Peeping Tom?

For Banks, though, the problem was even more involved. He was a policeman; therefore, he was expected to set an example, to follow the letter of the law himself. In the past, he may have occasionally driven at a little over the speed limit or, worse, had perhaps one drink too many before driving home from a Christmas party, but he had never been faced with such a conflict between professional and family duty before. Sandra and he had decided, though, over a long talk in bed, and that decision was final. They had also told the children, who had heard Sandra's scream, that she had thought someone was trying to break in but had been mistaken.

What bothered Banks was that if there was no investigation, then valuable clues or information might be sacrificed. To put that right as far as possible, Sandra had offered to talk to the neighbours discreetly, to ask if anyone had noticed any strangers hanging around. It wasn't much, but it was better than nothing.

So that was that. Banks shrugged and watched a red bus try to extricate itself from an awkward parking spot off the square. The gold hands against the blue face of the church clock said eleven-thirty. He had promised that they would be home for lunch by twelve.

Rounding up Brian and Tracy, who had fallen to arguing about the history of the castle, Banks ushered them towards the exit.

"Of course it's an ancient castle," Brian argued. "They've got dungeons with chains on the walls, and it's all falling to pieces."

Tracy, despite her anachronistic image of the period, knew quite well that the castle was built in the early part of the twelfth century, and she said so in no uncertain terms.

"Don't be silly," Brian shot back. "Look at what a state it's in. It must have taken thousands of years to get so bad."

"For one thing," Tracy countered with a long-suffering sigh, "it's built of stone. They didn't build things out of stone as long ago as that. Besides, it's in the history book. Ask the teacher, dummy, you'll see if I'm not right."

Brian retreated defensively into fantasy: he was a brave knight and Tracy was a damsel in distress, letting down her hair from a high, narrow window. He gave it a long, hard pull and swaggered off to fight a dragon.

They wound their way down to the market square, which, though it had seemed to move as slowly and silently as in a dream from high up, buzzed with noisy activity at close quarters.

The vendors sold everything from toys, cassette tapes and torch batteries to lace curtains, paintbrushes and used paperbacks, but mostly they sold clothes—jeans, jackets, shirts, lingerie, socks, shoes. A regular, whom Banks had christened Flash Harry because of his pencil-thin moustache, flat cap and spiv-like air, juggled with china plates and cups as he extolled the virtues of his wares. Tourists and locals clustered around the draughty stalls handling goods and haggling with the red-faced holders, who sipped hot Oxo and wore fingerless woollen gloves to keep their hands warm without inhibiting the counting of money.

After a quick look at some children's shoes—as cheap in quality as they were in price—Banks led Brian and Tracy south along Market Street under the overhanging second-floor bay windows. About a quarter of a mile further on, beyond where the narrow street widened, was the cul-de-sac where they lived. It was five to twelve.

"Superintendent Gristhorpe called," Sandra said as soon as they got in. "About fifteen minutes ago. You're to get over to number 17 Clarence Gardens as soon as you can. He didn't say what it was about."

"Bloody hell," Banks grumbled, buttoning up his donkey-jacket again. "Can you keep lunch warm?"

Sandra nodded.

"Can't say how long I'll be."

"It doesn't matter," she said, and smiled as he kissed her. "It's only a casserole. Oh, I almost forgot, he invited us to Sunday dinner tomorrow as well."

"That's some consolation, I suppose," Banks said as he walked out to the garage.

II

"It's a bloody disgrace, that's what it is," Maurice Ottershaw announced, hands on hips. Banks wasn't sure whether he meant the burglary itself or the fact that the police hadn't managed to prevent it. Ottershaw was a difficult character. A tall, grey-haired man, deeply tanned from his recent holiday, he seemed to think that all the public services were there simply for his benefit, and he consequently treated their representatives like personal valets, stopping just short of telling Banks to go and make some tea.

"It's not unusual," Banks offered, by way of meagre compensation for the mess on the walls, carpet and appliances. "A lot of burglars desecrate the places they rob."

"I don't bloody care about that," Ottershaw went on, the redness of his anger imposing itself even on his tan. "I want these bloody vandals caught."

"We're doing our best," Banks told him patiently. "Unfortunately, we don't have a lot to go on."

Richmond and Hatchley had already talked to the neighbours, who had either been out or had heard nothing. Manson had been unable to find any fingerprints except for those of the owners and their cleaning lady, who had been in just the other day to give the place a thorough going-over. There was no way of telling exactly on what day the robbery had taken place, although it must have happened between Tuesday, the day of the cleaner's visit, and the Ottershaws' return early that Saturday morning.

"Can you give me a list of what's missing?"

"One hundred and fifty-two pounds seventy-five pence in cash, for a start," Ottershaw said.

"Why did you leave so much cash lying around the place?"

"It wasn't lying around, it was in a box in a drawer. It was just petty cash for paying tradesmen and such. I don't often have cash on me, use the card most of the time."

"I see you're an art lover," Banks said, looking towards the large framed prints of Bosch's *Garden of Earthly Delights* and Botticelli's *The Birth of Venus* hanging on the walls. Banks wasn't sure whether he could live with either of them.

Ottershaw nodded. "Just prints, of course. Good ones, mind you. I have invested in one or two original works." He pointed to a rough white canvas with yellow and black lines scratched across it like railway tracks converging and diverging. "London artist. Doing very well for herself, these days. Not when I bought it, though. Got it for a song. Poor girl must have been starving."

"Any pictures missing?"

Ottershaw shook his head.

"Antiques?" Banks gestured towards the standard lamp, crystalware and bone china.

"No, it's still all there and in one piece, thank the Lord."

"Anything else?"

"Some jewellery. Imitation, but still worth about five hundred pounds. My wife can give you descriptions of individual pieces. And there's all this of course. My wife won't watch this TV again, nor will she touch the hi-fi. It'll all have to be replaced. They've even spilled the Rémy."

This last remark seemed a bit melodramatic to Banks, but he let it slip by. "Where is your wife, sir?" he asked.

"Lying down. She's a very highly strung woman, and this, on top of being stuck at the bloody airport for a whole night... it was just too much for her."

"You were supposed to be home yesterday?"

"Yes. I told you, didn't I? Bloody airport wallahs went on strike."

"Did anyone know you were away?"

"Neighbours, a couple of friends at work and the club."

"What club would that be, sir?"

"Eastvale Golf Club," Ottershaw announced, puffing out his chest. "As you probably know, it's an exclusive kind of place, so it's very unlikely that any criminal elements would gain access."

"We have to keep all possibilities open," Banks said, managing to avoid Ottershaw's scornful glare by scribbling nonsense in his notebook. There was no point in getting involved in a staring match with a victim, he thought.

"Anyone else?"

"Not that I know of."

"Would your wife be likely to have told anyone?"

"I've covered everyone we know."

"Where do you work, sir?"

"Ottershaw, Kilney and Glenbaum."

Banks had seen the sign often enough. The solicitors' offices were on Market Street, just a little further south than the police station.

"Who's going to clear all this up?" Ottershaw demanded roughly, gesturing around the disaster area of his living-room.

The faeces lay curled on the rug, staining the white fibres around and underneath it. The TV, video and stereo looked as if they'd been sprayed with a hose, but it was quite obvious what had actually happened. Amateurs, Banks thought to himself. Kids, probably, out on a lark. Maybe the same kids who'd done the old ladies' houses, graduating to the big time. But somebody had told them where to come, that the Ottershaws were away, and if he could find out who, then the rest would follow.

"I really don't know," Banks said. Maybe forensic would take it away with them. Perhaps, with a bit of luck, they'd be able to reconstruct the whole person from the faeces: height, weight, colouring, eating habits, health, complexion. Some hope.

"That's fine, that is," Ottershaw complained. "We go away for a ten-day holiday, and if it's not enough that the bloody wallahs choose to go on strike the day we leave, we come home to find the house covered in shit!" He said the last word very loudly, so much so that the lab men going over the room smiled at each other as Banks grimaced.

"We're not a cleaning service, you know, sir," he chided Ottershaw mildly, as if talking to a child. "If we were, then we'd never have time to find out who did this, would we?"

"Shock could kill the wife, you know," Ottershaw said, ignoring him. "Doctor said so. Weak heart. No sudden shocks to the system. She's a very squeamish woman—and that's her favourite rug, that sheepskin. She'll never be able to manage it."

"Then perhaps, sir, you'd better handle it yourself," Banks suggested, glancing towards the offending ordure before walking out and leaving the house to the experts.

III

The Oak turned out to be one of those huge Victorian monstrosities—usually called The Jubilee or The Victoria—curving around the corner where Cardigan Drive met Elmet Street about half a mile north of Gallows View. It was all glossy tiles and stained glass, and it reminded Banks very much of the Prince William in Peterborough, outside which he used to play marbles with the other local kids while they all waited for their parents.

Inside, generations of spilt beer and stale cigarette smoke gave the place a brownish glow and a sticky carpet, but the atmosphere in the spacious lounge was cheery and warm. The gaudy ceiling was high and the bar had clearly been moved from its original central position to make room for a small dance floor. It now stretched the whole length of one of the walls, and a staff—or what looked more like a squadron—of buxom barmaids flexed their muscles on the pumps and tried to keep smiling as they rushed around to keep up with the demand. The mirrors along the back, reflecting chandeliers, rows of exotic spirits bottles and the impatient customers, heightened the sense of good-natured chaos. Saturday night at The Oak was knees-up night, and a local comedian alternated with a pop group whose roots, both musical and sartorial, were firmly planted in the early sixties.

"What on earth made you bring me to a place like this?" Jenny Fuller asked, a puzzled smile on her face.

"Atmosphere," Banks answered, smiling at her. "It'll be an education."

"I'll bet. You said there's been a new development, something you wanted to tell me."

Banks took a deep breath and regretted it immediately; the air in The Oak wasn't of the highest quality, even by modern pollution standards. Fortunately, both the comedian and the pop group were between sets and the only noise was the laughter and chatter of the drinkers.

When Banks had phoned Jenny after he'd left the Ottershaws' house, he hadn't been sure why he wanted her to meet him at The Oak, or what he wanted to say to her. He had brought the *Tosca* cassettes that he had promised to lend her, but that wasn't excuse enough in itself. She had been obliging, but said she had to be off by nine as there was a small party honouring a visiting lecturer at the university. Banks also wanted to be home early, for Sandra's sake, so the arrangement suited him.

"Last night we had a visit from the peeper," he said finally. "At least Sandra did."

"My God!" Jenny gasped, wide-eyed and open-mouthed. "What happened?"

"Not much. She spotted him quite early on and he ran off down the back alley. I went out there but he'd already disappeared into the night."

"How is she?"

"She's fine, taking it all very philosophically. But she's a deep one, Sandra. She doesn't always let people know what her real feelings are—especially me. I should imagine she feels like the others—hurt, violated, dirty, angry."

Jenny nodded. "Most likely. Isn't it a bit awkward for you as far as your job's concerned?"

"That's something else I wanted to tell you. I haven't reported it."

Jenny stared at Banks far too long for his comfort. It was an intense, curious kind of look, and he finally gave in by going to the bar for two more drinks.

The crowd was about five deep with what looked like at least two local rugby teams, and Banks was smaller and slighter than most of the men who waved their glasses in the air and yelled over the heads of others—"Three pints of black and tan, Elsie, love, please!"... "Vodka and slimline, two pints of Stella, Cherry B, and a brandy and crème de menthe,"... "Five pints of Guinness...Kahlua and Coke, and a gin-and-it for the wife, love!" Everybody seemed to be placing such large orders.

Fortunately, Banks spotted Richmond, tall and distinctive, closer to the bar. He caught the constable's attention—the man was on duty, after all—and asked for one-and-a-half pints of bitter. Surprised but immediately compliant, Richmond added it to his own order. Rather than demand waiter service of his young constable, Banks waited till Richmond had got the drinks, paid him and made off.

"What are you thinking?" he asked, sitting next to Jenny again.

Jenny laughed. "It wasn't anything serious. Remember the other night?"

So the ice was broken; the subject wasn't taboo, after all. "Yes," he answered, waiting.

"I said I knew how you'd behave, even though I hoped it would be different?"

"Something like that."

"Well, I was just trying to work out where I'd have placed my bet. Reporting or not reporting. I think I'd have been wrong. It's not that I think you're a slave to duty or anything like that, but you like to do things right...you're honest. I'd guess that if you don't do things the way you know they should be done, you suffer for it. Conscience. Too much of it, probably."

"I never asked for it," Banks replied, lighting his second cigarette of the evening.

"You weren't born with it, either."

"No?"

"No. Conditioning."

"I didn't ask for that either."

"No, you didn't. None of us do. You've surprised me this time, though. I'd have guessed that you would report the incident no matter how much embarrassment it might cause."

Banks shook his head. "There would be too much unfavourable publicity all round. Not only for Sandra but for the department, too. That Wycombe woman would just love to get her hands on something like this. If it were made public and we solved the case quickly, according to her it would only be because a policeman's wife was among the victims. No, I'd rather keep it quiet."

"But what about interviews, questioning people?"

"Sandra and I will do that locally. We'll ask if anyone has seen any strangers hanging around."

Jenny looked at him quizzically. "I'm not judging you, you know. I'm not the authorities."

"I know," Banks said. "I needed to tell someone. I couldn't think of anyone else who'd . . ."

"Automatically be on your side?"

"I was going to say 'understand,' but I suppose you're right. I did count on your support."

"You have it, whether you need it or not. And your secret's safe with me."

"There is something a bit more technical I want to ask you, too," Banks went on. "This new incident, the fact that it was Sandra, *my* wife. Do you think that means anything?"

"If he knew who it was, and I think he probably did, then yes, I do think it's a development."

"Go on."

"It means that he's getting bolder, he needs to take greater risks to get his satisfaction. Unless he's some kind of hermit or human ostrich, he must have read about reactions to what he's been doing, probably with a kind of pride. Therefore, he must know that you've been heading an investigation into the case. He does a bit of research on you, finds you have an attractive blonde wife—"

"Or knows her already?" Banks cut in.

"What makes you think that? He could simply have watched the house discreetly, seen her come and go."

"It's just a feeling I've got."

"Yes, but what basis does it have? Where does it come from?"

Banks thought as deeply as he could, given that the pop group had started its set with a carbon copy of the ancient Searchers' hit, "Love Potion Number Nine."

"We were talking about the Camera Club Sandra belongs to," he answered slowly. "Sometimes they have nude models, and I said that most of the men probably don't even have films in their cameras. It was just a joke at the time, but could there be any connection?"

"I'm not sure," Jenny replied. "A Camera Club does grant permission for its members to look at the models, though if someone really didn't have a film in his camera, it might give the illusion of peeping, of doing something vaguely wrong. That's a bit far-fetched, I'm afraid, but then so is your theory. We can at least expect our man to be interested in naked women, although it's spying on them that gives him his real thrills. What happened about this other fellow you got onto?"

"Wooller?"

"If that's his name."

"Yes, Wooller. Lives on Gallows View. We did a bit of very discreet checking, and it turns out that he was on a two-week library sciences course in Cardiff when two of the incidents took place. That lets him out, however much pornography he's got hidden away."

"Sorry," Jenny said, glancing at her watch, "but I've got to dash. The department head will have apoplexy if I'm not there to greet our eminent visitor." She patted Banks's arm. "Don't worry, I think you made the right decision. And one more point: I'd say that our man's recent actions also show that he's got a sense of humour. It's a bit of a joke to him, leaving you with egg on your face, wouldn't you say? Call me after the weekend?"

Banks nodded and watched Jenny walk away. He noticed Richmond glancing over at him and wondered how bad it looked— a Detective Chief Inspector spending Saturday evening in The Oak with an attractive woman. He saw Jenny in his mind's eye just as she had looked on Thursday night after telling him she knew he wouldn't sleep with her. Was it being predictable that annoyed him so much? If so, he could console himself with thoughts of having won a small victory this time. Or was it guilt over what he had really wanted to do? Maybe he would do it anyway, he thought, sauntering out into the chilly October evening. It wasn't too late yet. Surely a man, like a woman, could change his mind? After all, what harm would it do? "No strings," Jenny had said.

Banks turned up his collar as he walked back to the Cortina. He needed cigarettes, and fortunately there was an off-licence next door to the pub. As he picked up his change, he paused for a moment before pocketing it. Hatchley might have questioned the barmaids at The Oak, but he hadn't said anything about talking to the local shop-keepers.

Banks identified himself and asked the owner's name.

"Patel," the man answered cautiously.

"What time do you close?"

"Ten o'clock. It's not against the law, is it?" Mr Patel answered in a broad Yorkshire accent.

"No, not at all. It's nothing to do with that," Banks assured him. "Think back to last Monday night. Did you notice anybody hanging around outside here during the evening?"

Mr Patel shook his head.

It had probably been too early in the evening for the peeper and too long ago for the shopkeeper to remember, as Banks had feared.

"A bit later, though," Mr Patel went on, "I noticed a bloke waiting at the bus stop for a bloody long time. There must have been two or three buses went by and 'ee were still there. I think that were Monday last."

"What time was this?"

"After I'd closed up. 'Ee just sat there in that bus shelter over t'street." Banks looked out of the window and saw the shelter, a dark rectangle set back from the road.

"Where were you?" he asked.

"Home," Mr Patel said, turning up his eyes. "The flat's above t'shop. Very convenient."

"Yes, yes indeed," Banks said, getting more interested. "Tell me more."

"I remember because I was just closing t'curtains when a bus went by, and I noticed that bloke was still in t'shelter. It seemed a bit odd to me. I mean, why would a chap sit in a bus shelter if 'ee weren't waiting on a bus?"

"Why, indeed?" Banks said. "Go on."

"Nothing more to tell. A bit later I looked again, and 'ee were still there."

"What time did he leave?"

"I didn't actually see him leave, but 'ee'd gone by eleven o'clock. That were t'last time I looked out."

"And the time before that?"

"Excuse me?"

"When was the last time you looked out and saw him?"

"About 'alf past ten."

"Can you describe the man?"

Mr Patel shook his head sadly. "Sorry, it were too dark. I think 'ee were wearing a dark overcoat or a raincoat, though. Slim, a bit taller than you. I got the impression 'ee were youngish, some'ow. It was 'ard to pick him out from the shadows."

"Don't worry about it," Banks said. At least the colour of the coat matched the description that Sandra and the other victims had given. It had to be the man. They could talk to other people in the street: shopkeepers, locals, even the bus drivers. Maybe somebody else would have noticed a man waiting for a bus he never caught on Monday night.

"Look," Banks said, "this is very important. You've been a great help." Mr Patel shrugged and shook his head shyly. "Have you ever seen the man before?"

"I don't think so, but how would I know? I couldn't recognize him from Adam, could I?"

"If you see him again, or anyone you think looks like him, anyone hanging about the bus stop without catching a bus, or acting oddly in any way, let me know, will you?" Banks wrote his number on a card and passed it to Mr Patel, who nodded and promised to keep his eyes skinned.

For the first time in days, Banks felt quite cheerful as he drove home to the delightful melodies of *The Magic Flute*.

TEN

I

On Sunday morning, Banks paid his visit to Robin Allott, who lived in his parents' modest semi about ten minutes walk away.

A tiny, bird-like woman answered his knock and fluttered around him all the way into the living-room.

"Do sit down, Inspector," she said, pulling out a chair. "I'll call Robin. He's in his room reading the Sunday papers."

Banks looked quickly around the room. The furniture was a little threadbare and there was no VCR or music centre, only an ancient-looking television. Quite a contrast from the Ottershaws' opulence, he thought.

"He's coming down," Mrs Allott said. "Can I make you a cup of tea?"

"Yes, please," Banks said, partly to get her out of the way for a while. She made him nervous with her constant hovering. "I hope I'm not disturbing you and Mr Allott," he said.

"Oh no, not at all." She lowered her voice. "My husband's an invalid, Inspector. He had a serious stroke about two years ago and he can't get around much. He stays in bed most of the time and I look after him as best I can."

That explained the badly worn furnishings, Banks thought. Whatever help the social services gave, the loss of the breadwinner was a serious financial setback for most families.

"It's been a great help having Robin home since his divorce," she added, then shrugged. "But he can't stay forever, can he?"

Banks heard footsteps on the stairs, and as Robin entered the room, Mrs Allott went to make the tea.

"Hello," Robin said, shaking Banks's hand. He looked an almost unnaturally healthy and handsome young man, despite the unmistakable signs of his chestnut-brown hair receding at the temples. "Sandra said you might call."

"It's about Alice Matlock," Banks said. "I'd just like to find out as much as I can about her."

"I don't really see how I can help you, Inspector," Robin said. "I told Sandra the same, but she seemed quite insistent. Surely you'll have found out all you want to know from her close friends?"

"She only had one, it seems: a lady called Ethel Carstairs. And even they haven't been friends for long. Most of Alice's contemporaries appear to have died."

"I suppose that's what happens when you reach her age. Anyway, as I said, I don't know how I can help, but fire away."

"Had you seen her recently?"

"Not for a while, no. If I remember correctly, the last time was about three years ago. I was interested in portrait photography and I thought she'd make a splendid subject. I have the picture somewhere—I'll dig it out for you later."

"And before that?"

"I hadn't seen her since my gran died."

"She and your grandmother were close friends?"

"Yes. My father's mother. They grew up together and both worked most of their lives in the hospital. Eastvale's not such a big place, or it wasn't then, so it was quite natural they'd be close. They went through the wars together, too. That creates quite a bond between people. When I was a child, my gran would often take me over to Alice's."

Mrs Allott appeared with the tea and perched at the opposite end of the table.

"Can you tell me anything about her past?" Banks asked Robin.

"Nothing you couldn't find out from anyone else, I don't think. I did realize later, though, when I was old enough to understand, what a fascinating life she'd led, all the changes she'd witnessed. Can you imagine it? When she was a girl cars were few and far between and people didn't move around much. And it wasn't only technology. Look at how our attitudes have changed, how the whole structure of society is different."

"How did Alice relate to all this?"

"Believe it or not, Inspector, she was quite a radical. She was an early struggler for women's rights, and she even went so far as to serve with the International Brigade as a nurse in the Spanish Civil War."

"Was she a communist?"

"Not in the strict sense, as far as I know. A lot of people who fought against Franco weren't."

"What were your impressions of her?"

"Impressions? I suppose, when I was a child, I was just fascinated with the cottage she lived in. It was so full of odds and ends. All those alcoves just overflowing with knick-knacks she'd collected over the years: tarnished cigarette lighters, Victorian pennies and those old silver three-penny bits—all kinds of wonderful junk. I don't imagine I paid much attention to Alice herself. I remember I was always fascinated by that ship in the bottle, the *Miranda*. I stared at it for hours on end. It was alive for me, a real ship. I even imagined the crew manning the sails, doing battle with pirates."

Mrs Allott poured the tea and laughed. "He always did have plenty of imagination, my Robin, didn't you?"

Robin ignored her. "How did it happen, anyway? How was she killed?"

"We're still not sure," Banks said. "It looks like she might have fallen over in a struggle with some kids come to rob her, but we're trying to cover any other possibilities. Have you any ideas?"

"I shouldn't think it was kids, surely?"

"Why not?"

"Well, they wouldn't kill a frail old woman, would they?"

"You'd be surprised at what kids do these days, Mr Allott. As I said, they might not have killed her intentionally."

Robin smiled. "I'm a teacher at the College of Further Education, Inspector, so I'm no great believer in the innocence and purity of youth. But couldn't it have happened some other way?"

"We don't know. That's what I'm trying to determine. What do you have in mind?"

"Nothing, I'm afraid. It was just an idea."

"You can't think of anyone who might have held a grudge or wanted her out of the way for some other reason?"

"I'm sorry, no. I wish I could help, but..."

"That's all right," Banks said, standing to leave. "I wasn't expecting you to give us the answer. Is there anything else you can think of?"

"No. I can dig out that portrait for you, though, if you're interested."

Out of politeness' sake, Banks accompanied Robin upstairs and waited as he flipped through one of his many boxes of photographs. The picture of Alice, when he found it, was mounted on mat and still seemed in very good shape. It showed a close-up of the old woman's head in semi-profile, and high-contrast processing had brought out the network of lines and wrinkles, the vivid topography of Alice Matlock's face. Her expression was proud, her eyes clear and lively.

"It's very good," Banks said. "How long have you been interested in photography?"

"Ever since I was at school."

"Ever thought of taking it up professionally?"

"As a police photographer?"

Banks laughed. "I didn't have anything as specific as that in mind," he said.

"I've thought of trying it as a freelance, yes," Robin said. "But it's too unpredictable. Better to stick to teaching."

"There is one more thing, while I'm here," Banks said, handing the photograph back to Robin. "It's just something I'm curious about. Do you ever get the impression that anyone at the Camera Club might be...not too serious...might be more interested in the models you get occasionally than in the artistic side?"

It was Robin's turn to laugh. "What an odd question," he said. "But, yes, there's always one or two seem to turn up only when we've got a model in. What did Sandra say?"

"To tell the truth," Banks said, "I didn't like to ask her. She's a bit sensitive about it and I've probably teased her too much as it is."

"I see."

"Who are these people?"

"Their names?"

"Yes."

"Well, I know..." Robin said hesitantly.

"Don't worry," Banks assured him, "you won't be getting them into trouble. They won't even know we've heard their names if they've done nothing wrong."

"All right." Robin took a deep breath. "Geoff Welling and Barry Scott are the ones who spring to mind. They seem decent enough sorts, but they hardly ever turn up and I've never seen any examples of their work."

"Thank you," Banks said, writing down the names. "What do they look like?"

"They're both in their late twenties, about my age. Five-ten to six feet. Barry's got a bit of a beer belly but Geoff seems fit enough. What's all this about? That Peeping Tom business?"

"Robin!" Mrs Allott shouted from the bottom of the stairs, "Can you come and take your dad up his tea and biscuits?"

"Coming," Robin yelled back, and followed Banks down the stairs.

"Another cup of tea, Inspector?" Mrs Allott asked.

"No, I won't if you don't mind," Banks said. "Have to get home."

As he walked the short distance back home, Banks tried to pinpoint exactly what it was that Robin had said to increase his uneasy feeling about the Alice Matlock killing.

II

Apart from the immediate shock, which had made her scream, Sandra felt very calm about her experience. One minute she had been undressing for bed, as she had done thousands of times before, absorbed in her own private rituals, and the next moment that world was in tatters, would probably never really be the same again. She realized that the idea of such permanent ruin was melodramatic, so she kept it to herself, but she could think of no other way to express the complex sense of violation she had experienced.

She wasn't scared; she wasn't even angry after the shock had worn off and the adrenalin dispersed. Surprisingly, her main feeling was pity—Harriet's compassion—because Sandra did feel sorry for the man in a way she found impossible to explain, even to herself.

It was something to do with the unnaturalness of his act. Sandra had always been fortunate in having a healthy attitude towards sex.

She had neither needed nor wanted the help of manuals, marital aids, awkward positions or suburban wife-swapping clubs to keep her sex life interesting, and it was partly because of this, her own sexual healthiness, that she felt sorry for the pathetic man who could only enjoy sex in such a vicarious, secretive way. Her pity was not a soft and loving feeling, though; it was more akin to contempt.

That Sunday morning as she rang Selena Harcourt's doorbell, which played a fragment of "Lara's Theme" from *Doctor Zhivago*, she thanked her lucky stars for the hundredth time that she had managed to persuade Alan not to report the incident. It had gone against all his instincts, and the task had required all of Sandra's rhetorical expertise, but she had done it, and here she was, about to fulfill her part of the bargain.

"Oh, hello, Sandra, do come in," Selena said in her cooing voice. "Excuse the mess."

There was, of course, no mess. Selena's living-room was spick and span, as always. It smelled of pine air-freshener and lemon-scented disinfectant, and all the souvenir ashtrays and costume-dolls from the Algarve, the Costa del Sol and various other European resorts simply glowed with health and shone with cleanliness.

The only new addition to the household was a gloomy poodle, called Pépé, who turned around slowly from his spot by the fireplace and looked at Sandra as if to apologize for his ridiculous appearance: the clippings and bows that Selena had inflicted on him in the hope that he might win a prize in the upcoming dog show. Sandra duly lavished hypocritical praise upon the poor creature, who gave her a very sympathetic and conspiratorial look, then she sat uneasily on the sofa. She always sat uneasily in Selena's house because everything looked as if it were on show, not quite real or functional.

"I was just saying to Kenneth, we haven't seen very much of you lately. You've not been to one of our coffee mornings for simply ages."

"It's the job," Sandra explained. "I work three mornings a week for Dr Maxwell now, remember?"

"Of course," Selena said. "The dentist." Somehow or other, she managed to give the word just the right shade of emphasis to imply that although dentists might be necessary, they were certainly not desirable in respectable society.

"That's right."

"So what else have you been up to since we last had a little chat?"

Sandra couldn't remember when that was, so she gave a potted history of the last month, to which Selena listened politely before offering tea.

"Have you heard about this Peeping Tom business?" she called through from the kitchen.

"Yes," Sandra shouted back.

"Of course, I keep forgetting your hubby's on the force. You must know all about it, then?" Selena said as she brought in the tray bearing tea and a selection of very fattening confectionery.

"On the force, indeed!" Sandra thought. Selena knew damn well that Alan was a policeman—in fact, that was the only reason she had ever talked to Sandra in the first place—and her way of digging for gossip was about as subtle as a Margaret Thatcher pep speech.

"Not much," Sandra lied. "There's not much to know, really."

"That Dorothy Wycombe's been having a right go at Alan, hasn't she?" Selena noted, with so much glee that the lah-de-dah inflection she usually imposed on her Northern accent slipped drastically around "having a right go."

"You could say that," Sandra admitted, gritting her teeth.

"Is it true?"

"Is what true?"

"That the police aren't doing much. Now, you know I'm no women's libber, Sandra, but we do get treated just a teeny bit unfairly sometimes. It is a man's world, you know."

"Yes. As a matter of fact, though, they're doing quite a lot. They've brought in a psychologist from the university."

"Oh?" Selena raised her eyebrows. "What's he supposed to do?"

"*She* helps tell the police what kind of person this peeper is."

"But surely they know that already? He likes to watch women undress."

"Yes," Sandra said. "But there's more to it than that. Why does he like to watch? What does he do while he's watching? Why doesn't he have a normal sex life? That's the kind of thing the psychologists are working on."

"Well, that's not much use, is it?" Selena observed. "Not until they've caught him, anyway."

"That's what I came to see you about," Sandra said, forging ahead. "They're worried that he might not stop at looking—that might be just the beginning—so they're really stepping up the investigation. They've already got enough information to know that he checks out his areas before he strikes, so he knows something about the layout of the house. He probably finds out when people go to bed, whether the woman goes up alone first, that kind of thing. So I suggested that it would be a good idea if we all kept our eyes open for strangers, or anyone acting strangely around here. That way we could catch him before he did any real harm."

"Good lord!" Selena exclaimed. "You don't really think he'd come around here, do you?"

Sandra shrugged. "There's no telling where he'll go. They've not found any rhyme or reason to his movements yet."

Selena's hand shook slightly as she poured more tea, and she bit her bottom lip between her teeth. "There was something," she started. "It was last week—Wednesday, I think—it startled me at the time but I never really gave it much thought later."

"What was it?"

"Well, I was walking back from Eloise Harrison's. She lives on Culpepper Avenue, you know, two streets down, and it's such a long way around if you go right to the main road and along, so I cut through the back here. There's a little snicket between the houses in the next street, you know, so I just go out of our back gate into the alley, then cut through the snicket, cross the street, do the same again, and I'm right in Eloise's back garden.

"Coming back on Wednesday, it was quite dark and wet, a nasty night, and when I cut into our back alley I almost bumped into this man. It was funny, I thought, because he looked like he was just standing there. I don't know why, but I think if we'd both been moving we'd have really bumped into each other. Well, it made me jump, I can tell you that. There's no light out there except what shines from the houses, and it's a lonely sort of place. Anyway, I just hurried on through the back gate and into the house, and I never really thought much more of it. But if you ask me, I'd say he was just standing there, loitering."

"Do you remember what he looked like?"

"I'm sorry, dear, I really didn't get a good look. As I said, it was dark, and what with the shock and all I just hurried on. I think he was wearing a black raincoat with a belt, and he had his collar turned up. He was wearing a hat, too, because of the rain, I suppose, so I couldn't have seen his face even if I'd wanted to. It was one of those . . . what do you call them? Trilbies, that's it. I think he was quite young, though, not the dirty-old-man type."

"What made you think that?"

"I don't know, really," Selena answered slowly, as if she was finding it difficult to put her instincts and intuitions into words. "Just the way he moved. And the trilby looked too old for him."

"Thank you," Sandra said, anxious to get home and make notes while it was all still fresh in her mind.

"Do you think it was him?"

"I don't know, but the police will be thankful for any information about suspicious strangers at the moment."

Selena fingered the plunging neckline of her dress, which revealed exactly the right amount of creamy skin to complement her peroxide curls, moon-shaped face and excessive make-up. "If it was him, then he's been watching us. It could be any of us he's after. Me. You. Josephine. Annabel. This is terrible."

"I shouldn't worry about it that much, Selena," Sandra said, taking malicious pleasure in comforting the woman for worries that she, herself, had raised. "It was probably just someone taking a short cut."

"But it was such a nasty night. What normal person would want to stand out there on a night like that? He must have been up to something. Watching."

"I'll tell Alan, and I'm sure the police will look into it. You never know, Selena, your information might lead to an arrest."

"It might?"

"Well, yes. If it is him."

"But I wouldn't be able to identify him. Not in a court of law, or one of those line-ups they have. I didn't really get a good look."

"That's not what I mean. Don't worry, nobody's going to make you do that. I just meant that if he's been seen in the area, the police will know where to look."

Selena nodded, mouth open, unconvinced, then poured more tea. Sandra refused.

Suddenly, at the door, Selena's face brightened again. "I keep forgetting," she said, putting her hand to her mouth to stifle a giggle. "It's so silly of me. I've got nothing to worry about. I live right next door to a policeman!"

III

Sunday afternoon at Gristhorpe's farmhouse was a great success, though it did little for Banks's emotional confusion. On the way, he was not allowed to play opera in the car and instead had to put up with some dull, mechanical pop music on Radio One—mostly drum-machine and synthesizer—to keep Brian and Tracy happy. It was a beautiful day; the autumn sky was sharp blue again, and the season's hues glowed on the trees by the riverbank. In daylight, the steep dale sides showed a varied range of colour, from the greens of common grazing slopes to the pink, yellow and purple of heather and gorse and the occasional bright edge of a limestone outcrop.

Gristhorpe greeted them, and almost immediately the children went off for a pre-dinner walk while the three adults drank tea in the cluttered living-room. The conversation was general and easy until Gristhorpe asked Banks how he was getting on with the "lovely" Jenny Fuller.

Sandra raised her dark eyebrows, always a bad sign as far as Banks was concerned. "Would that be the Dr Fuller you've been spending so much time with lately, Alan?" she asked mildly. "I knew she was a woman, but I'd no idea she was young and lovely."

"Didn't he tell you?" Gristhorpe said mischievously. "Quite a stunner, our Jenny. Isn't she, Alan?"

"Yes," Banks admitted. "She's very pretty."

"Oh, come on, Alan, you can do better than that," Sandra teased. "Pretty? What's that supposed to mean?"

"All right, beautiful then," Banks growled. "Sexy, sultry, a knock-out. Is that what you want?"

"Maybe he's smitten with her," Gristhorpe suggested.

"I'm not smitten," Banks countered, but realized as he did so that he was probably protesting too forcefully. "She's being very helpful," he went on quickly. "And," he said to Sandra, "just so that I don't get accused of being chauvinistic about this, let me put it on record that Dr Fuller is a very competent and intelligent psychologist."

"Brains and beauty?" Sandra mocked. "How on earth can you resist, Alan?"

As they both laughed at him, Banks slumped back into the armchair, craving a cigarette. Soon the talk changed direction and he was off the hook.

The dinner, presented by a proud Mrs Hawkins, was superb: roast beef still pink in the middle, and Yorkshire puddings, cooked in the dripping, with exactly the right balance of crispness outside and moistness within, smothered in rich gravy.

After a brief post-prandial rest, Brian and Tracy were off playing Cathy and Heathcliffe again on the moorland above Gristhorpe's few acres of land, and Sandra took a stroll with her camera.

"Do you know," Gristhorpe mused as they stood in the back garden watching Sandra and the children walk up the grassy slope, "millions of years ago, this whole area was under a tropical sea? All that limestone you see was formed from dead shellfish." He swept out his arm in an all-embracing gesture.

Banks shook his head; geology was definitely not his forte.

"After that, between the ice ages, it was as warm as equatorial Africa. We had lions, hyenas, elephants and hippopotami walking the Dales." Gristhorpe spoke as if he had been there, as if he was somehow implicated in all he said. "Come on." He took Banks by the arm. "You'll think I'm turning into a dotty old man. I've got something to show you."

Banks looked apprehensively at the embryonic dry-stone wall and the pile of stones to which Gristhorpe led him.

"They amaze me, those things," he said. "I can't imagine how they stand up to the wind and rain, or how anyone finds the patience to build them."

Gristhorpe laughed—a great booming sound from deep inside. "I'll not say it's easy. Wall-building's a dying art, Alan, and you're right about the patience. Sometimes the bugger runs me to the end of my tether." Gristhorpe's voice was gruff and the accent was clearly North Yorkshire, but it also had a cultured edge, the mark of a man who has read and travelled widely.

"Here," he said, moving aside. "Why don't you have a go?"

"Me? I couldn't," Banks stammered. "I mean, I wouldn't know where to start. I don't know the first thing about it."

Gristhorpe grinned in challenge. "No matter. It's just like building a case. Test your mettle. Come on, have a go."

Banks edged towards the heap of stones, none of which looked to him as if it could be fitted into the awesome design. He picked some up, weighed them in his hand, squinted at the wall, turned them over, squinted again, then picked a smooth, wedge-shaped piece and fitted it well enough into place.

Gristhorpe looked at the stone expressionlessly, then at Banks. He reached out, picked it up, turned it around and fixed it back into place.

"There," he said. "Perfect. A damn good choice."

Banks couldn't help but laugh. "What was wrong with the way I put it in?" he asked.

"Wrong way around, that's all," Gristhorpe explained. "This is a simple wall. You should have seen the ones my grandfather built— like bloody cathedrals, they were. Still standing, too, some of them. Anyway, you start by digging a trench along your line and you put in two parallel rows of footing stones. Big ones, square as you can get them. Between those rows you put in the hearting, lots of small stones, like pebbles. These bind together under pressure, see. After that, you can start to build, narrowing all the time, two rows rising up from the footing stones. You keep that gap filled tight with hearting and make sure you bind it all together with plenty of through-stones.

"Now, that stone you put in fit all right, but it sloped inwards. They have to slope outwards, see, else the rain'll get in and soak the hearting. If that happens, when the first frost comes it'll expand, you see." He held his hands close together and moved them slowly apart. "And that can bring the whole bloody thing tumbling down."

"I see." Banks nodded, ashamed at how such basic common sense could have been beyond him. Country wisdom, he guessed.

"A good dry-stone wall," the superintendent went on, "can stand any weather. It can even stand bloody sheep scrambling over it. Some of these you see around here have been up since the eighteenth century. Of course, they need a bit of maintenance now and then, but who doesn't?" He laughed. "You and that lass, Jenny," he asked suddenly. "Owt in it?"

Surprised at the question coming out of the blue like that, Banks blushed a little as he shook his head. "I like her. I like her a lot. But no."

Gristhorpe nodded, satisfied, placed a through-stone and rubbed his hands together gleefully.

That evening, back at home, Alan and Sandra shared a nightcap after they had sent Tracy and Brian off to bed. The opera ban was lifted, but it had to be quiet. Banks played a tape of Kiri te Kanawa singing famous arias from Verdi and Puccini. They snuggled close on the sofa, and as Sandra put her empty glass down, she turned to Banks and asked, "Have you ever been unfaithful?"

Without hesitation, he replied, "No." It was true, but it didn't feel true. He was beginning to understand what Jimmy Carter's predicament had been when he said that he had committed adultery in his mind.

ELEVEN

I

By midday on Monday, DC Richmond had not only discovered from the Eastvale census records and electoral lists that there were almost eight hundred men aged between twenty and thirty-five living either alone or with a single parent, but he also had a list of their names.

"Marvellous what computers can do these days, sir," he said to Banks as he handed over the report.

"Keen on them, are you?" Banks asked, looking up and smiling.

"Yes, sir. I've applied for that course next summer. I hope you'll be able to spare me."

"Lord knows what'll be going on next summer," Banks said. "I thought I was all set for the quiet life when I came up here, and look what's happened so far. I'll bear it in mind, anyway. I know the super's keen on new technology—at least as far as the workplace is concerned."

"Thank you, sir. Was there anything else?"

"Sit down a minute," Banks said as he started reading quickly through the list. The only names he recognized at first glance were those he had heard from Robin Allott the previous day: Geoff Welling and Barry Scott.

"Right," he said, shoving the papers towards Richmond. "There's a bit more legwork to be done. First of all, I want you to check into the two names I've ticked here. But for God's sake do it discreetly. I don't want anyone to know we're checking up on private citizens on so little evidence." He grinned at Richmond. "Use your imagination, eh? First thing to find out is if they have alibis for the peeping incidents. Clear so far?"

"Yes, sir."

"The next job might take a bit more doing." Banks explained about Mr Patel's observations, hoping that he might also relieve any anxieties Richmond had about his being in The Oak with Jenny on Saturday evening. "Someone else might have seen him in the area, so talk to the residents and local shopkeepers. Also, see if you can find out who the bus drivers were on the routes past The Oak that night. Talk to them, find out if they noticed our man. All right?"

"Yes, sir," Richmond said, a bit more hesitantly.

"What is it, lad?"

"I'm not complaining, sir, but it's going to take a long time without help."

"Get Sergeant Hatchley to help you if he's not too busy."

When Richmond hardly appeared to jump with joy, Banks suppressed a smile. "And ask Sergeant Rowe if he can spare you a couple of uniformed boys."

"Yes, sir," Richmond said more cheerfully.

"Right. Off you go."

Banks had no great hopes for the enquiry, but it had to be carried out. It was the same with every case; thousands of man-hours seemed to amount to nothing until that one fragment of information turned up in the most unexpected place and led them to the solution.

He remembered his mental note to visit Alice Matlock's cottage again and see if he could nose out what it was that had bothered him since his talk with Robin.

As it was a pleasant, if chilly, day, he put on his light overcoat and set off. Turning left into the market square, then left again, he walked through the network of old cobbled streets to King Street, then wound his way down through Leaview Estate to Gallows View.

Alice Matlock's house was exactly as the police had left it almost a week ago, and Banks wondered who was going to inherit the mess. Ethel Carstairs? If there was anything of value, would it have been worth killing for? No will had been discovered so far, but that didn't mean Alice hadn't made one. She had no next of kin, so the odds were that at some point she had considered what to do about bequeathing her worldly goods. It was worth looking into.

As he stood in the small, cluttered living-room, Banks tried to work out exactly what it was that bothered him. Again, he made the rounds of the alcoves, with their hand-painted figurines of nursery-rhyme and fairy-tale figures like Miss Muffet and Little Jack Horner, their old gilt-framed sepia photographs and teaspoons from almost every coastal resort in Britain.

He picked up a glass-encased Dales scene and watched the snow fall on the shepherd and his sheep as he shook it. Moving on, he found an exquisitely engraved silver snuff-box, dented on one edge. Opening it up, he noticed the initials A.G.M. on the inside of the lid. Alice? Surely not. Still, Robin Allott had said she was a radical, a fighter for women's rights, and Banks had seen photographs of pioneer feminists smoking cigars or pipes, so why not take snuff, too? On the other hand, he was certain she had no middle name, but there had been a boyfriend who had died in the Great War. Perhaps the snuff-box had been his. The dent might even have been caused by the bullet that killed him, Banks found himself thinking. There was something about Alice's house that made him feel fanciful, as if he were in a tiny, personal museum.

Next he peered closely at the ship in the bottle. Banks could easily imagine a young boy populating the ship with sailors and inventing adventures for them. Its name, *Miranda*, was clear on its side, and all the details of deck, mast, ropes and sails were reproduced in miniature. There was even a tiny figurehead of a naked woman with streaming hair—Miranda herself, perhaps.

As he moved back to the centre of the room and looked around again at Alice's carefully preserved possessions, he realized exactly what it was that had been nagging away at the back of his mind.

When Robin had mentioned the ship, Banks had visualized it clearly, just as he had been able to remember many of the other articles in the room. True, the place had been a mess—cupboards and sideboards had been emptied and their contents scattered over the floor—but there had been no gratuitous damage.

One of the features of the Ottershaw burglary that led Banks to believe it was the work of the same youths who had been robbing the old women was the wanton destruction of property: the urine and faeces that had defaced Ottershaw's paintings, music centre, television and VCR.

It was slim evidence to base a decision on, Banks realized, but it confirmed the hunch he already had about the Matlock killing. If the same youths had been responsible, they would, according to form, have smashed the ship in the bottle, the snowstorm and any other fragile object on display. But no, this thief had only made a straightforward utilitarian search for cash and such things as could be easily translated into money; the gratuitous element was entirely missing.

Pulling his collar up against the breeze, Banks set off, deep in thought, back to the station.

II

"I'm worried, Gray," Andrea said as they dipped into a dessert of cherry pie and ice cream after a main course of lasagne and salad. It was Monday evening—Andrea's husband was off in Bristol for the week and it was Trevor's youth-club night—so Graham and Andrea could actually have dinner together like a normal couple. The romantic peace of their candle-lit dinner was spoiled, however, by her obvious distress.

"What is it?" Graham asked, spooning up another mouthful of pie. "Don't tell me Ronnie's getting suspicious?"

"No, it's not that," Andrea reassured him quickly. "But it could lead to that."

She looked beautiful across the table. Her breasts pushed at the tight black blouse, which revealed tiny ovals of olive skin between the buttons, and her glossy hair, equally black, swept down across her shoulders and shimmered every time she tossed her head. Her red lipstick emphasized her full lips, and her dark eyes reflected the candle flames like brightly polished oak. Graham was excited, and Andrea's preoccupied mood irritated him.

"What's happened, then?" he asked, sighing and putting his spoon down.

Andrea leaned forward on the table, cupping her chin with her hands. "It's that man next door."

"Wooller?"

"Yes, him."

"What about him? I know he's a bit of a creep, but..."

"Remember last week I told you I thought he'd been looking at me funny?"

"Yes."

"Well, he actually spoke to me this morning. I was just going to the shops and he caught up with me at the end of the street and walked along beside me."

"Bloody cheek! Go on," Graham prompted her, curious. "Did he try to pick you up?"

"No, it wasn't like that. Well, not really like that." She shivered. "He makes my skin crawl, those thin, dry lips of his, and that weird smile he's always got on his face, as if he knows something you don't. He knows about us, Gray, I'm sure of it."

"Did he say so?"

"Not in so many words. He wasn't direct about it. First he just went on about how lonely it must be with my husband away so much, then he said it was so nice that I'd found a friend, that nice Mr Sharp from the shop. He said he'd seen you coming and going out of the back window, and he thought it was so good of you to keep me company, especially when you had a son to look after, too. It was the way he said it, though, Gray. His voice. His tone. It was dirty."

"Is that all he said?" Graham asked.

"What do you mean?"

"About seeing me visit you."

"Yes. I told you, it wasn't what he said but the way he said it, as if he knew much more."

"Go on." Graham started chewing on his bottom lip as Andrea continued her story.

"He said that not everyone was as sympathetic as him, and maybe my husband wouldn't be so understanding—he might worry about people talking, for example, even though there was nothing really going on. But he was leering at me all the time, as if he was nudging me and saying, 'We both know there's something going on, don't we?' I just ignored him and tried to walk faster, but he kept up with me and even turned the corner when I did. He went on about what a pity it would be if my husband did find out and wasn't understanding—then I'd be all lonely again, and I'd never have any nice friends again, however innocent their intentions were. I asked him to get to the point, to tell me what he was getting at, and he pretended to take offence."

"What does he want?" Graham asked impatiently. "Money?"

"I don't think so, no. I think he wants to go to bed with me."

"He what?"

"He wants me himself. I couldn't bear it, Gray. I'd be sick, I know I would." She was almost in tears now.

"Don't worry," Graham comforted her. "It won't come to that, you can be certain. What did he say?"

"He just said that there was no reason why I shouldn't have another friend, like him, for example, and what a good friend he could be and all that. He never really said anything, you know, explicit, nothing you could put your finger on. But we both knew what he was talking about. He said how pretty he thought I was, what nice legs I had, and I could feel his eyes crawling all over my body while he spoke. Then he said we should all have tea together soon, and he'd be happy just to sit there and watch us—Oh, he's disgusting, Gray! What am I going to do?"

"You're not to worry," Graham said, moving his chair next to hers and stroking her hair. "I'll take care of him."

"Will you?" She turned her face so that it was close to his. He could smell the cherries on her breath. "What will you do?"

"Never you mind about that, love. I've told you I'll deal with him. Don't I always keep my word?"

Andrea nodded.

"Then you've nothing to worry about, have you? You won't hear anything from him again. He won't even so much as glance in your direction if he sees you in the street, I promise you that."

"You won't hurt him, will you Gray? I don't want you to get into trouble. You know what that might lead to."

"At least then," Graham said wearily, "we'd be out in the open. We could go away together."

"Yes," Andrea agreed. "But it wouldn't be a good start, would it? I want things to be better than that for us."

"I suppose so," Graham said, sitting back.

"But you'll really deal with him, will you? And not make any trouble?"

Graham nodded and smiled at her. Andrea caught his look and stood up to clear the table. "Not yet, you goat," she said. "Wait till I've cleared the dishes."

"They can wait," Graham said, reaching out for her. "I can't."

She moved away playfully and his hand caught the collar of her blouse. As she stepped back, the material ripped down the front and the buttons flew off, pinging against wine glasses and plates. The blouse hung open, revealing Andrea's semi-transparent black brassiere, the one that stood out in clear relief against her pale skin and exposed a great deal of inviting cleavage.

Graham froze for a second. He didn't know what her reaction would be. Perhaps it was an expensive blouse—it felt soft, like silk— and she would be angry with him. He was all set to apologize and offer to buy her another when she laughed and reached forward to pull at his shirt.

"Come on, then," she said, smiling at him. "If you really can't wait." And they rolled to the floor, laughing and tearing at each other's clothes.

Afterwards, sweaty and out of breath, they lay back and laughed again, then went up to the bedroom to continue making love in a more leisurely way for another two hours.

Finally, it was time to go. Trevor was due back in about half an hour, and Graham had promised to drop in on Wooller on his way home.

"Remember," Andrea said, kissing him as he left, "no trouble. Ask him nicely. Tell him there's nothing in it."

III

Graham Sharp knocked softly at the door of number six Gallows View, and a few seconds later, Wooller peered around the chain, squinting through his thick glasses.

"Mr Sharp!" he exclaimed. "What a pleasant surprise. Come in, come in!"

The messy room smelled of old socks and boiled cabbage. Wooller, obviously thinking that Sharp had come to make some arrangement about Andrea Rigby, scooped some newspapers from a straight-backed chair and bade him sit down.

"Tea? Or perhaps something a little stronger?"

"No, thanks," Graham said stiffly. "And I won't sit down either. I'll not be stopping long."

"Oh," said Wooller, standing in the kitchen doorway. "Sure I can't persuade you?"

"No," Sharp said, walking towards him. "You can't bloody persuade me. But I think I can persuade you."

Wooller looked puzzled until Graham grabbed him by the front of his pullover, bunching the wool in his fist and half-lifting the frail librarian from the floor. Sharp was much taller and in far better physical shape. He began to shake Wooller, gently at first, then more violently, against the kitchen door jamb. Each time Wooller's back hit the wood, Graham spat out a word. "Don't...you...ever... threaten...Andrea...Rigby...again...you...smelly...little... prick....Do...you...under...stand?" It was hard to tell if Wooller was nodding or not, but he looked scared enough.

"Stop it," Wooller whined, putting his hand to the back of his head. "You've split my skull. Look, blood!"

He thrust his open palm under Graham's eyes, and there was clearly blood on it. Sharp felt a sudden lurch of fear in his stomach. He let go of Wooller and leaned against the doorway, pale and trembling. Wooller stared at him with his mouth open.

Quickly, Graham made the effort to pull himself together. He grabbed a glass from the draining-board and, without even bothering to see if it was clean or not, filled it with cold water from the tap and gulped it down.

Feeling a little better, he ran his hand through his hair and faced a confused Wooller, grasping the front of his pullover again. "I'm not going to tell you again," he said, injecting as much quiet menace into his tone as he could manage. "Do you understand me?"

Wooller swallowed and nodded. "Let me go! Let me go!"

"If you say one more word to Mrs Rigby," Graham went on, "even if you so much as look at her in a way she doesn't like, I'll be back to finish what I started. And don't think of talking to her husband, either. True, you might cause a bit of trouble if you do, but not half as much trouble as you'll be causing for yourself. Get it?"

Again Wooller's Adam's apple bobbed as he nodded. "Let me go! Please!"

Graham relaxed his grip a bit more, but didn't quite let go of Wooller's bunched-up pullover. "I want to hear you say you understand me, first," he said. "I want you to tell me you won't talk to anyone about this—not her husband, not the police, not anyone. Because if you do, Wooller, I swear it, I'll break every fucking bone in your stinking little body."

Wooller was shaking. "All right," he whimpered, trying to wriggle free. "All right, I'll say nothing, I'll leave her alone. I only wanted to be her friend, that's all I wanted."

Graham raised his fist, angered again by Wooller's pathetic lie, but he made the effort and restrained himself. He had almost gone too far, and he was certain now that Andrea and he would have no more trouble from Wooller.

IV

As soon as the back door cracked open, Trevor felt the thrill; it set his blood dancing and made the sweat prickle on his forehead and cheeks. The rough wool of the balaclava scratched at his face and made it itch like mad. The two of them entered the house cautiously, but all was as they had expected—dark and quiet. The narrow beams of their torches picked out dishes piled up for washing, a table littered with shadowy objects, a newspaper open at a half-finished crossword puzzle. Again, they were in a kitchen, but it seemed much less clean and tidy than the one they'd been in a few days ago.

The living-room, too, turned out to be in a bit of a mess: Sunday's paper lay scattered on the carpet, and Trevor's beam picked out a half-full coffee mug on the mantelpiece.

They'd been tipped by Lenny that the woman who lived there kept a lot of expensive jewellery, which he could easily fence in London, so they ignored the living-room and, keeping their torch beams pointed towards the floor, headed up the stairs. The first room they entered was empty except for a single bed—a guestroom, most likely—and two others were similarly ascetic. It felt eerie, as if the woman had once had family and now they were gone and the house was empty and bare. You could tell from the downstairs that she couldn't be bothered much any more; yet she was supposed to be well off.

Finally, after more false starts in the bathroom and airing-cupboard, they found what seemed to be her bedroom. At first they couldn't make it out, but by running the torches over a wider area they discovered that a large, four-poster bed stood at the centre of the room. Mick sat on the edge of the mattress and bounced up and down for a while before pronouncing it too lumpy. Then they began their search.

Again, there was an assortment of clothes, this time all female, and Trevor noticed that this woman's underwear was far more exotic than the other's. There were brassieres cut so low that they were practically non-existent; skimpy, see-through panties; a garter belt with roses embroidered on it; stockings with dark borders around the tops; and short, lacy nightdresses. The lingerie was all clean and it smelled of something faintly exotic: jasmine, Trevor thought it was. His mother had bought some jasmine tea once, many years ago, and the smell took him back and made him think of her. He remembered that none of them had liked the tea and his mother had laughed at their lack of adventurous spirit.

They found the jewellery in a lacquered box with a Chinese land-scape painted on it. The box was locked but it broke open easily and they pocketed its contents. They poked around the room a bit longer, looking for cash, but found none. That made Trevor angry, because with cash he didn't have to rely on Lenny's spurious deals.

They set off back downstairs, and just as they were about to turn the final bend into the front hallway, the door opened and closed, the hall light came on and a woman began to take off her sleek fur coat.

Cautiously, Mick led the way down. The last stair creaked and the woman turned, but Mick got his hand over her mouth before she could scream. They dragged her into the living-room and switched on the standard-lamp. The curtains were already closed. Mick took the woman's head-scarf and fastened it tight, like a bit between her teeth, then he took the belt from her raincoat and tied her hands crudely behind her back.

"We need time to get away," he said to Trevor. "We've got to make sure she keeps quiet for long enough. Bring me that candlestick over there."

Trevor looked and saw an old brass candlestick with a heavy base. The woman whimpered behind her gag and struggled to free herself.

"No," he said.

"Come on," Mick urged him. "We've got to. We can't risk getting caught now."

Slowly, Trevor walked over to the mantelpiece, picked up the candlestick, felt its weight, then dropped it on the floor. "No," he said again. "You'd probably kill her. You don't know how little strength it takes."

"So what," Mick argued, stretching out his hand scornfully. "Give us it here."

"I've got a better idea," Trevor said.

"What?"

Trevor looked at the woman sprawled awkwardly on the sofa. She was about thirty-eight, forty maybe, but very well preserved. Her hair was blonde, but the dark roots showed, and perhaps she was wearing just a little too much mascara. But apart from that, she looked very tasty indeed to Trevor. Her breasts jutted behind the polo-necked sweater and her skirt had already slipped up high enough to show a spread of thigh. He got an eerie feeling that his moment had come at last.

"You must be mad," Mick gasped, realizing what Trevor meant. "We can't hang around here."

"Why not? We know she lives alone. She's here. So who else is going to come?"

Mick thought for a moment, licking his lips. "All right, then," he agreed, and began to move forward.

Trevor stood in front of him and nudged him gently out of the way. "Me first."

There was something determined in his tone, so Mick just shrugged and moved back. Trevor manoeuvred the woman awkwardly onto the floor. She didn't struggle, but she seemed to have gone limp and heavy. He pulled the sweater up around her breasts but couldn't get it off while here hands were tied. There were some scissors by the stack of magazines on the coffee table, so he picked them up and carefully cut the material. Underneath, her bra was pink, and the hard nipples poked at its cups. Trevor grabbed the elastic in the middle and tried to tear it off, but it proved stronger than it looked. Again, he used the scissors. The whole thing was beginning to seem a lot harder than he'd imagined.

"For fuck's sake, hurry up," Mick urged him. "Get on with it!"

Trevor squeezed the woman's breasts. They were soft and slack and he didn't like the feel of them. Slowly, he cut off the rest of her clothes. Again, she didn't struggle; she just lay there like a sack of potatoes.

Finally, he pushed her legs apart, unbuckled his belt and unzipped his trousers. It was his first time, but it felt right; he knew what to do.

He tried to avoid looking her in the face. Because of the scarf between her teeth she seemed to be grinning maliciously, and when he caught her eyes he thought he saw mockery in them, not just fear. He'd soon teach her. When he started, he thought he heard her grunt with pain behind her gag as she whipped her head from side to side, and he could see her eyes were blurred with tears now.

The pressure was strong in Trevor and he could manage no more than three or four rough thrusts before it was all over. Exhausted even by such a meagre effort, he got to his knees and pulled up his pants. The woman just lay there. She wasn't crying now; her eyes were far away and the taut scarf still made her appear to grin.

"Your turn," he said, turning to Mick.

"Not on your bleeding Nelly! If you think I'm taking your sloppy seconds, you've got another bloody think coming, mate. Let's piss off out of here."

Before they left, Mick gave the woman a hard kick to the side of her head and told her there'd be more of that if she didn't keep her mouth shut. Trevor noticed a thin trickle of blood shining in her hair before he turned and followed Mick out through the kitchen.

TWELVE

I

After a dull, elementary talk by Fred Barton on the properties of the medium telephoto lens, the Tuesday evening Camera Club was devoted to mutual criticism of work produced at the session two weeks earlier when a nude model had been the subject. As expected, some ribald remarks came from less mature male amateurs, but on the whole the brief, informal session was productive.

Sandra looked over Norman's work and had to admit, if only to herself, that she liked it. It was far more experimental than anyone else's, she imagined, and she felt some sympathy because she, too, liked to take risks, though she rarely went as far as Norman. He had used a fast film and blown up the prints to give them a very coarse grain; consequently, the photographs did not look like shots of a naked woman; they looked more like moonscapes.

The usual crowd gathered at The Mile Post later. The pub was busier than usual; rock 'n' roll on the jukebox and bleeping video games made conversation difficult. There was also a group of local farmers celebrating something with a great deal of laughter and the occasional song, and some of the lads from the racing stables in Middleham were out enjoying a night on the town.

"Have you seen that new Minolta?" Norman asked, getting comfortable in his chair and arranging pipe and matches neatly in front of him on the varnished table.

"That's not a camera," Robin said. "It's a computer. All you have to do is programme it and it does everything for you, including focus."

"What do you think you're doing when you set your shutter speed and your aperture?" Norman asked. "You're programming your camera then, aren't you?"

"That's different."

"As far as I'm concerned," Sandra chipped in, "anything that makes the technical side easier and allows me to concentrate more on the photograph is fine by me."

Norman smiled indulgently. "Well put, Sandra. Although I would add that the 'technical side,' as you term it, is an integral part of the photograph."

"I know the selections are important," Sandra agreed, "and I'd always want a manual override—but the easier the better as far as I'm concerned."

"I've never found it particularly difficult to set the camera," Robin said. "Or to focus. I don't really see what all the fuss is about."

"Typical reactionary attitude," Norman sneered. "You can't ignore the new technology, lad. You might as well make good use of it."

"I've really nothing against it," Robin argued quietly. "I just don't think I need one, that's all. No more than I need an electric toothbrush."

"Oh, you'd be happy with a bloody pinhole camera, you would," Norman sighed.

"My excuse is that I can't afford one," Sandra said.

"I don't think any of us can," Harriet echoed. "It's a very expensive hobby, photography."

"True enough," Norman agreed. "I'd have to sell all the camera equipment I've already got. It might be worth it, though. I'll look into it a bit more closely. Another round?"

When Norman came back with the drinks, the conversation had shifted subtly to the evening's session. Sandra complimented him on his photos and he grudgingly admitted that hers, though they were in colour and had obviously been cropped, were fine compositions. He told her that she had done particularly interesting and unusual things with skin tone.

"Where are yours?" Norman asked Robin. "I don't think any of us had a look at them."

"They're not back yet. I took slides and I didn't finish the film. I only sent it off a couple of days ago."

"Slides!" exclaimed Norman. "What an odd thing to do."

"I used an Ektachrome 50," Robin argued. "It's very good for that kind of thing."

"But all the same," Norman repeated, *"slides* in a studio nude session? I'll bet you never even had a film in your camera, eh, Robin? I'll bet that's why you've got nothing to show us."

Robin ignored him and looked over to Sandra. "I talked to your husband," he said, "but I can't see how I was any help."

Sandra shrugged. "You never know. He's got to gather all the information he can. I should imagine it's like counting the grains of sand on a beach."

"I think I'd find that too frustrating."

Sandra laughed. "Oh, I'm sure Alan does, too. Especially when there's so many cases going at once and they keep him out till all hours. Still, that's not all there is to it."

"'A policeman's lot,'" quoted Norman "'is not a happy one.'"

"I wouldn't agree with that," Sandra said, smiling. "Alan's usually perfectly happy unless he's dealing with particularly unpleasant crimes, like the killing of a defenceless old woman."

"And a Peeping Tom," Norman added. "Let's not forget our Peeping Tom."

"No, let's not," Sandra said. "Anyway, Robin, you might have been helpful. Alan says it's often hard to know exactly where the solution comes from. Everything gets mixed in together."

"When are we going to see these slides, then?" Norman asked Robin impatiently.

"They should be back soon."

"I'll bet you don't even have a slide projector."

"So what? I could always borrow one."

"Not from me, you couldn't. I haven't got one either. I haven't even been able to show anyone last year's holiday pictures yet."

"Surely Robin must have one if he's been taking slides?" Harriet said.

"No, I don't," Robin mumbled apologetically. "I'm afraid I've never done transparencies before. I do have a small viewer, of course, but that's not much use."

"Well, I *do* have a projector and a screen," Sandra told them. "And if any of you want to borrow it, you're quite welcome. Just drop around sometime. You know where I live."

"Is that an invitation, Sandra?" Norman leered.

"Oh, shut up," she said, and pushed him playfully away.

"Don't you think there's something unnatural about taking pictures of nudes at the Camera Club?" Harriet asked suddenly. "I mean, we're all talking about it as if it's the most normal thing in the world."

"Why?" demanded Norman. "It's the only chance some of us get."

"What?" Sandra joked. "A gay, young blade like yourself, Norman. Surely they're just flocking to your studio, dying to take their clothes off for you?"

"Less of the 'gay,' if you please, love. And I don't have a studio. What about you, Robin?"

"What about me?"

"Do you agree with Harriet, that it's unnatural to photograph nudes in a studio?"

"I wouldn't say it's unnatural, no. I don't think my mother would approve, though," he added in an attempt at humour. "I sometimes have a devil of a job keeping things to myself."

At about ten o'clock, there was a general movement homewards, but Sandra managed to catch Harriet's eye and signal discreetly for her to stay. After the others had gone, Harriet moved her chair closer. "Another drink?" she asked.

"Please." Sandra said. She needed it. She also needed somebody to talk to, and the only person she could think of was Harriet. Even then, it would take another drink to make her open up.

The empty seats at the table were soon taken by a noisy but polite group of stable-lads. When she had adjusted to the new volume level, Harriet, who drove a mobile library around some of the more remote Dales villages, began to talk about work.

"Yesterday I got a puncture near the Butter Tubs Pass above Wensleydale," she said. "A car full of tourists came speeding round the corner, and I had to pull over quick. Some of those stones by the side of the road are very sharp, I can tell you. I was stuck there for ages till a kind young vet stopped to help me. When I got to Angram, old Mrs Wytherbottom played heck about having to wait so long for her new Agatha Christie." She paused. "Sandra, what's wrong? You haven't listened to a word I've said."

"What? Oh, sorry." Sandra gulped down the last of her vodka and slimline and took the plunge. "It happened to me, Harriet," she said quietly. "What we were talking about last week. It happened to me on Friday."

"Good Lord." Harriet whispered, putting her hand on Sandra's wrist. "What...how?"

"Just like everyone else. I was getting ready for bed and he was watching through the bottom of the curtains."

"Did you see him?"

"I saw him before I'd got too far, fortunately. But he was off like a shot. I didn't get a good look at him. The thing is, Harriet, this has got to be in strict confidence. Alan didn't report it because of the embarrassment it would cause us both. He feels bad enough about that, but if he thought anyone else knew..."

"I understand. Don't worry, Sandra, I won't tell a soul. Not even David."

"Thank you."

"How do you feel?"

"Now? Fine. It seems very distant already. It was a shock at first, and I certainly felt violated, but I wanted to tell you that I also felt some sort of pity for the man. It's odd, but when I could first think about it rationally, it just seemed so childish. That's the word that came to mind: childish. He needs help, not punishment. Maybe both, I don't know. It depends which gets the better of me, anger or pity. Every time I think about it they seem to be fighting in me."

"It was silly of me to say what I did last week," Harriet apologized. "About feeling sorry for him. I'd no idea...I mean, I've still no idea what it actually feels like. But they're closer than you think, aren't they, anger and pity?"

"Yes. Anyway, it's not as bad as you'd imagine," Sandra said, smiling. "You soon get over it. I doubt that it leaves any lasting scars on anyone, unlike most sex crimes." Even as she spoke the words, they sounded too glib to be true.

"I don't know. Has Alan got any leads yet?"

"Not much, no. A vague description. One of our neighbours saw a man hanging around the back alley a few days ago. He was dressed pretty much the same as the man I saw, but neither of us could give a clear description. Anyway, keep an eye on your neighbourhood, Harriet. It seems that he does a bit of research before he comes in to get his jollies."

"Yes, I read about that in the paper. Superintendent Gristhorpe gave a press release."

"Anyway," Sandra said, "there's a lot of women in Eastvale, so I would think the odds against you are pretty high."

Harriet smiled. "But why you?"

"What do you mean?"

"The odds against you must have been high, too."

"Alan thinks it's because of who I am. He says the man's getting bolder, more cocky, throwing down the gauntlet."

"A Peeping Tom with a sense of humour?"

"Why not? Plenty of psychos have one."

"You don't think he's looking for someone, do you?"

"Looking for someone? Who? What do you mean?"

"Someone in particular. You know, like Jack the Ripper always said that woman's name."

"Mary Kelly? That's just a rumour, though. Why would he be looking for someone in particular?"

"I don't know. It was just a thought. Somebody who reminds him of his first time, his first love or someone like that."

"You're quite the amateur psychologist, aren't you?" Sandra said, looking at Harriet through narrowed eyes.

"It's just something I thought of, that's all." Harriet shrugged.

"They've brought a professional psychologist in," Sandra said. "Woman called Fuller. Dr Jenny Fuller. According to Gristhorpe she's quite a looker, and Alan's been working late several evenings."

"Oh, Sandra," Harriet exclaimed. "You surely can't think Alan . . .?"

"Relax," Sandra said, laughing and touching Harriet's arm. "No, I don't think anything like that. I do think he fancies her, though."

"How do you know?"

"A woman can tell. Surely you could tell if David had his eyes on another woman?"

"Well, I suppose so. He is rather transparent."

"Exactly. I wouldn't use that word to describe Alan, but it's in what he doesn't say and how he reacts when the subject's brought up. He's been very cagey. He didn't even tell me it was an attractive woman he was working with."

"Does it worry you?"

"No. I trust him. And if he does yield to temptation, he wouldn't be the first."

"But what would you do?"

"Nothing."

"Would he tell you?"

"Yes. Eventually. Men like Alan usually do, you know. They think it's because they're being honest with you, but it's really because the guilt is too much of a burden; they can't bear it alone. I'd probably rather not know, but he wouldn't consider that."

"Oh, Sandra," Harriet snorted, "you're being a proper cynic. Don't you think you're being a bit hard on him?"

Sandra laughed. "I wouldn't be able to say it if I didn't love him, warts and all. And don't get upset. I don't think anything will come of it. If she's as beautiful as Gristhorpe says, Alan would hardly be normal if he didn't feel some attraction. He's a big boy. He can deal with it."

"You haven't met her, then?"

"No, he's not offered to introduce me."

"Maybe," Harriet suggested, leaning forward and lowering her voice, "you should get him to invite her for dinner? Or just suggest a drink together. See what he says."

Sandra beamed. "What a good idea! I'm sure it'd be a lot of fun. Yes, I think I'll get working on it. It'll be interesting to see how he reacts."

II

Police Constable Craig was one of the uniformed officers temporarily in plain clothes on the peeper case. It was his job to walk between as many pubs as possible within his designated area and to keep an eye open for any loiterers. The job was tiring and frustrating, as he was not allowed to enter any of the pubs; he simply had to walk the streets and pass each place more than once to see if anyone was hanging around for too long.

As he approached The Oak, near the end of his beat, for the second time that evening, he noticed the same man standing in the shadows of the bus shelter. From the few details that Craig could make out, the man was slim, of medium height and wearing a dark, belted raincoat and a flat cap. It wasn't a trilby, but there was no law against a man's owning more than one hat. Craig also knew that at least two buses must have stopped there since he had last walked by The Oak.

Following instructions, he went inside the noisy pub and sought out DC Richmond, who was by now sick to death of spending every evening—duty or no—in that loud, garish gin-palace. Richmond, hearing Craig's story, suggested that they call the station first, then check once more in about fifteen minutes. If the man was still there, they would approach him for questioning. Gratefully, Craig accepted a half of Guinness and the chance to sit down and take the weight off his feet.

Meanwhile, Mr Patel, who had become quite the sleuth since Banks's visit, glanced frequently out of his shop window, and wrote down, in a notebook bought especially for the purpose, that a man resembling the suspect he had already described to the police had been standing in the shelter for forty-eight minutes. He timed his entry "Tuesday, 9:56 P.M.," then picked up the phone and asked for Detective Chief Inspector Banks.

Banks was not, at first, happy to take the message. He was enjoying a pleasant evening with the children—no opera, no television—helping Brian construct a complicated extension of track for his electric train. Tracy was stretched out on her stomach, too, deciding where to place bridges, signal boxes and papier-mâché mountains. Everyone pulled a face when the phone rang, but Banks became excited when Sergeant Rowe passed on Mr Patel's information.

Back at The Oak, the fifteen minutes was up. Richmond had reported in, as arranged, and now it was time to approach the suspect and ask a few questions. As he and Craig headed for the pub's heavy smoked-glass and oak doors, Banks was just arriving at Mr Patel's shop, walking in as casually as any customer.

"Is that him?" he asked.

"I can't say for certain," Mr Patel answered, scratching his head. "But 'ee looks the same. 'Ee weren't wearing an 'at last time, though."

"How long did you say he's been there?"

Mr Patel looked first at his watch, then down at his notebook. "Sixty-three minutes," he answered, after a brief calculation.

"And how many buses have gone by?"

"Three. One to Ripon and two to York."

The bus shelter stood at the apex of a triangle, the base of which was formed by a line between Mr Patel's shop and The Oak itself. Banks was already at the door, keeping his eyes on the suspect across the road to his right, when Craig and Richmond, walking much too purposefully towards their man, were spotted, and the dark figure took off down the street.

But what could have been a complete disaster was suddenly transformed into a triumphant success. As the man sprinted by Mr Patel's shop with a good lead on his pursuers, Banks rushed out and performed the best rugby tackle he could remember making since he'd played scrum-half in a school game over twenty years ago.

The quartet returned to Eastvale station at ten-thirty, and the suspect, protesting loudly, was led into the interview room: a stark place with three stiff-backed chairs, pale green walls and a metal desk.

Richmond and Craig thought they were in for a telling-off, but Banks surprised them by thanking them for their help. They both knew that if the man had got away things would have been very different.

The suspect was Ronald Markham, age twenty-eight, a plumber in Eastvale, and apart from the headgear, his clothing matched all earlier descriptions of the peeper's. At first he was outraged at being attacked in such a violent manner, then he became sullen and sarcastic.

"What were you doing in the shelter?" Banks asked, with Richmond standing behind him instead of Hatchley, whom nobody had thought to disturb.

"Waiting for a bus," Markham snapped.

"Did you get that, Constable Richmond?"

"Yes sir. Suspect replied that he was 'waiting for a bus,'" Richmond quoted.

"Which bus?" Banks asked.

"Any bus."

"Where were you going?"

"Anywhere."

Banks walked over to Richmond and whispered in his ear. Then he turned to Markham, said "Won't be a minute, sir," and the two of them disappeared, leaving a uniformed constable to guard the room.

About forty-five minutes later, when they returned after a hastily grabbed pint and sandwich at the Queen's Arms, Markham was livid again.

"You can't treat me like this!" he protested. "I know my rights."

"What were you doing in the shelter?" Banks asked him calmly.

Markham didn't answer. He ran his thick fingers through his hair, turned his eyes up to the ceiling, then glared at Banks, who repeated his question: "What were you doing in the shelter?"

"Keeping an eye on my wife," Markham finally blurted out.

"Why do you think you need to do that?"

"Isn't it bloody obvious?" Markham replied scornfully. "Because I think she's having it off with someone else, that's why. She thinks I'm out of town on a job, but I followed her to The Oak."

"Did she enter alone or with a man?"

"Alone. But she was meeting him there, I know she was. I was waiting for them to come out."

"What were you going to do then?"

"Do?" Markham ran his hand through his thin, sandy hair again. "I don't know. Hadn't thought of it."

"Were you going to confront them?"

"I told you I don't know."

"Or were you just going to keep watching them, spying on them?"

"Maybe."

"Why would you do that?"

"To make sure, like, that they were having it off."

"So you're not sure?"

"I told you I'm not sure, no. That's what I was doing, trying to make sure."

"What would it take to convince you?" Banks asked.

"What do you mean?"

"What kind of evidence were you hoping to get?"

"I don't know. I wanted to see where they went, what they did."

"Did you hope to watch them having sex? Is that what you wanted to see?"

Markham snorted. "It's hardly what I *wanted* to see, but I expected it, yes."

"How were you going to watch them?"

"What do you mean?"

"The logistics. How were you going to spy on them? Use binoculars, climb a drainpipe, what? Were you going to take photographs, too?"

"I said before, I hadn't thought that far ahead. I was just going to follow them and see where they went. After that..." He shrugged. "Anyway, just what the hell are you getting at?"

"After that you were going to watch them and see what they did. Right?"

"Perhaps. Wouldn't you want to know, if it was your wife?"

"Have you done this kind of thing before?"

"What kind of thing?"

"Followed people and spied on them."

"Why would I?"

"I'm asking you."

"No, I haven't. And I don't see the point of all these questions. By now they're probably at it in some pokey bungalow."

"Bungalow? You know where he lives, then?"

"No. I don't even know who he is."

"But you said 'bungalow.' You know he lives in a bungalow?"

"No."

"Why did you say it, then?"

"For God's sake, what's it matter?" Markham cried, burying his long face in his hands. "It's over now, anyway."

"What's over?"

"My marriage. The cow!"

"Have you ever watched anybody getting undressed in a bungalow?" Banks persisted, though he was quickly becoming certain that it was all in vain now, that they had the wrong man.

"No," Markham answered, "of course I haven't." Then he laughed. "Bloody hell, you think I'm that Peeping Tom, don't you? You think I'm the bloody peeper!"

"Why did you run away when you saw my men approaching you?"

"I didn't know they were police, did I? They weren't wearing uniforms."

"But why run? They might simply have been walking to the bus stop, mightn't they?"

"It was just a feeling. The way they were walking. They looked like heavies to me, and I wasn't hanging around to get mugged."

"You thought they were going to mug you? Was that the reason?"

"Partly. It did cross my mind that they might be pals of the bloke my wife was meeting—that I'd been seen, like, and they wanted to warn me off. I don't know. All I can say is they didn't look like they were coming to wait for a bus."

It was almost midnight. Markham said that he was expected home late, at about one o'clock. He had arranged it that way so that he could give his wife enough time, enough rope to hang herself with. Banks suggested that to clear things up once and for all, they should return to Markham's house and wait for her.

The house, on Coleman Avenue about a mile northwest of the market square, was so spacious and well furnished that Banks found himself wondering if it was true that plumbers earned a fortune. The predominant colours were dark browns and greens, which, Banks thought, made the place seem a little too sombre for his taste.

At a quarter to one, the key turned in the door. Markham's wife had told him that she was visiting a friend and that if he did get home before her he shouldn't be surprised if she was a bit late. Curious about the light in the living-room, she peered around the door and walked in slowly when she saw her husband with a stranger.

Mrs Markham was a rather plain brunette in her late twenties, and Banks found it hard to imagine her as the type to have an affair. Still, it took all sorts, he reminded himself, and it never did to pigeon-hole people before you knew them.

After identifying himself, Banks asked Mrs Markham where she had spent the evening.

She sat down stiffly and started strangling one of her black leather gloves. "With a friend," she answered cautiously. "What's all this about?"

"Name?"

"Sheila Croft."

"Is she on the phone?"

"Yes."

"Would you call her, please?"

"Now? Why?"

"This is very important, Mrs Markham," Banks explained patiently. "Your husband might be in serious trouble, and I have to verify your story."

Mrs Markham bit her thin lower lip and glanced over at her husband.

There was fear in her eyes.

"The number?" Banks repeated.

"It's late, she'll be in bed now. Besides, we weren't at her house," Mrs Markham dithered.

"Where were you?"

"We went to a pub. The Oak."

"You weren't with no Sheila Croft, either, you bloody lying cow," Markham cut in. "I saw you go in there by yourself, all tarted up. And look at yourself now. Couldn't even be bothered to put a bit of make-up on again after."

Mrs Markham paled. "Call Sheila, then," she shouted. "Just you ask her. She was already there. I was late."

"Sheila would lie her pants off to protect you, and you bloody well know it. Who is he, you bitch?"

He got to his feet as if to strike her, and Banks stepped forward to push him back down.

"It's all right," Markham said bitterly. "I wouldn't hit her. She knows that. Who is he, you slut?"

At this point, Mrs Markham started weeping and complaining about being neglected. Banks, depressed by the entire scene and angry that it had not been the peeper they had caught, made his exit quietly.

III

A chill wind blew through Glue-Sniffers' Ginnel, where Mick and Trevor stood, jackets buttoned uptight, smoking and chatting.

"Did you like it, then, last night?" Mike asked.

"Not much," Trevor answered. "I suppose it was all right, but..."

"What? Too tight?"

"Yeah. Hurt a bit. Dry as a bone at first."

"Just wait till you get one that's willing. Slides in easy, then, it does. Plenty of 'em like it the hard way, though. You know, they like you to show 'em who's boss."

Trevor shrugged. "Where's the loot?"

"Got it hidden at my place. It's safe. Looks like we've struck the jackpot there, too, mate. Never seen any that sparkled so much."

"That depends on Lenny, doesn't it?"

"I told you, he's got the contacts. He'll get us the best he can. Probably a few G, there."

"Sure. And how much of that will we see?"

"Oh, don't go on about it, Trev," Mick grumbled, shifting from one foot to the other as if he had ants in his pants. "We'll get what's coming. And you did get a little bonus, didn't you?" he leered.

"What's Lenny doing?"

"Still in The Smoke setting up a business deal. Bit tight-lipped about it, right now."

"When's he coming back?"

"Don't know. Few days. A week."

"When are we going to get rid of the stuff?"

"What the bloody hell's wrong with you tonight, Trev? Nothing but fucking moan, moan, moan. You haven't spent all your readies yet, have you?"

"No. I just don't like the idea of that jewellery lying about, that's all."

"Don't worry. I told you it's safe. He'll be back soon."

"Heard from him, have you?"

"Got a letter from him this morning. Careful, our Lenny is. Thinks the blower might be tapped. He said he thought it'd be a good idea if we laid off on the jobs for a while. Just till things cool down, like."

"I've not noticed any heat."

"Bound to be going on, though, ain't it, behind the scenes. Stands to reason. There's been a lot of bother lately, and the rozzers must be getting their bleeding arses flayed. Mark my words, mate, they'll be working their balls off. Best lay off for a few weeks. We've got plenty to be going on with."

It wasn't the money that interested Trevor so much; it was the thrill of breaking in, the way it made his heart beat faster and louder in the darkness, pen-lights picking out odd details of paintings on walls or bottle-labels and family snapshots on tables. But he couldn't explain that to Mick.

"Well, what do you think?" Mick asked.

"I suppose he's right," Trevor answered, his mind wandering to the possibility of doing jobs alone. That would be much more exciting. The privacy, too, he could savour. Somehow, Mick just seemed too coarse and vulgar to appreciate the true joy and beauty of what they were doing.

"So we lie low, then?"

"All right."

"Till we hear from Lenny?"

"Yes."

A train rumbled over on the tracks above the ginnel. Mick looked at his watch and grinned. "Late."

"What is?"

"Ten-ten from 'Arrogate. Twenty minutes late. Typical bloody British Rail."

THIRTEEN

I

Banks spent most of the week in his office brooding on the three cases and smoking too much, but the figures refused to become clear; the shadowy man in the dark, belted raincoat seemed to float around in his mind with the two faceless youths, watching them watching the sailors on the deck of Alice Matlock's ship in a bottle, the *Miranda*. And somewhere among the crowd were all the people he had talked to in connection with the cases: Ethel Carstairs, the Sharps, "Boxer" Buxton the headmaster, Mr Price the form-master, Dorothy Wycombe, Robin Allott, Mr Patel, Alice Matlock herself, dead on the cold stone flags, and Jenny Fuller.

Jenny Fuller. Twice during the week he picked up the phone to call her, and twice he put it down without dialling. He had no excuse to see her—nothing new had happened—and he felt he had already misled her enough. When, on Wednesday evening, Sandra suggested that they invite Jenny to dinner, a silly argument followed, in which Banks protested that he hardly knew the woman and that their relationship was purely professional. His nose grew an inch or two, and Sandra backed down gracefully.

Richmond and Hatchley were in and out of his office with information, none of it very encouraging. Geoff Welling and Barry Scott appeared to be normal enough lads, and they had gone off on holiday to Italy the day before the Carol Ellis incident, so that let them out.

Sandra continued talking to the neighbours, but none of them had anything to add to Selena Harcourt's information.

The search continued for passers-by, shopkeepers and bus drivers

who might have been near The Oak the night Mr Patel saw the loi-
terer. Yes, one of the bus drivers remembered seeing him, but no, he
couldn't offer a description; the man had been standing in the shadows and the driver had been paying attention to the road. All the
shopkeepers had closed for the night and none of them lived, like Mr
Patel, above their premises. So far, no pedestrians had come forward,
despite the appeal in the *Yorkshire Post.*

Richmond had conducted a thorough search of Alice Matlock's
cottage, but no will turned up. Alice had nothing to her name but a
Post Office Savings Account, the balance of which stood at exactly
one hundred and five pounds, fifty-six pence on the day of her death.
She seemed to be one of that rare breed who do not live beyond their
means; all her life, she had made do with what she earned, whether it
was her nurse's salary or her pension. Ethel Carstairs said she had
never heard Alice talk of a will, and the whole motive of murder for
gain crumbled before it was fully constructed.

On Friday morning, Banks walked into the station, absorbed in
Monteverdi's *Orfeo.* Orpheus was pleading with Charon to allow him
to enter the underworld and see Eurydice.

> *Non viv'io, no, che poi de vita è priva*
> *Mia cara sposa, il cor non è più meco,*
> *E senza cor com'esser può ch'io viva?*

sang the man who could tame wild beasts with music: "I am no
longer alive, for since my dear wife is deprived of life, my heart
remains no longer with me, and without a heart, how can it be that
I am living?"

He didn't notice the woman waiting by the front desk to see him
until the desk-sergeant coughed and tapped him on the arm as he
drifted by, entranced. The embarrassed sergeant introduced them,
then went back to his duties as Banks, awkwardly removing his headphones, led the woman, Thelma Pitt, upstairs to his office.

She seemed very tense as she accepted the chair Banks drew out
for her. Though her hair was blonde, the dark roots were clearly visible, and they combined with the haggard cast of her still-attractive,
heart-shaped face and a skirt too short for someone of her age to give

the impression of a once gay and beautiful woman going downhill fast. Beside her right eye was a purplish-yellow bruise.

Banks took out a new file and wrote down, first, her personal details. He vaguely recognized her name, then remembered that she and her husband, a local farm labourer, had won over a quarter of a million pounds on the pools ten years ago. Banks had read all about them in the Sunday papers. They had been a young married couple at the time; the husband was twenty-six, Thelma twenty-five. For a while, their new jet-setting way of life had been a *cause célèbre* in Eastvale, until Thelma had walked out on her husband to become something of a local *femme fatale*. (Why, wondered Banks, were these delicate phrases always in French, and always untranslatable?) Thelma's legendary parties, which some said were thinly disguised orgies, involved a number of prominent Eastvalers, who were all eventually embarrassed one way or another. When the party was over, Thelma retreated into well-heeled obscurity. Her husband was later killed in an automobile accident in France.

It was a sad enough story in itself; now the woman sat before Banks looking ten years older than she was, hands clasped over her handbag on her lap, clearly with another tale of hard times to tell.

"I want to report a robbery," she said tightly, twisting a large ruby ring around the second finger of her right hand.

"Who was robbed?" Banks asked. "I assume it was..."

"Yes, it was me."

"When did it happen?"

"Monday evening."

"At your home?"

"Yes."

"What time?"

"It was just after ten. I got home early."

"Where had you been?"

"Where I usually go on Mondays, the Golf Club."

"Are you a player?"

"No," she smiled weakly, relaxing a little. "Just a drinker."

"You realize it's Friday now?" Banks prompted her, eager to set her at ease but puzzled about the circumstances. "You say the robbery took place on Monday.... It's a long time to wait before reporting it."

"I know," Thelma Pitt said, "and I'm sorry. But there's something else..."

Banks looked at her, his wide-open eyes asking the question.

"I was raped."

Banks put his pen down on the table. "Are you sure you wouldn't like to see a policewoman?" he asked.

"No, it doesn't matter." She leaned forward. "Inspector, I've lived with this night and day since Monday. I couldn't come in before because I was ashamed to. I felt dirty. I believed it was all my fault— a punishment for past sins, if you like. I'm a Catholic, though not a very good one. I haven't left the house since then. This morning I woke up angry, do you understand? I feel angry, and I want to do whatever I can to see that the criminals are caught. The robbery doesn't matter. The jewels were worth a great deal but not as much... not as much..." She gripped the sides of her chair until her knuckles turned white, then struggled for control of her emotions again.

Banks, who had been thinking that now the peeper had escalated to more serious crimes, was surprised by Thelma's description.

"Criminals?" he asked. "You mean there was more than one?"

"There were two of them. Kids, I think. They were wearing balaclavas. Only one of them raped me. The other said he didn't fancy 'sloppy seconds.' That's the way he put it, Inspector, his exact words—'sloppy seconds.'" She pointed to her bruise. "He's the one that kicked me."

Banks didn't know what to say, and into the uneasy silence Thelma dropped what turned out to be the best lead of all.

"There's another thing," she said, looking away from him towards the wall as if she were examining the idyllic autumn scene on the calendar. "I've got VD."

II

Over the next half-hour, Banks listened to the details of Thelma Pitt's story as PC Susan Gay transcribed them.

Every Monday night Thelma went to the bar of the Eastvale Golf Club, where she kept up her association with some of the people she had got to know in earlier, better days. There was one man in particular, a Lewis Micklethwaite, with whom she had been going out for several weeks.

During a long weekend in London with a female friend a couple of weeks ago, Thelma had, while not entirely sober, allowed herself to be picked up by a younger man in a pub and had subsequently spent the night with him. She didn't remember much about the experience, but the following morning she felt terrible: physically and emotionally hungover. The young man lived in a small flat off the Brixton Road, and Thelma rushed outside as fast as she could and, unable to find a taxi, took the first bus into central London, returning to her friend at the hotel.

"To cut a long story short," she said, "I found out just over a week later that the bastard had kindly passed on his disease to me—gonorrhoea."

That was why she had left the Golf Club early. She didn't want to tell Lewis, nor did she want to infect him. They argued. He seemed unusually perturbed about her going, but she ran off anyway. And as a result of that, she had disturbed the burglars and got herself raped.

"Can you describe them at all?" Banks asked. "You said they were wearing balaclavas?"

"Yes."

"What colour?"

"Grey. Both grey."

"Any idea how old they were?"

"By the way they spoke and acted, I'd say they were both in their teens."

"How can you be sure?"

"The one who raped me was inexperienced. It was all over mercifully fast. I'd say it was his first time. A woman can tell these things, you know, Inspector."

"What about the other?"

"I think he was scared. He talked tough, but I don't think he dared do anything. He was smaller, more squat, and he had a very ugly voice. Raspy. And piggy eyes. He was edgy. I think he might have been on drugs. The one who raped me was leaner and taller. He didn't say an awful lot. I noticed nothing peculiar about his voice. His eyes were blue, and his breath didn't smell too good."

"Did they call each other by name?"

"No. They were careful not to do that."

"What about the rest of their clothing? Anything distinctive?"

Thelma Pitt shook her head. "Just what lots of kids wear these days. Bomber jackets, jeans..."

"There's nothing else you can remember?"

"Oh, I remember it all quite vividly, Inspector. I've replayed it over in my mind a hundred times since Monday. But that's all there is that's likely to help you. Unless it's of any use to know that the boy who raped me was wearing white Y-fronts. Marks and Sparks, I think," she added bitterly. Then she put her head in her hands and started to weep. Susan Gay comforted her, and after a few moments, Thelma Pitt again made the effort to control her feelings.

"I'm sorry," she apologized. "That was uncalled for."

Banks shrugged. "It must have been a terrifying experience," he said, feeling completely inadequate. "Would you recognize them again?"

"Yes, I think so. In the same circumstances. But that wouldn't help you because I can't identify their faces."

"That might not be necessary."

"I'd recognize the squat one's voice and eyes any time. As for the other... I do remember that he had a bit of decay between one of his front teeth and the one next to it, as if a filling had come out. But I couldn't give you a positive identification. I couldn't swear to anything in court."

She was remarkably calm as she relived it, Banks thought, trying to imagine the inner strength and courage it took to deal with such horror.

Finally, she described the jewellery that had been stolen, along with a valuable camera, then Banks let her leave, promising to get in touch as soon as anything happened. He also suggested, though it was much too late, that she see a doctor and have him look for and record any signs of assault for the purposes of evidence.

As soon as PC Gay had escorted Thelma Pitt from his office, Banks phoned Dr Glendenning. He was with a patient, so his receptionist said, but would call back in about ten minutes.

"What is it?" the old doctor asked brusquely about twenty minutes later.

"VD," Banks said. "Gonorrhoea, to be specific. What do you know about it?"

"Ah, gonorrhoea," Glendenning said, warming to the subject like a general admiring a brave opponent. "More commonly known as the clap, Cupid's revenge."

"What are the symptoms?"

"Discharge, a burning sensation while urinating. Inspector Banks, I hope you're not trying to tell me that you—"

"It's not me," Banks snapped, adding "you silly old sod" under his breath. "How soon do the symptoms appear?"

"It varies," Glendenning went on, unruffled. "Three to ten days is about usual."

"Treatment?"

"Penicillin. There have to be tests first, of course, just to make sure it isn't something else—particularly syphilis. The early symptoms can be similar."

"Where would a person find treatment?"

"Well, in the old days, of course, he'd go to his GP or perhaps to the infirmary. But nowadays, what with all the sexual promiscuity and what not, there are specialized VD clinics all over the place. Confidential treatment, naturally."

Banks had, indeed, heard of such places. "There's one here in Eastvale, right?" he asked. "Attached to the hospital?"

"Yes. And one in York."

"None nearer?"

"Not unless you count Darlington or Leeds."

"Thank you, doctor," Banks said hurriedly. "Thank you very much."

As soon as he'd hung up, he called in Hatchley and Richmond, and after explaining the situation, had them phone all the clinics within a fifty-mile radius and ask about a lean, tall teenager with decay between his front teeth, who would probably be very vague about where he had contracted the disease.

Fifteen minutes later, he was informed that nobody fitting the description had been into any of the clinics, which meant either that the suspect had not experienced the symptoms yet or that he was still worrying about what to do. Hatchley and Richmond had also requested that the staff of each clinic be on the lookout, and that they call their nearest police station if they became suspicious about anyone looking for treatment. After that, Hatchley phoned the local police in each area and asked them to detain the boy if he appeared at the clinic and to call Banks immediately.

Later, Banks talked to Jenny Fuller at her York University office and told her about Thelma Pitt. It wasn't part of the peeper case, but it was a sexual crime and he needed a woman's advice.

"Have you sent her for any help?" Jenny asked.

"I suggested she see a doctor. Mostly for our own official purposes, I have to admit."

"That won't do her a lot of good, Alan. There's a Rape Crisis Centre in York, a place where people can talk about their problems. I'm surprised you don't know about it. A lot of women find it hard to get on with their lives after an experience like that. Some never recover. Anyway, these people can help. They're not just doctors—a lot of them have been rape victims themselves. Just a minute and I'll get you the number."

Banks wrote down the telephone number and assured Jenny that he would pass it on to Thelma Pitt.

"Are we going to meet again soon?" she asked.

"Of course. I've got a lot on with this Thelma Pitt business at the moment, though, and there are no real developments on our case. I'll give you a call."

"The brush-off!" Jenny cried melodramatically.

"Don't be stupid," he laughed. "See you soon. And you never know," he added, "you might even get invited to dinner." Then he hung up before Jenny could respond.

The next job was to get Mr Lewis Micklethwaite in. Banks pulled the local directory out of his rattling desk drawer and reached for the phone again.

III

Micklethwaite was reluctant to drop in at Eastvale police station after work. He was also unwilling to have Banks call on him at home. In fact, Micklethwaite wanted to avoid all contact with the local constabulary, and when he finally did come to the office under threat of arrest, Banks immediately knew why.

"If it isn't my old pal Larry Moxton," Banks said, offering the man a cigarette.

"I don't know what you mean. My name's Micklethwaite."

But there was no mistaking him—the receding hairline, dark beady eyes, black beard, swarthy skin, fleshy lips—it was Moxton all right.

"Come on, Larry," Banks urged him. "You remember me, surely?"

"I've told you," Micklethwaite repeated, squirming in his chair. "I don't know what you're talking about."

Banks sighed. "Larry Moxton, ex-accountant. I put you away about ten years ago in London, remember, when you swindled that divorcée out of her savings? What was it—prime Florida real estate? Or was it gilt-edged securities?"

"It was a bloody frame-up, that's what it was," Moxton burst out. "It wasn't my fault my bloody partner took off with the funds."

Banks stroked his chin. "Bit of bad luck, that, Larry, I agree. We never did find him, did we? Probably sunning himself in Spain now. Still, that's the way it goes."

Moxton glared at him. "What do you want this time? I'm straight. Have been ever since I came out and moved up north. And the new name's legit, so don't waste your time on that."

It was hard to believe that such a surly, sneaky man had enough charm to cheat intelligent women out of their money, but that had been Moxton's specialty. For some reason, inexplicable to Banks, women found him hard to resist.

"Thelma Pitt, Larry. I want to know about Thelma Pitt."

"What about her?"

"You do know her, don't you?"

"So what if I do?"

"What are you after, Larry? A rich widow this time?"

"You've no right to make accusations like that. I've served my time—for a crime I didn't commit—and it's no bloody business of yours who I spend my time with."

"When was the last time you saw her?"

"Hey, what is this?" Moxton demanded, grasping the flimsy desk and half rising. "Nothing's happened to her, has it?"

"Never mind that. And sit down. When did you last see her?"

"I want to know. I've got a right to know."

"Sit down! You've got a right to know nothing, Larry. Now answer my questions. You wouldn't want me to lose my temper like last time, would you? When did you see her last?"

Moxton, like many others, had learned from experience that it was no use arguing with Banks, that he had the patience and persistence of a cat after a bird. He might not actually hit you, but you'd go away thinking it would have been easier if he had.

"Monday night," he answered sullenly. "I saw her on Monday night."

"Where?"

"Eastvale Golf Club."

"You a member, Larry?"

"'Course I am. I told you, I'm a respectable businessman. I *am* a CA, you know."

"You're an effing C, too, as far as I'm concerned, Larry. But that's beside the point, isn't it? How long have you been a member?"

"Two years."

"Two years." And to think that Ottershaw had told him it was an exclusive place—no riff-raff. "I don't know what the world's coming to, Larry, I really don't," Banks said.

Moxton glowered at him. "Get to the point, Inspector," he snapped, looking at his watch. "I've got things to do."

"I'll bet you have. All right, so you know Thelma Pitt. What's your relationship with her?"

"None of your business."

"Good friends, business partners, lovers?"

"So we go out together, have a bit of fun. What's it to you? What's happened to her?"

He did seem genuinely concerned about the woman's welfare, but Banks considered it unethical to tell him that Thelma Pitt had been robbed and raped. If she wanted him to know, she would tell him herself.

"What time did you leave her on Monday?" Banks pressed on.

"I didn't. She left me. It was earlier than usual—about a quarter to ten. I don't know why. She was upset. I suppose you could say we argued."

"Could I? What about?"

"None of your... Oh," he sighed and turned up his hands, "why not? She wanted to be alone, that's all. I wanted her to come with me as usual."

"Where did the two of you usually go?"

"To my place."

"Did you spend the night there?"

"Sometimes, yes."

"Why didn't you go there last Monday?"

"I told you. She wouldn't. Said she had a headache. You know women."

"But you pressed her to stay at the club?"

"Of course I did. I was enjoying her company."

"Even though she didn't feel very well?"

"It didn't look like anything to me. I think it was just an excuse. She seemed fine physically, just a bit upset about something."

"Any idea what?"

"No. She wasn't very communicative. She just stormed off."

"After you'd tried very hard to persuade her to stay and to accompany you to your house? Is that right?"

"What are you getting at?"

"Nothing. I'm just trying to establish the facts, that's all."

"Well, yes. Naturally, I wanted her to stay with me. I'm a man, like any other. I enjoy the company of attractive women."

"So Thelma Pitt isn't the only one?"

"We're not engaged to be married or anything, if that's what you're getting at. Come on, I've had enough of this pussyfooting around. What's it all about?"

"Know anyone else at the Golf Club?"

"One or two. It is a social place for professional men, you know."

"Maurice Ottershaw?"

A look of fear flashed in Moxton's eyes. It didn't last long, but Banks saw it.

"Maurice Ottershaw?" he repeated. "I know him. I mean, we've had a few drinks together. I wouldn't really say I know him. What is it you're getting at?"

"I'll tell you, Larry," Banks said, leaning forward on the desk and holding Moxton's eyes with his. "I think you've been fingering jobs for someone, that's what I think. You know when your rich friends at the club are likely to be away, and you tip someone the wink. But it went wrong with Thelma Pitt, didn't it? You couldn't keep her away from home long enough."

Moxton looked really frightened now. "What's happened to her? You've got to tell me. She isn't hurt, is she?"

"Why would she be?"

"After what you said...I thought..."

"Don't worry about it."

"You can't prove anything, you know."

"I know," Banks admitted. "But I also know you did it."

"Look, I wouldn't shit on my own doorstep, would I?"

"A creep like you would shit anywhere, Moxton. We're going to be watching you, keeping an eye on you. You won't be able to crap anywhere without being watched, understand?"

"That's intimidation, harassment!" Moxton yelled, jumping to his feet in exasperation.

"Oh, piss off," Banks said, and pointed to the door.

FOURTEEN

I

When Trevor awoke on Monday morning, he knew something was wrong.

"Trevor!" his father shouted as usual. "Breakfast's on the table! If you don't hurry up you'll be late for school."

At least he knew there would be no row over the table this morning. All day Sunday he had stayed in like a dutiful son; he'd helped his dad with the stock and had even done some homework. Such gestures as that could earn him a few days' peace, if not more.

Pity about the homework, he thought. It was a waste really because he wouldn't be there to hand it in. He was taking the afternoon off to go and discuss future plans with Mick. Just because Lenny had told them to lay off the break-ins for a while didn't mean they couldn't find some other ways of amusing themselves—perhaps out of town.

But something was wrong. He didn't feel right. He lay there with the sheets pulled up and looked at the glossy posters of pop stars on his walls, wondering if the stickiness he felt meant that he'd had a wet dream. Cautiously, he pushed the bedclothes aside and sat up on the edge of the bed. The front of his pyjamas was stained, and when he looked more closely he noticed a kind of yellowish discharge.

Alarmed, Trevor rushed to the bathroom and washed himself. When he stood to urinate, the fear really took hold of him. It hurt like hell. It felt as if he was pissing red-hot needles. He leaned against the wall in a cold sweat, pressing his forehead against the tiles. When he'd finished, the pain faded and all that remained was a lingering throb, the echo of an ache.

Trevor washed his face and stared at himself in the mirror. The dark patch between his teeth was spreading quickly, and he had two spots: one, still embryonic, wedged between the edge of his nostril and his upper lip; the other, yellow and juicy, exactly at the point where his chin curved under to become his throat. But they were the least of the worries. He was pale and his eyes were dull. He knew what he'd got; he'd got the clap. That flicking cunt had given him the clap.

With a great effort, Trevor pulled himself together. He finished washing, then returned to his bedroom to get dressed.

"Hurry up, our Trev!" his father called. "Your bacon and eggs are going cold!"

"Coming, dad," he yelled back. "Won't be a minute."

He pulled his white shirt and grey slacks on, picked out a sleeveless, V-neck pullover with a muted pattern of grey and mauve, and he was ready. They ate breakfast together quickly, Graham beaming at his son.

"It was a good day we had yesterday, wasn't it?" he asked.

"Yes," Trevor lied.

"Got a lot of work done."

"We did, didn't we?"

"And all your homework, too."

"That's right."

"Believe me, Trevor, it's worth it. You might not think so now, but you'll be grateful in the future, mark my words."

"I suppose so," Trevor mumbled. "Look at the time! I'll be late."

"Off you go, then," Graham said, ruffling Trevor's hair and smiling at him. "And don't forget to hand that homework in."

"Don't worry, I won't," Trevor said, forcing a grin and picking up his satchel.

"And you'd better get that tooth seen to, too, lad," Graham added, "or it'll only get worse. See if you can get an appointment with the school dentist."

"All right, dad," Trevor replied, and rushed off.

He had no intention of making any appointment with the school dentist, or with any other dentist, for that matter. It was Dr Himmler, as he called the school dentist, and his assistant Griselda who had put

Trevor off dentists in the first place. The man was grubby and his National Health glasses were stuck together across the bridge with Elastoplast. Griselda stood by, white-faced and red-lipped, like some mediaeval witch passing him the instruments of torture. He never gave anaesthetics for fillings; you simply had to grip the chair. For extractions he administered nitrous oxide, and Trevor would never forget that feeling of suffocation as the mask was finally pressed over his nose and mouth, like a polythene bag clinging to the pores, keeping all the air out. And afterwards, he would stand up groggily and stagger to the next room, where the previous patients were still standing around water fountains spitting or swilling the blood from their mouths.

Trevor set off in the right direction for school. He walked up through Leaview Estate, which was already busy with the postman, the milkman and wives seeing husbands off to work, then turned onto King Street with its cobbles and trendy tourist shoppes. The places all had looking-glass windows and black-leaded railings leading down to basements stuffed with mildewed books, spinning wheels, bobbins and other relics of the woollen industry, which were now sold as antiques.

The school was at the bottom of a narrow street to his left, and Trevor could see the white tips of the rugby posts and the dirty red-brick Victorian clocktower. Instead of turning down School Drive, though, he took the narrow, winding streets to the market square. On the eastern side of the square, between the National Westminster Bank and Jopling's Newsagent's, a short flight of worn stone steps led down to the El Toro Coffee Bar, a dim room with bullfight posters, castanets and maracas on the walls. Trevor slumped into the darkest corner, ordered an espresso coffee, and settled down to think.

He knew he had VD because he'd heard other kids talking and joking about it at school. Nobody ever thought it would happen to them, though. And because Trevor's intelligence was imaginative rather than scientific, his ideas about the consequences of the disease were far-fetched, to say the least. He pictured his penis turning black and rotten, the flesh coming away in great gobbets in his hands the next time he had to go to the toilet. He was convinced that it would drop off altogether within hours. There was treatment, he knew, though he had no idea what it was. But anything was better than dying that way; even the school dentist would be better than that.

He could not go to his GP, Dr Farmer, because his father would find out. He could bear the embarrassment, but not disclosure. Too many awkward questions would be asked. There were special clinics, or so he'd heard people say, and he figured that one of those was his best bet. There had been nothing in the papers about the woman he had raped, so Trevor assumed that Mick's boot had done the trick and she was keeping quiet for fear of worse reprisals. Still, the police didn't publicize everything they knew, so it would be best to avoid Eastvale, just in case. Trevor asked the owner for the phone directory and looked up hospitals and clinics. As he had guessed, there was a place in York. He scribbled down the address on a page torn out of a school exercise book and left the El Toro.

At the bus station, he put his satchel and school blazer in a locker, wearing only his duffle-coat over his shirt and pullover. That way he didn't look at all like a schoolboy. The next bus for York was due to leave in fifteen minutes. He bought a copy of *Melody Maker* at the newsstand and sat on the cracked green bench to wait.

II

All day Monday Banks seethed with impatience. He had made great efforts to put the Thelma Pitt business out of his mind over the weekend, mostly for the sake of his family. On Saturday, they had driven into York to do some shopping and on Sunday they had all gone on a vigorous walk from Bainbridge to Semerwater, in Wensleydale. It was a brisk day, sunny and cool, but they were all warm enough in their walking gear.

On Monday morning, though, Banks took off his Walkman, hardly having noticed which opera he'd been listening to, slammed it shut in the drawer and shouted for Hatchley.

"Sir?" the sergeant said, red-faced with the effort of running upstairs.

Banks looked at him sternly.

"You'd better do something about the shape you're in, Sergeant," he said first. "You'd not be much use in a chase, would you?"

"No, sir," Hatchley replied, gasping for breath.

"Anyway, that's not what I want to see you about. Anything from the clinics?"

"No, sir."

"Damn!" Banks thumped the desk.

"You did ask us to let you know, sir," Hatchley reminded him. "I'm sure you'd have heard if there'd been any news over the weekend."

Banks glared at him. "Of course," he said, scratching his head and sitting down.

"It can take up to ten days, sir."

"When would that take us to?"

"Wednesday or Thursday, sir."

"Thursday," Banks repeated, tapping a ruler against his thigh. "Anything could happen before then. What about Moxton?"

"Moxton, sir?"

"Micklethwaite, as he calls himself now."

"Oh, him. Nothing there either, I'm afraid."

Banks had ordered surveillance on Moxton, assuming that he might try to warn his partner, whoever that was.

"He didn't do much at all," Hatchley added, "though he did go and visit the woman."

"Thelma Pitt?"

"Yes, sir."

"And?"

"And nothing, sir. Stayed about fifteen minutes, then drove home. Seemed a bit pissed off, if you ask me. Slammed the car door. He stayed in all Saturday night, went for a walk on Sunday morning, washed his car, dropped in for a quick drink at that posh place, the Hope and Anchor, about nine o'clock, then went home and stayed there."

"Did he talk to anyone at the Hope and Anchor?"

"Only the landlord, sir."

"Anyone we know?"

"No, sir. Straight as a die. Never even sold short measure, far as we can tell."

Banks took a deep breath. "All right, Sergeant. Thank you," he said, softening his tone a little to mollify Hatchley. "Have some coffee sent up, will you?"

"Sir?"

Banks grinned. "I know it's awful muck, but I need it all the same."

"Will do," Hatchley said, lingering. "Er...Sir?..."

"What is it?"

"Have you got any idea who it was, sir? The rapist?"

"I'm not sure, Sergeant. It could be that Sharp kid and his mate or a pair very much like them. It's the same ones who robbed the old ladies and pissed on the Ottershaws' VCR—that I am sure about."

"And the Matlock killing?"

Banks shook his head. "I don't think so. That's something different. Another problem altogether."

"Why not bring the Sharp kid in for questioning?"

"Because I can't prove anything. Do you think I wouldn't have had him in before if I had something on him? Besides, I'm not certain yet that he is the one, I just got the feeling there was something wrong when I talked to him and his father."

"That bit about the bad tooth, sir. If he—"

Banks waved his hand as if to brush aside a fly. "By itself it's nothing. You know that as well as I do. On the other hand, if he's got the clap..."

"We could always bring him in, just to shake him up a bit."

"No good. His father would insist on being present. He'd probably send for a bloody solicitor, too, then they'd just clam up on us. If Sharp's our lad, we need evidence before we tackle him again or we'll lose him for good."

Hatchley scratched the seat of his pants. "What about the woman?" he asked.

"Thelma Pitt?"

"Yes."

"She said she couldn't positively identify them. We don't want to take any risks on this. When we get him, I want him to stay, not walk off on some technicality. Besides, I'd rather not put her through it until we've got a bit more to go on. If it's Sharp, we know he's got the clap. Sooner or later, he'll turn up at one of the clinics. Then we'll haul him in."

Hatchley nodded and went back downstairs.

When the coffee came, Banks realized all over again why he usually took his breaks in the Golden Grill. He sat with his chair turned to face the window, smoked and stared blankly over the market square, watching the first activities of the morning. Delivery vans double parked outside the shops; the minister, glancing at his watch, hurried into the church; a housewife in a paisley headscarf rattled the door of Bradwell's Grocery, which didn't appear to be open yet.

But all this was mere activity without meaning to Banks. He was close to solving the robberies and the rape of Thelma Pitt—he knew that, he could feel it in his bones—but there was nothing he could do to hurry things along. As so often in his job, he had to be patient; this time he literally had to let nature take its course.

Slowly, while he smoked yet another cigarette, the market square came to life. As the first tourists stepped into the Norman church, Bradwell's Grocery finally opened its doors and took delivery of boxes of fruit from an orange van with a sombrero painted on its side. The woman in the paisley headscarf was nowhere to be seen.

By mid-morning, Banks was sick of being cooped up in his office. He told Sergeant Rowe he was going out for half an hour or so, then went for a walk to burn off some of his impatience.

He hurried across the market square, fastening his overcoat as he went, then cut down the narrow backstreets and through the flower gardens to the riverside.

The slowly increasing cloud cover had not yet quite blotted out the sun, but it had drawn a thin veil over it that weakened the light and gave the whole landscape the look of a water-colour in pale greens, yellows, orange, brown and red. The scent of rain came on a chilling wind, which seemed to be blowing from the northwest, along the channel of Swainsdale itself. The breeze hurried the river over the terraced fulls and set up a constant skittering sound in the trees that lined the banks. Leaves were already falling and scraping along the ground. Most of them ended up in the water.

Across the Swain was another pathway, and behind that more trees and flowerbeds. The houses that Banks could just see through the waving branches were the ones fronting The Green, which separated them from the East Side Estate. Banks knew that Jenny's house was among them, but he couldn't tell which one it was from that distance and angle.

He pushed his hands deep into his overcoat pockets, hunched his shoulders and hurried on. The exercise was doing the trick, driving chaotic thoughts from his mind and helping him work up an appetite for lunch.

He doubled back around the castle to the market square. Hatchley and Richmond were lunching in the Queen's Arms when he got there, and Hatchley stopped in mid-sentence when he saw his boss enter. Banks remembered that he had been rude to the sergeant that morning and guessed that they were complaining about him. Taking a deep breath, he joined them at their table and set things right again by buying both his men a pint.

III

The York bus arrived at the station by the Roman wall at ten-thirty. Trevor walked along the wall, passed the railway station, then crossed the Ouse over Lendal Bridge by the ruins of St Mary's Abbey and the Yorkshire Museum. After that, he wandered in a daze around the busy city until he felt hungry. Just after opening time, he found a pub on Stonegate—with his height and out-of-school dress he certainly looked over eighteen—where he ate a steak-and-mushroom pie along with his pint of keg beer.

He lingered there for almost two hours, nursing his pint and reading every word (including the "Musicians Wanted" column) in his *Melody Maker*, before venturing out into the streets again. Everywhere he walked he seemed to stumble across pairs of American tourists, most of them complaining because they were inadequately dressed for the cool weather.

"Goddamn sun's out," he heard one fat man in thin cotton slacks and a blazer grumble. "You'd think there'd be some goddamn heat, for Christ's sake."

"Oh, Elmer," his wife said. "We've been in Yoorp for a month now. You oughtta know it never gets hot north of Athens."

Trevor sneered. Silly sods, he thought. Why even bother to come here and litter up the streets if they were too soft to take a bit of autumn chill. He imagined America as a vast continent baking in the sun—pavements you could fry eggs on; people stripped to the waist all the time having barbecues; enormous, uninhabitable stretches of desert and jungle.

About an hour later, he knew he was lost. He seemed to have wandered outside the city walls. This was no tourist area he was in; it was too working-class. The long straight rows of tiny back-to-backs built of dusty pink bricks seemed endless. Washing flapped on lines hung across the narrow streets. Trevor turned back, and at the end of the street saw the Minster's bright towers in the distance. He started walking in their direction.

He'd put it off for long enough, he decided. If he didn't want his penis to shrivel up and drop off, he'd better go for treatment, however frightening the prospect seemed.

In a newsagent's, he found time to look up the location of the clinic in a street guide before the suspicious owner told him to clear off if he wasn't going to buy anything.

"Bleeding Paki," Trevor muttered under his breath as he found himself being ushered out. But he'd got what he'd come for.

The clinic, not very far from the hub of the city, was a squat, modern building of windowless concrete with a flat, asphalt roof. Trevor presented himself at reception, where he was told to take a seat and wait until a doctor became available. There were two other people before him, a middle-aged man and a scruffy female student, and both of them looked embarrassed. As they waited, nobody spoke and they all avoided even accidental eye contact.

About an hour later, it was Trevor's turn. A bald, long-faced doctor led him into a small room and bid him sit in front of the desk. Trevor shifted anxiously, wishing to God the whole thing was over and done with. The place smelt of Dettol and carbolic; it reminded him of the dentist's.

"Right," the doctor said brightly, after scribbling a few notes on a form. "What can we do for you, young man?"

What a stupid question, Trevor thought. What the hell does he think I'm here for, to have my bunions seen to?

"I've got a problem," he mumbled, and gave the doctor the details.

"What's your name?" the doctor asked, after umming and ahing over Trevor's description of his symptoms.

"Peter Upshaw," Trevor answered smartly. It was something he'd had the foresight to work out in advance, a name he had picked out from the columns of *Melody Maker*.

"Address?"

"Forty-two Arrowsmith Drive."

The doctor glanced at him sharply: "Is that here, in York?"

"Yes."

"Whereabouts?" He scratched his shiny pate with his ballpoint pen. "I don't believe I know it."

"It's by the Minster," Trevor blurted out, reddening. He hadn't anticipated that the quack would be so inquisitive.

"The Minster? Ah, yes…" The doctor made an entry on the form. "All right, Peter," he said, putting down his pen. "We'll have some tests to do, of course, but first I have to ask you where you caught this disease, who you caught it from."

Trevor certainly hadn't bargained for this. He couldn't tell the truth, he couldn't name anyone he knew, and he certainly couldn't answer, "Nobody."

"A prostitute," he replied quickly. It was the first thing that came into his mind.

The doctor raised his thin eyebrows. "A prostitute? Where was this, Peter?"

"Here."

"In York?"

"Yes."

"When?"

"About a week ago."

"What was her name?"

"Jane."

"Where does she live?"

It was all going too fast for Trevor. He began to stumble over his answers. "I…I…don't know. I was with some other boys. We'd had a bit too much to drink, then we walked around and she just came up to us."

"In the street?"

"Yes."

"But you must have gone somewhere."

"No. I mean yes."

The doctor stared at him.

"In an alley," Trevor went on. "We went in an alley. There was nobody around. We stood up, leaning against a wall."

"What about your friends? Did they... er?"

"No," Trevor assured him hastily. He realized that he would be asked to name anybody else he implicated.

The doctor frowned. "Are you sure?"

"Yes. It was only me. It was my birthday."

"Ah," the doctor said, smiling benignly. "I understand. But you don't know where this woman lived?"

"No."

"Have you been with anyone else since it happened?"

"No."

"Very well, Peter. If you'll just walk down the corridor to the room at the end, you'll find a nurse there. She'll take a blood sample—just to make sure. After that, come back here and we'll get on with it."

The room was like the school chemistry laboratory, with glass-fronted cupboards full of labelled jars and long tables covered with retorts, bunsen burners, pipettes and racks of test tubes. It made Trevor nervous.

The nurse was quite pretty. "Relax," she said, rolling up his sleeve. "It won't hurt."

And it didn't. He couldn't feel the needle going in at all, but he turned his head away so he wouldn't see the blood running into the syringe. He felt a slight prick as it came out.

"There," the nurse said, smiling and wiping the spot with cotton-wool soaked in alcohol. "All done. You can go back to Doctor Willis now."

Trevor went back to the small examination-room, where Doctor Willis greeted him.

"I want you to sit back on that chair over there and relax, Peter," he said in a soft hypnotic voice. "This won't take very long. Just another little test."

Willis turned his back to Trevor and picked up something shiny from a white kidney-shaped tray.

"Just remove your trousers, Peter. Underpants, too. That's right," the doctor said, and came towards him. Willis held in his hand what looked like a sewing-needle. He seemed to be holding it by the point, though, and the angled eye was larger than normal.

Trevor tensed as Willis came closer. For a moment the doctor seemed to be wearing a dirty smock, and his National Health glasses were held together at the bridge by Elastoplast.

"Now, relax, Peter," he said, bending forward. "I'm just going to insert this gently inside..."

IV

The phone call came through at 4:17.

"Chief Inspector Banks?" It was an unfamiliar voice.

"Yes."

"This is Inspector MacLean here. York CID."

Banks tightened his grip on the receiver, his palms sweating, slippery against the black bakelite: "Yes, go on."

"It's about your request. The local clap-shop called us a few minutes ago. Seems they've got a kid down there. Looks about eighteen but could be younger and doesn't appear to know York very well. He was very vague about how he picked up the disease. Some claptrap—excuse the pun—about having a prossie in a back alley. Doctor got the distinct impression that he was making it up as he went along. Sound like your laddie?"

"It certainly does," Banks said, drumming on his desk with excitement. "Tell me more."

"Not a lot more to tell," MacLean went on in his deadpan voice. "Some decay between the front teeth, all right, but most kids have rotten teeth these days. I was over in the States two years ago on an exchange, and they think it's criminal there the way the British treat their teeth—or don't treat them, if you catch my drift. They say you can always spot a Brit by his teeth. You know—"

"Inspector..." Banks cut in.

"Sorry," MacLean said. "You must be eager to get your mitts on him."

"I am, rather. Where is he?"

"Still at the clap-shop. We're holding him there. Got a couple of uniforms on the job. We let him have his treatment, of course. You realize he'll need a few more shots yet? Do you want him delivered?"

"No, thanks. I'll pick him up myself."

"I'm glad you said that. We're a bit short of staff down here."

"What name did he give?"

"Upshaw. Peter Upshaw. Ring a bell?"

"No, but it'd be false, wouldn't it?" Banks took down the address of the clinic. "Be there in about an hour—and thank you, Inspector MacLean."

"You're welcome," MacLean said, and hung up.

"Sergeant Hatchley!" Banks bellowed, jumping up and flinging open his door.

For the second time that day, Hatchley arrived red-faced and breathless. But Banks made no comment on his physical condition. His dark eyes glittering with success, he clapped his hand gleefully on the sergeant's broad, well-padded shoulder and said, "Fancy a ride to York?"

V

Trevor, meanwhile, sat glumly in the examination room under the bored eyes of a fresh-faced constable no more than three or four years his senior. The other officer, of similar age and appearance (so much so that locals on their beat called them the Bobbie Twins) stood in the reception area waiting for the CID bigwig.

After the slight discomfort and great humiliation of his examination, Trevor had been told to await the test results. He felt edgy and afraid, but not of the police; there was room only for one worry at a time in his youthful mind. It was with great surprise, then, that he noted the arrival of Constable Parker, who preceded Dr Willis through the door.

"Sorry about this," Willis said embarrassedly, taking off his glasses and cleaning them on his smock. "A little misunderstanding, I'm sure. Soon have it straightened out, eh?" And under the policeman's eyes, he administered the first injection in Trevor's course of treatment.

After that, there was nothing to do but wait, and one worry very quickly replaced another in Trevor's mind.

It was closer to six o'clock when Banks and Hatchley arrived at the clinic. They hadn't reckoned on the rush-hour snarl-up in York's maze of one-way streets. Constable Spinks led them to the examination room, and Trevor sneered when he saw Banks walk in.

"Well, Trevor," Banks greeted him. "I see you've lost a filling since we last talked."

Trevor said nothing, but got sullenly to his feet and followed the two men out to their car. The drive back to Eastvale in the dark passed in silence.

The law stated that a juvenile could not be charged unless his parents were present, and as a charge was likely, Banks had to call Graham Sharp in as soon as the trio arrived back at the Eastvale station.

Nobody said a word to Trevor until his father arrived.

When Graham Sharp was shown into the already crowded office by PC Gay, Banks was just finishing his call to Sandra, letting her know that he would be late home again that evening.

Finally, with both Trevor and his father sitting opposite him at the desk and Sergeant Hatchley standing by the window with his notebook, gazing down on the quiet, darkening market square, Banks was ready to begin. He tidied the files on his desk, arranged the pencils in front of him, and caught Trevor's eye.

"What were you doing at that clinic?" he opened.

"What do you think?" Trevor mumbled scornfully.

"Well, you weren't having your filling replaced, that's for certain."

"What's all this?" Graham Sharp butted in. "What clinic? What are you talking about?"

"Mr Sharp," Banks said patiently, "according to the law, you have to be present if charges are likely to be laid, but I'm the one who's asking the questions, all right?"

"I've got a right to protect my son."

"Yes, you have. You're perfectly at liberty to advise him not to answer if you wish. But please bear in mind that he hasn't been charged with anything *yet*."

Graham Sharp settled back in his chair, looking angry and confused.

"Why didn't you go to the Eastvale Clinic?" Banks asked Trevor.

"Didn't know there was one."

"How did you find out about York?"

"A schoolmate told me."

"Who did you get the clap from?"

"Now, wait a minute!" Sharp interrupted again. "This is going too far. What clap? Who's got VD?"

"Your son has gonorrhoea, Mr Sharp. Haven't you, lad?"

Trevor said nothing.

"There's no point denying it," Banks pressed. "The doctor did the tests. We can easily call him and have him talk to your dad."

Trevor tamed away from his father and nodded. Graham Sharp put his head in his hands.

"Let's get back to my original question," Banks continued. "Where did you get this disease? You don't catch it from toilet seats, you know."

"It was like I told the doctor," Trevor answered.

"Ah yes," Banks said, speaking up so that Graham Sharp could hear him clearly. "You had a prostitute against a wall down a back alley in York. Is that right?"

Trevor nodded, pale.

"When was this?"

"About a week ago. Last Monday."

"You were in York last Monday?"

"Yes."

"What time did he get home, Mr Sharp?"

Sharp snapped to attention at the sound of his name. "What?"

"What time did your son get home last Monday night?" Banks repeated.

"About eleven. He always has to be in by eleven. It's his bedtime, see."

"Did you know where he was?"

"He said he was going to York, yes," Sharp said.

"Who did he go with?"

"I don't know. A friend. He didn't say."

"A friend?"

"I suppose so."

"Not friends?"

"For God's sake, I don't know."

"You see, the thing is, Mr Sharp, he told the doctor he went with a group of friends to celebrate his birthday, and that his friends got together and bought him, so to speak, a prostitute as a present. Was it your son's birthday last Monday, Mr Sharp?"

"Yes. Yes, it was, as a matter of fact."

"You realize," Banks said, "that we can always check the records?"

"Well, it wasn't officially his birthday, no. But it was his mother's birthday. He always used to celebrate his mother's birthday. He was very attached to her."

"Is that really what happened, Trevor?" Banks asked. "To celebrate your mother's birthday you had a prostitute up against a wall in a back alley in York? She said her name was Jane and you've no idea where she lives?"

Trevor nodded.

"Do you know, Trevor, that we can question every prostitute in York if we have to? It's not as big as Leeds or Bradford, and there aren't very many of them. The police know them all. They're on good terms—you know, you scratch my back, I'll scratch yours, that kind of thing? It wouldn't take us long to find out whether your story's true or not."

"All right," Trevor said defiantly. "Ask them. Bloody well ask them for all I care."

"Mind your language, Trevor," his father said.

Sergeant Hatchley, who had remained as impassive as a Buddha throughout the interrogation, suddenly moved away from the window and began pacing around the small office, making the floor creak. Trevor shot nervous glances at him and seemed to tense up when Hatchley walked behind him.

"Care to tell us the names of your friends, Trevor? Just so we can corroborate your story," Banks asked.

"No." Trevor glanced sideways at Hatchley, who leaned against the wall for a moment and cracked his knuckles before turning another page in his notebook.

"Where were you a week last Thursday evening?"

"He was at home with me," Graham Sharp answered quickly.

"I asked Trevor."

"Like he says." Trevor looked at his father.

"Doing what?"

"Watched a bit of telly, read a bit, did some homework."

"What about Tuesday, Wednesday, Friday, Saturday, Sunday?"

"Same thing."

"Don't have much of a social life, do you Trevor? When I was a lad I was all over the place. My mother and father couldn't keep track of me."

Trevor shrugged.

"Look," Graham Sharp cut in, eyeing Hatchley, who moved casually away from the wall and back over to the window, "this has gone far enough. What's it all about? What's my Trevor supposed to have done?"

"When?"

"What do you mean, 'when'?"

"I mean that we think Trevor's done a lot of things. I was asking you which night you meant."

"Don't be ridiculous. Trevor's a good kid. He's doing well at school and he'll be going on to university. He's going to make something out of his life."

Banks shook his head. "He's not doing so well at school, you know. I've checked."

Sharp's mouth dropped open, then he pulled himself together. "All right, so he's having one or two problems at the moment. We all go through difficult phases, Inspector, you must know that?"

"Yes, I know that," Banks replied evenly. "But I'm afraid that in your Trevor's case it's something more serious."

"What is it?" Sharp pleaded. "What on earth is he supposed to have done?"

Hatchley turned from the window and startled everybody with his gruff voice. He spoke, however, with a quiet intensity that enthralled his audience completely.

"Last Monday," he said, "two lads broke into a woman's house. They thought she was out and wouldn't be back till late. As it happened, she had a fight with her fancy man and came home early. She caught them at it, burgling her house. They tied her up, then one of them raped her and the other kicked her in the head. We think the crime was committed by the same two youths who also burgled a Mr Maurice Ottershaw's house, assaulted and robbed four old ladies and, possibly," he glanced at Banks, who nodded, "killed your neighbour, Alice Matlock."

"And you're saying my Trevor had something to do with this?" Sharp cried, getting to his feet. The veins on his temples stood out, throbbing wildly. "You must be insane!" He banged on the flimsy desk. "I want my solicitor here! I want him here now, before you say another word."

"You're perfectly at liberty to request that, of course, sir," Banks said mildly, giving Hatchley the signal to fade into the woodwork again. "But, I must repeat, your son hasn't been charged with anything yet. He's simply helping us with our enquiries."

The cliché seemed to calm Sharp down a little. He eased himself slowly back into his chair and brushed back the hair from his forehead. "I thought your man here just accused my son of rape, burglary, and murder," he snarled, glaring at Hatchley's back.

"Nothing of the sort," Banks assured him. "He simply gave details of the crimes we think your son might be able to help us with."

Though he no longer linked the robberies with the death of Alice Matlock, Banks knew how to exploit an unsolved killing in his favour. If Trevor thought he was going to get Alice's murder pinned on him, too, there was a slim chance he might confess to the other offences.

"What makes you think my Trevor knows anything about it?" Sharp asked.

"Because the woman who was raped had just discovered that she had contracted gonorrhoea," Banks said, directing his words at Trevor, who stared down at his knees. "And your son has just returned from a VD clinic in York, where he was diagnosed as having gonorrhoea. The symptoms show up, so I'm told, anywhere between three and ten days. I'd say that seven days fits into that time scale quite well, wouldn't you?"

"But surely," Sharp objected, "there are other people visiting these clinics? If Trevor really did go with a prostitute and catch VD from her as he says—and I believe him—then that's no crime. It's just youthful high spirits. I was a bit of a lad myself at his age."

"Are robbery, rape, assault and murder just youthful high spirits, too?" Banks asked sarcastically.

"Now, look here, you said you weren't accusing my son of anything."

"I'm not accusing him, I'm trying to get to the truth. I never said he wasn't a suspect, though. Are you sure he went to York last Monday?"

"That's where he said he was going."

"When did you lose that filling, Trevor?" Banks asked.

"Wednesday," Trevor replied. But not before his father had said, "Thursday."

"You see," Banks went on, "the woman who was raped said she remembered the kid's front teeth, that there was some decay between them, as if he had a missing filling. She said she'd recognize it again. She said she'd know his voice, too. And," here he directed his words at Trevor, "she'd know his technique. She said she could tell he was just an inexperienced kid because he shot his load almost as soon as he stuck it in."

Trevor flushed with anger and grasped the edge of the desk. Graham put a restraining hand on his shoulder.

"We'll bring her in, Trevor. She's not afraid to give evidence, you know, despite what your friend did to her. And we'll question all the prostitutes in York. We'll talk to the bus drivers and see if any of them remember you, and if you tell us you went by train we'll talk to the ticket collectors and train crews. We'll find out who else went to York that night and we'll ask if any of them saw you and your friends. Seeing as there were a few of you, I should imagine you were quite noisy—youthful high spirits and all that—and someone in whatever pub you were in is bound to remember. So why don't you make it easier for us, Trevor? Make it easier for everyone. It's up to you. We'll nail you in the end anyway."

"Come on, Trev," Hatchley piped up, putting a fatherly hand on the boy's shoulder. "Before it goes too far. It'll go easier on you this way."

Trevor shook his hand off.

"I refuse to believe this," said Sharp. "My son isn't capable of such actions. He can't be. I raised him myself after his mother left. Gave him everything he wanted. If he's done anything wrong—and I don't think he has—then he was led on. He was led on by that bloody Mick Webster. It's him you want, not my Trevor."

"Shut up, dad!" Trevor snapped. "For God's sake, shut up!" And he lapsed back into sullen silence.

Banks got to his feet and smiled down at Trevor, who caught his eye before turning away. Both of them knew, in that split second of eye contact, that Banks had won. He had nowhere near enough evidence yet to make a conviction, but if Mick Webster thought that Trevor had snitched on him...

"Where does he live, this Webster?" Banks asked Graham.

"On the East Side Estate. That first street, the one that faces The Green."

"I know it. Number?"

"I don't know, but it's the fifth house down after the tobacconist's. I've seen him coming and going a few times when I've been picking up stock."

"Got that?" Banks asked Hatchley, who nodded. "Take Richmond, and hurry up. Bring in Mick Webster."

FIFTEEN

I

After Alan's phone call, Sandra packed Brian off to the Lifeboys and Tracy to the Guides. They hadn't been interested in such organizations back in London, but since they'd started school in Eastvale and discovered that many of the other children were members, they decided it would be a good way to make friends. Tracy was still quite happy with it, but Brian was already chafing at the bit. He complained that he didn't like drill, and that he liked the leader, who spat as he shouted, even less. Sandra, having been a loner as a child, thought the whole network of Scouts, Cubs, Brownies and the rest rather silly, but she would never say anything about that in front of the children.

When they had finally gone, she took a deep breath and looked around the living-room, wondering what to do first. Though she managed to be a fairly efficient housewife, she wasn't an obsessive cleaner. Alan also helped out on the weekends, taking on jobs she didn't like, such as Hoovering the staircase and cleaning the bathroom.

It was seven o'clock. She didn't know when Alan would be back; he'd said he was questioning a suspect. Sandra was trying to decide between doing some dark-room work or settling down with the biography of Alfred Hitchcock she had taken out of Eastvale Library that morning, when there was a knock at the door.

Puzzled, she went to answer it, expecting perhaps Selena Harcourt wanting to borrow a cup of sugar. But it was Robin Allott from the Camera Club.

"You told us you were willing to lend out your slide projector, remember?" he said, standing in the doorway.

"Oh, of course, Robin," Sandra said. "I'm so sorry, it slipped my mind. I must have looked quite unwelcoming for a moment. Please come in."

"I hope I've not called at an inconvenient time."

"Not at all. I've just sent the children off and I was wondering what to do."

"Yes, I saw them," Robin said, smiling. "Lifeboys and Guides. It reminds me of my own childhood."

He wiped his feet carefully on the doormat and Sandra hung up his navy-blue raincoat in the hall closet, then directed him into the front room, which he admired politely. He unslung his old, heavy Pentax from his shoulder and put it on the table by the front window.

"Silly habit," he said. "But I always carry it with me. You never know."

Sandra laughed. "That's the sign of a true professional. Do sit down, Robin. Can I get you a drink?"

"Yes, please, if it's no trouble."

"None at all. Gin or scotch? I'm afraid that's all we've got."

"Quite all right. Scotch'll do fine."

"Water? Ice?"

"No, just as it comes, for me, please."

Sandra poured his drink, mixed herself a gin and slimline tonic, then sat in the armchair opposite him. He seemed more shy than he usually did in The Mile Post, as if he was embarrassed to be alone with her in the house, so Sandra broke the ice and asked him if he'd done anything interesting over the weekend.

Robin shook his head. "Not really. I did take a ride to the coast on Sunday, but it clouded over there, so I couldn't get any good shots."

"What about the evenings?" Sandra asked. "Don't you go to clubs or concerts?"

"No, I don't do much of that. Oh, I drop in at the local for the odd jar, but that's about all."

"That's not much of a social life, is it? What about girlfriends? Surely there must be someone?"

"Not really," Robin answered, looking down into his drink. "Since my divorce I've been, well, a bit of a hermit, really. It wouldn't feel right going out with anybody else so soon."

"It's not as if you're a widower, you know," Sandra argued. "When you get divorced it's all right to go out and have fun if you feel like it. Was it mutual?"

Robin nodded hastily, and Sandra sensed that he felt uncomfortable with the subject. "Anyway," she said, "you'll get over it. Don't worry. I'll just nip upstairs and fetch the projector."

"Would you like me to help?" Robin offered awkwardly. "I mean, it must be heavy."

"No, not at all," Sandra said, waving him back onto the sofa. "They're all made of light plastic these days."

Robin was gazing at the books on the shelves by the fireplace when Sandra came back down with the slide projector.

"Here it is," she said. "It's easy to work. Do you know how?"

"I'm not sure," Robin said. "Outside of cameras I'm not very mechanically minded. Look," he went on, "I've got those slides back, the ones I took at the Camera Club. Would you like to see them? You can show me how to set up the machine."

"Why not?"

Sandra set up the projector on the table at the far end of the room and fetched the screen from upstairs. She then drew the curtains and placed it in front of the window. Finally, she showed Robin how to switch on the power and fit the slides he gave her into the circular tray.

"It's automatic," she explained. "Once you've got it all set up you just press this button when you want to move on to the next slide. Or this one if you want to go back. And this is how you focus." She showed him the controls.

Robin nodded. "Excuse me," he said. "I think I would like some ice and water with my whisky after all."

Sandra moved forward to take his glass.

"No, it's all right," he said. "I can get it myself. You set up the show." And he went into the kitchen.

Sandra adjusted the height of the projector and turned off the light. Robin came back with his whisky as the first slide zoomed into focus.

It really was quite remarkable. The model was sitting with her legs tucked under her, gazing away from the camera. The lines drew the eye right into the composition and Robin had obviously used one of the 81-series filters to bring out the warm flesh tones. What was especially odd about the whole thing was that the model didn't seem to be posing; she looked as if she were staring into space thinking of a distant memory.

"It's excellent," Sandra remarked over the hum of the projector. "I really didn't think a modelling session like that would work out well on slides, but it's really amazing. Beautiful."

She heard the ice tinkling in Robin's glass. "Thank you," he said in a far-off voice. "Yes, they did work out well. She's not as beautiful as you, though."

Something in the way he said it sent a shiver of fear up Sandra's spine, and she froze for a moment before turning slowly to look at him. It was too dark to see anything except his silhouette, but in the light that escaped from the edges of the lens, she could see the sharp blade of one of her kitchen knives glinting.

Robin was on his feet, quite close to her. She could hear him breathing quickly. She backed away and found herself between the projector and the screen. The projection of the nude model distorted as it wrapped around her figure like an avant-garde dress design, and she froze again as a transformed Robin moved closer.

II

Mick gobbled up another mouthful of pills and went over to the window again. It was dark outside and the tall sodium lights glowed an eerie red the way they always did before they turned jaundice yellow.

Still no sign. Mick started pacing the room again, one batch of amphetamines wearing off and the new ones beginning to take effect. Sweat prickled on his forehead and skull, itching between the spikes of hair. His heart was pounding like a barrage of artillery, but he didn't feel good. He was worried. Where the hell was Trevor? The bastard was supposed to arrive two hours ago.

As the lights yellowed like old paper, Mick got more edgy and jittery. The room felt claustrophobic, too small to contain him. His muscles were straining at his clothes and his brain felt like it was pushing at the inner edges of his skull. Something was going on. They were onto him. He looked out of the window again, careful not to be seen this time.

There was a man in a homburg walking his Jack Russell. He'd been walking that dog for hours up and down the street by the edge of The Green, under the lights, and Mick was sure he kept glancing covertly towards the house. A little further into The Green, where the lights of the posher houses at the other side seemed to twinkle between the leaves and branches that danced in the breeze, a young couple stood under a tree. The girl was leaning against the tree and the boy was talking to her, one arm outstretched, supporting his weight on the trunk above her head. Sure, they looked like lovers, Mick thought. That was the idea. But he wasn't fooled. He could see the way she kept looking sideways at him when she should have been paying closer attention to her man. He was probably speaking into a walkie-talkie or a microphone hidden in his lapel. They were communicating with the dog-walker. And they weren't the only ones. Deeper in the trees, what he had thought to be shadows and thick tree trunks turned into people, and if he listened closely enough he could hear them whispering to each other.

He put his hands over his ears and retreated into the room. He put a loud rock record on the stereo to shut out the noise of the whisperers, but it didn't work; they were in his head already, and even the music seemed part of a sinister plot. It was meant to put him off-guard, that was it. He snatched at the needle, scratching the record, and returned to the window. Vigilance, that was what was called for.

Nothing had changed. The man with the dog was walking back down the street. He stopped by a tree, holding the leash loosely and looking up at the sky as the dog cocked its leg. The couple on The Green were pretending to kiss now.

Perhaps there was time to get away, Mick thought, licking his lips and wiping his forehead with the back of his hand. He had to get himself ready. They probably didn't even know he was there yet. To escape, though, meant leaving the window for a few minutes, something he couldn't bear to do. But he had to. He couldn't let them catch him unprepared.

He dashed upstairs to Lenny's room first and pulled out the heavy gun from under the mattress; then he went into his own messy room and took all his cash out of its hiding place, a hollowed-out book called *The Practical Way to Keep Fit*. He had almost a hundred pounds. It should be enough.

Rushing back downstairs, he grabbed his parka from the hook in the hall, shoved the gun and money into its deep pockets and went back to watch from the window. Now he was ready. Now he could take on anybody. The familiar effect of the pills was returning. He felt the weight of the big gun in his pocket and waves of adrenalin surged through his veins, flooding him with a sense of power and well-being. But he had to do something; he had so much energy it was boiling over.

The man with the dog had gone and the young couple had moved to another tree. They thought they could fool him, but he wasn't that stupid. The Green was full of young couples now. They leaned against every tree, pretending to be kissing and feeling each other up. Mick felt a jolt of energy in his loins as he watched the erotic tableau of shadows.

When the police car finally came, he was ready. He saw its headlights approaching slowly, dispersing the watchers on The Green as its beams sought the right house, and he left softly by the back door. He had a plan. There was only one sensible thing he could do, and that was get out of Eastvale, disappear, go down to join Lenny in London for awhile. To get out of Eastvale, he had to cross The Green, then the river, and walk up around the castle to the bus station at the back of the market square. It was no good running east; in that direction there was nothing but fields and the long flat vale; he would be an easy target out in the open there.

Cautiously, he edged down the back alley to the end of the block, where a narrow snicket separated two terraces. As he crept out into the street again, he was about four houses north of the police. Now all he had to do was disappear quietly into the trees and he was home free.

He crossed the street without attracting any attention and stood on the verge of The Green. The police were still knocking at his door and trying to peer in through the windows, the fools. A few more paces and he would be among the shadows, the shadows that belonged to him again.

Suddenly, a voice called out behind him and for a moment he stopped dead in his tracks, feeling the adrenalin prickle inside him.

"Hey, you!" the voice called again. "Stop where you are! Police!"

For a second he thought it was all over, that they had him, but then he remembered he had an edge—the gun and the power he felt crackling inside him. The new plan came as a brainstorm, and he laughed out loud at the beauty of it as he ran across The Green with the police close behind, still shouting. He would never make it to the bus station, he knew that now, and even if he did they would be waiting for him, talking to each other on the airwaves. So he had to improvise, try something different.

The light was on. That was a good sign. Without hesitating, he leaped up the steps three at a time and ran his shoulder into the front door. It didn't give at once. The police were clearing the trees now, only about seventy-five yards away. Mick took a few paces back and crashed into the door again. This time it splintered open. The woman, alarmed by his first attempt, was peering, frightened, through a door in the hallway. Mick rushed in, grabbed her by her hair and dragged her to the front window. The police were halfway across the street by now. Taking out his gun, Mick smashed the window and held Jenny up by the hair.

"Stop!" he screamed at them. "Don't move another inch! I've got a gun and I've got the woman, and if you don't do what I say I'll fucking shoot the bitch."

III

Even Robin's voice was different. It had lost its timbre of shy cheerfulness and become forced and clipped.

Sandra edged backwards until she could feel the screen against her back. She was almost perfectly lined up with the projected model, whose image was wrapped around her body, the girl's face superimposed on her own.

"Robin," she said as calmly and quietly as she could manage, "you don't really want to do this, do you? Don't let things go too far."

"I have to," Robin said tersely. "It's already gone beyond."

"Beyond what?"

"Beyond where I thought I could go."

"You can still stop it."

"No."

"Yes, you can," Sandra insisted gently.

"No! Can't you see? I have to go further, always further, or it's no good, there's no point. When I watched you, Sandra, watched you undressing in your bedroom, it was the best, it was just like . . . I didn't think I could go any further than that. I didn't think I could ever go any further. Do you know what I mean? The ultimate."

Sandra nodded. The model's face remained still and detached, fixed on that far-off memory. Sandra felt as if she were tied to the screen by the projection. She wanted to tell Robin to turn it off but she didn't dare. The way he was talking, he was beyond reason. There was nothing she could do but keep asking him calmly to put the knife down and stop. But she knew he wouldn't. He'd gone too far now, and he could only go further. He'd made his greatest step and the rest would have to follow.

He was coming closer, the projected model bending around the knife blade, throwing its shadow onto Sandra's chest. She was backed up as far against the screen as she could get.

Robin stopped, still at an angle so as not to block the image projected on her. "Take your clothes off," he ordered, twitching the knife.

"No," Sandra replied. "You can't mean it. Put the knife away, Robin. It's not too late."

"Take your clothes off," he repeated. "I do mean it. Do as I say."

It was futile to protest any more. Sandra clenched her teeth, holding back the tears, and brought her trembling hands to the buttons on her shirt.

"Don't hurry," Robin said. "Take your time. Do it slow."

Each button seemed to take an eternity, but finally the shirt was undone. She dropped it on the floor and waited.

"Go on," he said. "The jeans."

Sandra was wearing tight Levis. She undid the top button and pulled down the zipper. It wasn't easy, but she managed to fold them over her hips and get out of each leg while still standing up.

She stood before Robin in her white bra and panties, shaking all over. The image was still wrapped around her and now it seemed welcome, offering her a little covering, some protection. Robin pulled the slide out of its slot, and the bright, piercing light of the lens pinned Sandra to the screen. She put up a hand to shield her eyes.

Robin said nothing for a long time. He seemed to be just gazing at her, a slender figure with long, blonde hair and shapely long legs. He was awestruck. She could feel his eyes as they slid over her body, probing every curve, every shadow. She noticed that the hand that held the knife was trembling.

"Now the rest," he ordered in a voice that seemed caught deep in his throat.

Sandra started to obey.

"Slower," Robin commanded her.

Finally, she stood naked in the harsh glare of the slide projector. Now she made no pretence of not crying; her shoulders shook and the tears flowed down her cheeks, fell onto her chest and trickled across her breasts.

Suddenly, Robin gave a strangled cry, dropped the knife and hurled himself down on his knees in front of her. The abruptness of his action shocked Sandra out of her fear. He put his arms around her hips and buried his face in her loins. She could hear him sobbing and she could feel his warm tears. Quickly, she stretched out her left hand to grab the camera that Robin had left on the table beside the screen. Then, with both hands, she lifted it high in the air and brought it down hard on the top of his head.

IV

It was quiet in Banks's office. He sat smoking a cigarette, feeling very pleased with himself, waiting to hear from Hatchley and Richmond. Opposite, Trevor sat sullen and withdrawn, while his father seemed nervous, tapping on the edge of the desk and whistling between his teeth.

There was a soft knock at the door and Sergeant Rowe's grey-haired head popped around, indicating that he had something to say.

"Phone call," he said in the corridor, looking worried. "Your wife, sir. Said it was urgent. She sounded very upset." Banks had asked that all calls be intercepted while he was interrogating Trevor; he hadn't wanted to be interrupted.

Puzzled, and worried that something might have happened to Brian or Tracy, he told Rowe to keep an eye on the suspect for a few moments and ducked into the nearest empty room to take the call.

"Alan? Thank God," Sandra breathed. Rowe was right. Banks had never heard her sound like that before.

"What is it? What's wrong?"

"It was Robin, Alan. The peeper. He came here. He had a knife."

"What happened? Are you all right?"

"Yes, yes, I'm all right. A bit scared and shaky, but he didn't hurt me. Alan, I think I've killed him. I hit him with the camera. Too hard. I wasn't thinking. I was so frightened and angry."

"Stay there, Sandra," Banks told her. "Don't move. I'll be over in a few minutes. Understand?"

"Yes. Hurry, Alan. Please."

"I will."

Banks got Rowe out of his office again and told the sergeant that an emergency had arisen and he had to rush home.

"What about those two?" Rowe asked.

"I'll be back," Banks said, thinking quickly. "Have Sergeant Hatchley call me at home when they get back with Webster. And don't, under any circumstances, let the two kids see each other."

"Right, sir, got it," Rowe said. Banks could tell that he wanted to ask what was wrong or offer some sort of sympathy, but discretion got the better of him and he went back into Banks's office, shutting the door softly behind him.

Banks got as far as the front door before PC Craig, on temporary desk duty, shouted after him.

"Sir! Inspector Banks, sir!"

Banks turned. "What is it?" he snapped, still edging towards the door.

"A call, sir. Sergeant Hatchley. Says it's an emergency."

Banks was in two minds whether to take it or not, but his professional instinct made him reach for the phone. At least Sandra wasn't in immediate danger any longer. A minute or two more wouldn't hurt.

"What is it, Sergeant?"

"The kid, sir. Webster. He gave us the slip."

"Well, go after him."

"It's not as simple as that. We know where he is."

"Get to the bloody point, Sergeant," Banks growled. "I've got one bloody emergency on my hands already."

"He ran across The Green and broke into a woman's house, sir. He's got her held hostage there. He's got a gun."

Banks felt his stomach tighten. "Which house?"

"It's that doctor woman, sir. The one I saw coming out of the super's office."

"Christ," Banks gasped, rubbing his free hand over his eyes.

"But there's more, sir. He says he wants you there. He asked for you and said if you didn't get here in twenty minutes he'd kill the woman."

Banks had to think more quickly than he had ever done in his life. It was probably no more than a split second before he gave Hatchley his instructions, but in that period Banks felt as if he had been to hell and back. The two women flashed before his eyes. If he deserted Sandra when she needed him, he thought, things might never be right again; she would never fully trust him. If he didn't go to help Jenny, on the other hand, she would surely die. Banks reasoned that Sandra would, somehow, understand this if she knew, that his duty was to try to save a life rather than console his wife after she had already succeeded in freeing herself from a dangerous, terrifying situation. Though he was thinking specifically that it was Jenny in danger, that he couldn't let Jenny die, he knew he would also have to go even if it was a stranger Mick Webster had taken hostage. It was personal, yes, and this intensified his concern, but his job demanded that he do the same for anyone. Somebody, however, would have to go to Sandra. There was always the chance that the man would return to consciousness again. And if someone else dealt with it, then it would be official business. It was official anyway, he realized. It had gone too far to be covered up as easily as the peeper episode. No matter who went to Sandra now, all the details would have to come out.

"I'll be there, Sergeant," Banks said quickly. "Send DC Richmond over to my house. Got it? MY HOUSE. Immediately. I've not got time to explain, but it's urgent. Tell him to hurry and to explain to my wife about the situation here."

"Yes, sir," Hatchley said, sounding puzzled.

"And let the super know," Banks added. "We'll need him down there if there's any negotiating to be done."

"He's already on his way," Hatchley said, and hung up.

Not wasting another moment, Banks rushed through the desk area, picked up the keys to the same car he had driven to York, and, without signing for them, dashed out of the back into the yard where the vehicles were parked. In seven minutes, he was outside Jenny's house.

Hatchley and two uniformed men stood the low wall at the bottom of the garden, which sloped upwards quite steeply to the bay window. The light in the front room was on, and Banks could hear the strains of *Tosca* playing in the background.

"Any developments?" he asked Hatchley.

"No, sir," the sergeant replied. "Haven't seen hide nor hair of him since he told us to send for you. They're inside, though. I sent Bradley and Jennings round the back. Told them not to do nothing, just keep their eyes open."

Banks nodded. Hatchley had done well, considering that this was the first time he had had to deal with hostage taking. It was a difficult business, as Banks had found out for himself on one or two occasions down in London, but it was of chief importance to maintain as calm and reasonable an atmosphere as possible for negotiations.

Another car drew up by the kerb and Superintendent Gristhorpe got out. He looked like a bulky, absent-minded professor with his unkempt thatch of hair blowing in the breeze and his bushy eyebrows meeting in the middle of his frown.

Banks explained the situation to him as quickly as possible.

"Why does he want you here?" Gristhorpe asked.

"I don't know."

"Have you told him you've arrived?"

"Not yet."

"Better do it, Alan. He might be getting impatient."

"Is there a megaphone?" Banks asked.

Gristhorpe smiled wryly. "Now where the bloody hell would we get a megaphone, Alan?"

Banks acknowledged this fact, then simply spoke out loud towards the broken window.

"Mick! Mick Webster! I'm here. It's Inspector Banks."

There were sounds of scuffling inside, then Webster appeared at the window, gun pointed at the side of Jenny's head.

"What do you want?" Banks asked. "Why do you want me here?"

"I want you in here," Mick shouted back.

"Why do you want me? You've already got the girl."

"Just do as I say. Get in here. And no tricks."

"Mick, send the girl out. Send her out and then I'll come in."

"Nothing doing. Come in now or I'll blow her fucking head off."

"Come on, Mick, let's play fair. Let her go. We give a little and you give a little. Send her out and I'll come in."

"I told you, Banks. Either you come in now or she dies. I'll give you thirty seconds."

"Better do it, Alan," Gristhorpe said heavily. "He's not stable, you can't reason with him. Have you dealt with anything like this before?"

"Yes," Banks answered. "A couple of times. Usually with pros, though."

"But you know the ropes?"

Banks nodded.

"I'll try and keep him talking," Gristhorpe said, "keep negotiations open."

"Your time's running out, Banks," Mick yelled.

"All right," Banks said, climbing the steps, "I'm coming in, Mick." And as he walked, he thought of Sandra.

V

Mick Webster was in a dangerously unstable state. Banks could see that at once as he obeyed orders and emptied out his pockets. The boy was constantly edgy, always scratching, sweating, fidgeting, shifting from one foot to the other, and it didn't take Banks long to recognize the signs of an amphetamine user.

Jenny appeared to be calm enough. Her left cheek was inflamed, as if she had been hit, but she seemed to be trying to reassure him with the look in her eyes that all was well and that now he was here they had a chance to work together and get out alive. She was quick, Banks knew that, and he also felt that a certain intuitive bond had quickly been forged between them. If there was an opportunity, he thought, then they could probably do something about it between them. It was just a matter of waiting to see who took the initiative.

Mick's moods were shifting minute by minute. One moment he'd be joking, the next he'd become morose and say he had nothing to lose. And all that pacing and jittering was driving Banks crazy. *Tosca* still played in the background, well into the second act, and the cassette box lay on a pine table by the broken window.

"All right, Mick," Banks said quietly. "What is it you want?"

"What do you think?" Mick sneered. "I want out of here." He swaggered over to the window and shouted: "I want ten thousand quid and safe passage out of the country, or the girl and the cop die, got it?"

Outside in the cold evening, Gristhorpe whispered to Hatchley, "Not a snowball in hell's chance," and said back to Mick, "All right, we'll work on it. Stay in communication and we'll let you know."

"I don't want to talk to you fuckers," Mick yelled back. "I know you and all your games. Just get me what I asked for and fuck off out of the way." He kept the gun pointed at Jenny. "Hurry up, get back in those trees where I can't see you or I'll kill the girl now."

Reluctantly, Gristhorpe, Hatchley and the two uniformed men moved back across the road onto The Green.

"That's right," Mick shouted at them. "And fucking well stay there till you've got something to tell me."

Banks stood as close to Mick and Jenny as he dared. "Mick," he said, "they're not going to do it. You don't stand a chance."

"They'll do it," Mick said. "They don't want to see your brains splattered all over the garden. Or hers."

"They can't do it, Mick," Banks went on patiently. "They can't give in to demands like that. If they did, then every Tom, Dick and Harry would start taking hostages and asking for the world."

Mick laughed. "Maybe I'll start a trend then, eh? They'll do it, and you'd better hope they do, both of you."

The music went on quietly and the cool night air came in through the broken window. Outside, Banks could hear talking on a car radio. They would already have the street cordonned off, and should have evacuated the neighbours.

Mick licked his lips and looked from one to the other of them. "Well," he said, "what shall we do when the transport comes?" And his eyes stayed on Jenny, who stood by the tile fireplace. Banks stuck close to the table by the window.

"Don't make things worse, Mick," Banks said. "If you give up now, it'll be taken into consideration. Things wouldn't go too badly for you. But if you go any further..."

"You know as well as I do," Mick said, turning to Banks, "that I'm in about as deep as can be."

"That's not true, Mick. There's a way out of this."

"And what's going to happen to me then?"

"I can't make any promises, Mick. You know that. But it'll go in your favour."

"Yeah, it'll go in my fucking favour. I'll only get twenty years instead of twenty-five, is that what you're telling me?"

"You'll get a lot more if you hurt anyone, Mick. No one's been hurt yet. Remember that."

Mick turned to Jenny. "This is what we're gonna do," he said. "When they fix up my transport, you're coming with me and he's staying. He'll know if he lets his copper mates do anything to stop us, you'll be dead. *They* might not think I mean it, but he does."

"No," Jenny said.

"What do you mean, 'no,' you cunt? What the fuck do you think this is in my hand, a fucking cap-gun?"

Jenny shook her head. "I'm not going anywhere with you. I'm not going to let you lay one dirty finger on me."

Mick reddened and looked, to Banks, dangerously near the end of his tether. But Jenny was the psychologist, and she seemed to have taken the initiative; it was up to Banks to follow. While Mick glared at Jenny, Banks picked up the cassette box from the table and tossed it out through the broken window.

There was a sudden clattering sound on the path and Mick turned to aim the gun towards the noise. Banks was close enough to jump him when the gun was pointing out of the window. But before Banks could make his move, Mick actually fired into the garden. The gun made a dull explosion and they both heard Mick scream. Slowly, he turned back towards the room, his face white, mouth and eyes wide open with shock and pain. The blood from his hand dripped onto the clean pine table.

SIXTEEN

I

As soon as Hatchley and Gristhorpe heard the shot and the scream, they dashed out of the trees towards the house. Inside, Jenny rushed to help Banks, who had already ripped off Mick's shirt-sleeve to apply as a tourniquet.

"It's a mess," he said, tying the knot, then he caught Jenny's eye. "You did well," he told her. "But for a minute I thought you were going to push him too far."

"Me, too. The idea was just to confuse him, then attract his attention. The kid was so stoned he didn't know what was happening. I'm glad you caught the signal."

When Banks heard the others reach the steps, he walked over to the window to tell them it was all clear. Inside the house after that it was chaos—several people asking different questions at the same time, orders being given to uniformed men, phone calls being made for the ambulance and Scene-of-Crime Squad—and throughout it all, nobody thought to turn off the stereo; Tosca was still singing:

> *Nell'ora del dolore*
> *Perché, perché, Signor,*
> *Perché me ne rimuneri cosí?*

A still point for a moment at the centre of all the frenetic activity, Banks took in the familiar words: "In this, my hour of grief and tribulation, Why Heavenly Father, Why hast thou forsaken me?"

"Good work, Alan," Gristhorpe said, snapping Banks out of the music. "All right?"

"Fine."

"You look a bit pale."

"I always do when I've been in close contact with guns."

Gristhorpe looked down at Mick. "If all guns reacted the way that one did, Alan, it might be a better world. I'm not a religious man, as you know—too much of that pernicious Yorkshire Methodism in my background—but maybe sometimes God is there when we need him."

Banks looked over at Jenny, who was telling a constable what had happened. "*She* was certainly there."

He went on to explain about Sandra and asked permission to go home and skip the formalities until later.

"Of course," Gristhorpe said. "You should have told me earlier. Are you sure she sounded all right?"

"A bit shook up, but in control. Richmond's still with her."

"Off you go, then," Gristhorpe said, giving Banks a gentle push in the small of the back.

It was time to face Sandra.

As he walked to the door, he saw Jenny, neglected now, slumped on the sofa with her face in her hands. He looked around the room again—the cold night air coming in through the broken window, the blood on the table, the shards of glass on the floor.

"Jenny," he called softly, holding out his hand. "Come with me."

She did as she was asked, and on the way home Banks told her about Sandra's ordeal.

"Do you think it'll be all right?" she asked. "You know, me coming with you?"

"To tell you the truth, Jenny, I don't know what to expect. I couldn't leave you there, though. Don't worry, the superintendent will see that everything's taken care of."

Jenny shivered. "I don't think I could have stayed there. I'd have gone to a hotel. I still can. I shouldn't come with you."

"Don't be silly."

Banks drove on in silence.

Finally, they arrived at the house and hurried up the path. Sandra flung open the door. Banks winced as she ran towards him, but she threw her arms around him.

"Alan! Alan, thank God you're all right," she sobbed, burying her face in his shoulder.

He stroked her hair. "I'm all right, don't worry. Let's go inside. I could do with a drink."

Richmond stood up as they entered the living-room. The young DC stroked his moustache and cleared his throat. Banks suddenly remembered that it was Richmond he had seen that night in The Oak. Jenny had been with him then and they must have seemed very close. God only knew what he was thinking!

"There, I told you," Richmond said to Sandra. "I told you he'd be all right." He turned to Banks and gave him a nod, as if to signify that all was well. The two of them walked together to the door. "I've taken your wife's statement, sir. It's all very clear what happened. He's the peeper, no doubt about it."

"How is he?"

"Don't know yet, sir. It didn't look serious to me. They took him to the hospital about half an hour ago. Will that be all, sir?"

Banks could tell that Richmond was anxious to leave, that being involved with his inspector in such a personal way was exceedingly uncomfortable for him. "Yes," he said. "You can go now. And Detective Richmond…"

"Yes, sir?"

"Thanks."

Richmond blushed and muttered something about it being nothing before he took off at a fair pace down the path.

Banks closed the door and noticed Jenny and Sandra looking at each other. He knew that Sandra would be embarrassed at showing so much emotion in front of a stranger.

"I'm sorry," he apologized wearily, running his hand over his close-cropped hair. "I didn't introduce you, did I?"

After the introduction, Sandra offered Jenny a chair.

Banks went straight to the drinks cabinet.

"Something a bit stronger than tea, I think. Scotch all round?"

"Yes, please." The two women nodded.

It was hard to know what to do to break the ice, Banks realized as he poured them all generous measures of Macallan single malt. Jenny could hardly say to Sandra, "I heard you had a terrible ordeal tonight, dear?" nor could Sandra answer, "Oh yes, absolutely dreadful. I thought I was going to be raped, then murdered. You didn't have such an easy time, yourself, I hear?" So they sipped scotch and said nothing for a while and Banks smoked a much-needed cigarette.

"Look, if you'd rather I went," Jenny said, "I'm feeling much better now."

"Nonsense," Sandra told her. "You can't go back there. You're staying here, with us. I'll make up the spare bed. Oh, Alan, it's nearly time to pick the children up from the meetings. Shall I go?"

"No," Banks said, putting his hand on her shoulder. "You've had enough for tonight. Let me go. It's only down the road."

"You'll tell them?"

"I'll tell them that we had a break-in and you caught a burglar. You'll be a real heroine in their eyes then."

"It'll be in the papers, won't it, later?"

"Probably. We'll cross that bridge when we get there. Will you two be all right?"

"Of course we will," Sandra said, smiling at Jenny. "We're a couple of heroes, didn't you just say so?"

"I thought it was heroines?"

Sandra shook her head. "Somehow, 'heroines' doesn't have the right ring to it. I think heroines are always victims. They're pale and wan and they make a lot of noise. More scotch, Jenny?"

Banks walked to the car. On the way back from the church hall, he told Brian and Tracy that they had a guest for the evening and that they were to behave themselves and go to bed as soon as they'd had their cocoa. There seemed no point in even mentioning what had happened.

Back at the house, they interrupted Sandra and Jenny deep in conversation, and Brian and Tracy were bursting with comments about their evening. Brian announced that he was sick to death of the Lifeboys and he was never going again. Banks helped get them ready for bed, took them upstairs and tucked them in; then, yawning, he walked back downstairs.

"I have to go in," he said. "There's a few loose ends to tie up."

Sandra nodded. It was nothing new to her.

"I'll probably be late," he added, "so don't wait up."

It was confusing, saying goodbye to the two of them. He bent and kissed Sandra's cheek, then nodded at Jenny and hurried out. Even though he'd got his priorities sorted out, there was something disturbing about being with both women at once. It was extremely disconcerting, and the more Banks analyzed the feeling as he walked—Walkman-less, but grateful to be breathing the cool night air—the more he decided that it wasn't sexual. It had nothing at all to do with the beauty and desirability of both women, but everything to do with his sensing a strong bond between them that put him on the outside. They didn't even have to talk to make it clear. Banks had felt as if he were a clumsy, primitive beast in the presence of two alien creatures.

II

The station was humming with activity. Already, those on duty in plain clothes had been recalled from the pubs and were clustering around the duty roster trying to decide who should go home and who should stay. And downstairs, the phone kept ringing. Residents of the East Side Estate were still calling to report the gunshot.

Upstairs, things were quieter. The Sharps had been taken to an interview room, and Gristhorpe's door was open. As soon as Banks rounded the corner, the superintendent popped his head out and invited him in. One shaded table lamp provided the only illumination, and the bookcases and deep leather chairs gleamed in its dim light. The only thing Banks needed was another cigarette. As if reading his mind Gristhorpe took a Queen's Arms ashtray out of his bottom drawer and pushed it over to him.

"Just this once, Alan. I can see you need it. Though God knows why a person would crave something that's a proven carcinogen."

"There's none worse than ex-smokers," Banks joked. Everybody knew that Gristhorpe's anti-smoking campaign was of fairly recent origin.

"How are things, Alan?"

"Pretty good, considering. It's nice to be able to relax for a moment. I haven't really managed to bring my mind to bear on what happened yet."

"Plenty of time. Write it down in the morning. Sandra's well?"

"Yes. She's either tougher than I thought or she's a good actress."

"I think she's just got hidden depths, Alan. Strong reserves. You'd be surprised how many have. My wife, God bless her, was the mildest, gentlest woman on the face of the earth. Talk about frail— you'd think she'd faint at a cuss-word. But she was a nurse in the war, just like Alice Matlock, and she saw more than one member of her family from this world to the next. But she never once flinched or complained, even when the cancer got hold of her. 'Course, she was a Yorkshirewoman."

Banks smiled. "Of course."

"Many a copper would have run straight to his wife, Alan. You did the right thing. You weighed up both situations and decided where you could do the most good."

"It didn't seem as logical a process as that. When it comes down to it, there was only one place where I *had* to be."

"I know that, and so do you. But a lesser man might have let emotion confuse the issue."

"There were times when I thought I had. What's happened to Robin Allott?"

"Mild concussion. He'll be all right. Still at the hospital. If that camera had been out of its leather case, and if Sandra had hit him on the temple or the base of the skull, he might have been dead. It was an old one, metal body instead of that plastic they use nowadays. The young fellow was very lucky indeed."

"Sandra, too."

"No blame would have attached to her."

"But imagine how she'd feel, even so."

"Aye," Gristhorpe said, rubbing his prickly chin.

"Has he said anything?"

"Not a dicky bird, yet. Still too dazed. I don't think he'll hold back on us, though. Sandra made a very clear statement." His bushy brows knitted in a deep frown. "She went through a lot, you know."

"I know. At least I think I do. I don't know all the details yet."

One of the uniformed constables knocked softly at the half-open door before delivering a tray of coffee and biscuits.

"They're from downstairs, the biscuits, sir," he said. "We keep a few packets in, club together, like. Thought you might appreciate some."

"Thank you, Constable Craig," Gristhorpe said. "Much appreciated. You on late duty tonight?"

"Yes, sir. Me and Susan Gay."

There was something in the constable's clipped tone that prompted Gristhorpe to ask if anything was wrong.

"Well, sir," Craig said, "I don't mean to complain, but every time we're on duty together and something like this comes up—making coffee or delivering biscuits—she always manages to push me into doing it." His face reddened. "It's that blooming women's lib is what it is, sir."

Gristhorpe laughed. "It's what we call 'positive discrimination,' lad, and you'll just have to get used to it. Stick up for yourself. And I hope this coffee's a bit better than the usual muck we get around here."

"It should be, sir," Craig said proudly. "A satisfied customer presented us with one of those automatic drip-filter things earlier this evening, sir. I went across to that fancy tea and coffee shop in King Street and got some fresh-ground Colombian beans."

The superintendent turned his baby blue eyes on Craig. "Did you, now? Not only accepting gifts from the public but playing truant, eh?"

"Yes, sir. Sorry, sir," Craig replied, standing stiffly to attention.

"It's all right," Gristhorpe said. "Only joking, lad. Wherever it came from, it's most welcome. The chief inspector'll be able to drink it black. Off you go, lad."

The coffee was good, the best they'd tasted in a long time, and Banks had a fondness for McVities' Chocolate Digestives. Gristhorpe was on yet another diet, though, and refused to give in to his sweet tooth.

"How's Mick Webster?" Banks asked.

"He'll live. Lost a lot of blood, but that tourniquet of yours did the trick."

"His hand?"

"Lost two fingers, and the doc says he might lose another if surgery doesn't go well. Have you any idea where he got the gun from?"

"No. The first I heard of Webster was from Trevor Sharp earlier tonight. I think we should get a warrant and search his place."

"It's already being done. That's where Richmond and Hatchley are now. If I were you, Alan, I'd go home, take care of my wife and get some sleep."

"I want to talk to Sharp."

"It'll wait, Alan."

"No."

"I can do it."

"I started it, and I'd hate to have to begin all over again."

Gristhorpe tapped a pencil on his blotter. "You've got a point, I suppose. We don't want him fresh again after a night's sleep."

"Does he know about Webster?"

"No."

"Good."

"Sure you're up to it?"

"Yes. I wouldn't get any sleep for thinking about it anyway."

Gristhorpe pointed towards the corridor. "Interview room number three. I think Sergeant Rowe's still with them. He'll be worn out by now."

III

Banks took his second cup of black coffee into the small interview room.

Graham Sharp jumped to his feet. "You can't keep us here like this," he said. "We've been cooped up here for hours. It's not a police state yet, you know."

Banks sat down and spoke to Sergeant Rowe. "You can go now, Sergeant. Could you send someone in to take notes? Constable Craig will do."

He didn't speak until Craig arrived, then he lit a cigarette and took a long pull on his coffee.

"Right," he said, looking at Trevor. "We've got your mate Webster and he's told us all about your little capers."

"You're lying," Trevor said. "You must think I'm stupid to fall for that one."

"What one?"

"The one where the cops tell a suspect his accomplice has confessed and expect him to break down. I've seen it on telly."

"'Accomplice?' Accomplice in what?"

"It's just a word."

"Yes, I know. But words mean things. What's more, they imply things too. 'Accomplice' implies that you worked together in committing a crime."

"I told you, it's just a word."

"Stop beating around the bush," Graham Sharp said. "If we have to stay until you've finished, at least get on with it."

"It's true," Banks said to Trevor, and noticed that the boy had started to chew his bottom lip. "He told us all about the break-ins—first the old ladies, then the Ottershaws and Thelma Pitt. He told us how he tried to stop you from raping her but you were like a mad dog. Those were his words, 'mad dog.'"

"He's a liar," Trevor said.

"What do you mean, Trevor? That you weren't like a mad dog?"

"I didn't rape anybody."

"Why would he lie? We found Thelma Pitt's jewellery in his house, and some bits and pieces from the other robberies." Banks knew he was treading on very shaky ground by lying in the hope of getting a confession, but he kept his fingers crossed and trusted that Richmond and Hatchley would turn up something. "Why would he lie, Trevor? It's all up for him and he knows it."

"He's trying to put the blame on someone else, that's all."

"But there were two of you. We know that. A gangly one and a squat one. The gangly one had decay between his front teeth and caught the clap from Thelma Pitt. The squat one had piggy eyes and a raspy voice. You've got to admit that fits Mick to a tee. And your father told us about Mick, remember? He said Mick Webster was to blame if you'd done anything wrong. Now Mick says you're both to blame. What am I supposed to believe?"

"Believe what you want. I don't care."

"But you should, Trevor. Your father does. He cares enough to lie for you."

"Now just a minute—"

"Be quiet, Mr Sharp. You lied for your son and you know damn well you did. Well, Trevor?"

"Well what?"

"Why don't you admit it? That way we can say you helped us and it'll go easier for you in court. If we have to prove a case, we can, but it'll be more trouble for all of us."

"Admit what?"

"The truth."

"I've told you."

"Not the truth. Not like Mick did. He was on drugs, you know. Remember what he gets like? You can't trust him at all when he's on drugs."

"And you can't believe him, either."

"I do. A jury will. How about it, Trevor?"

"What?"

"Tell me what you did?"

"I didn't do nothing."

"Alice Matlock?"

"He never killed anyone," Graham Sharp protested.

"How do you know? He's lied to you about everything else."

Sharp looked at his son, who turned to face the wall. "He didn't. I just know. He couldn't. He's not capable of it."

"It didn't take much strength, you know," Banks said. "Probably an accident."

"You'll never prove it," Graham said.

Banks shrugged. "What do you think, Trevor?"

"Did Mick tell you that?"

"Tell me what?"

"That we killed the old bag down the street."

"What if he did?"

"Then you're lying," Trevor said, gripping the table edge and rising from his chair. "You're bloody lying. We didn't kill nobody. We didn't have nothing to do with Alice Matlock. If you say he told you that then you're a fucking liar."

"I'm right about the rest, though, aren't I?"

"You made it all up. You don't even have Mick. I'm not saying another word."

In the silence that followed, PC Craig answered the gentle tapping on the door and whispered to Banks, who left the room. In the corridor stood Hatchley and Richmond, both looking pleased as Punch.

"Don't just stand there like the cats that got the cream," Banks said. "What did you find?"

"We got back the Ottershaw and Pitt jewellery and one or two other trinkets."

"Prints?"

"Vic Manson says so. On the camera and a large brooch."

Banks breathed a sigh of relief.

"And," Hatchley added, "we've got a damn good idea who the fence is."

"Go on."

"There was a snapshot in one of the drawers, not a good one, a bit blurred, but as far as I could tell, it matched the sketch we got from Leeds," Hatchley explained. "And there was a letter from London, from a chap called Lenny. Apparently he's Webster's brother."

"Does he have a record?"

Hatchley shook his head. "Not up here. Not as far as we know. Spends most of his time down in The Smoke. I'll check with records."

"Do that. Have you got an address?"

"Yes."

"Excellent. Perhaps you'd better take your findings to Superintendent Gristhorpe. He'll get in touch with London CID and have Lenny Webster picked up. Then we'll see what we shall see." Banks yawned. "Sorry, lads. Afraid I'm tired. Go on up, the super's still in his office."

"Yes, sir," Richmond said, heading for the stairs. Hatchley hung back for a moment, shifting awkwardly.

"Something else, Sergeant?" Banks asked, his hand on the door handle.

"It's just what you did tonight, sir. I just wanted to say I admired you for it. It was a brave thing to do. I don't reckon I'm no softie myself, but I've never been stuck up with a gun. The very thought of it gives me the bloody collywobbles."

"Let's hope you never will be," Banks said. "It happens a lot less often up here than down south."

"I know," Hatchley agreed. "I never thought I'd see the day when I was glad we had a Southerner on the Eastvale force."

That final disclosure seemed too much for Hatchley's tight-lipped nature, and he rushed off, Banks thought, before he went too far and his boss could accuse him of sentimentality.

Smiling, Banks returned to the interview room. Graham Sharp was pale and Trevor wore his customary scowl. Though the father might never admit it, Banks knew that he now thought Trevor was guilty. The boy's reactions had convinced him just as they had confirmed beyond any doubt two things Banks already believed: that they had definitely not killed Alice Matlock, and that they had done everything else.

When Banks sat down and lit a cigarette, Trevor began to look apprehensive. Sipping tepid coffee, Banks let the silence stretch until both father and son were clearly as tense and anxious as he wanted them to be, then he turned to PC Craig and pointed at Trevor.

"Hold him, Constable. Suspicion of burglary, assault and rape will do for a start. I've had quite enough of his company for the time being. Get him fingerprinted immediately."

Graham Sharp tried to block his way as he left the room, but Banks pushed him gently aside: "The constable here will explain your son's rights," he said.

It was late, well after midnight, and the town outside was dark and quiet. Only the bell of the church clock broke the silence every fifteen minutes. Back in his office, Banks looked out through the slats of his venetian blinds. There wasn't a soul in sight; all the lights were out except for the old-style gas lamps around the market square and a shop window to the right, across Market Street, in which elegant mannequins modelled the kind of long, expensive dresses that Grace Kelly wore in *Rear Window*.

Banks lit another cigarette and drank some more hot coffee, then turned to the first buff folder on his desk. It was Sandra's statement. Not much of her personality came through in Richmond's precise, analytical prose, nor did any of her feelings. Banks could only imagine them, and he found himself doing so only too well. As he read of her being forced back towards the screen at knife-point and made to strip ("To what point?" an obviously embarrassed Richmond had asked) to her skin, tears burned his eyes and anger seethed in his veins. He closed the folder and slammed it with his fist.

At least from what Sandra had remembered of Robin Allott's words—and she had done well to remember so much—it sounded as if he was their man. It also sounded as if he had broken down at the end, that he couldn't go through with it. Banks recalled Jenny once saying that the man might have to keep going further and further to satisfy himself, but that he might also reach breaking point before doing any serious damage. Whether he had done any serious damage or not was a moot point.

It had been a long day. Banks yawned and felt his eyelids suddenly become heavy and scratchy. It was time to go home.

He pulled up his coat collar and stepped out into Market Street. The chill October air was invigorating, but Banks felt tired beyond revival. All the way home, something nagged at his mind, something about the Sharp interview. Trevor's reaction to the Alice Matlock business certainly confirmed his earlier suspicions, but that wasn't it, there was something else. It was no good trying to think, though, he decided. It would have to wait until tomorrow.

IV

Jenny and Sandra were still talking when Banks walked in the front door. They were drinking cocoa laced with scotch, and Sandra had lent Jenny one of her old dressing-gowns to wear.

"I thought you'd be in bed by now," Banks said, hanging up his overcoat.

"We didn't feel like sleeping," Sandra replied. "But now you mention it, I do feel tired."

"Me too," Jenny echoed.

"I've made up the bed," Sandra told her. "I hope it's comfortable enough for you."

"I could sleep on a slab of stone." Jenny smiled and stood up. "Goodnight, you two, and thanks very much."

She went upstairs and Banks flopped down on the sofa beside Sandra. Again he had noticed a strange atmosphere between them, as if they were in a world that excluded him, but he was too tired to delve into it. About ten minutes later, they followed Jenny up and slipped between the sheets.

"What were you talking about?" he asked as they snuggled close.

"Oh, this and that."

"Me?"

"A bit. Mostly what it felt like."

"What did it feel like?"

"You'll never know."

"You could try and describe it for me."

"I don't want to go through it all again tonight, Alan. Some other time."

"Maybe it felt something like being held up at gunpoint."

"Maybe it did. I'll tell you something, though. It's very odd. I was terrified and I hated him, but afterwards I felt sorry for him. He was like a little child when I hit him, Alan. He was down on his knees. He'd dropped his knife, and he was like a child. I couldn't handle the feelings at the time. I was scared, angry, hurt, and I hit him. I wanted to kill him, I really did. But it was pathetic. He was like a child crying out for his mother."

"You did the right thing," Banks said, holding her and feeling her warm tears on his shoulder.

"I know. But that's what I mean when I said you'd never understand. You never could. There are some things men could never grasp in a million years."

Banks felt shut out again, and it irked him that Sandra was probably right. He wanted to understand everything, and he had sympathy, feelings and imagination enough to do so, or so he had thought. Now Sandra was telling him that no matter how hard he tried, he could never fathom the bond that united her and Jenny and excluded him, simply because he was a man. They had both been victims, and he was a member of the sex that had the power to humiliate them. In a way, it didn't matter how gentle and understanding he was; he was guilty by association.

But perhaps, he thought, as he drifted into sleep, it was neither as important nor as devastating as it seemed at that moment. After all, he was tired out, and the evening's events had left their unassimilated residue in him, too. He was simply recognizing a chasm that had always existed, even before Sandra had been so abused. That unbridgeable gap had not interfered seriously with their happiness and closeness before, and it probably wouldn't do so in the future. The human spirit was a great deal more resilient than one imagined in one's darker moments. Still, the distance between them was more apparent now than ever, and it would have to be dealt with; he would have to make attempts to cross it.

He held Sandra tighter and told her he loved her, but she was already asleep. Sighing, he turned over and fell into his own dreamless darkness.

SEVENTEEN

I

When Banks met Robin Allott the next morning, he could see exactly what Sandra meant. He had expected to hate the man, but Robin, looking rather like a tonsured monk with the dressing fixed over the shaved centre of his skull, was pathetic. Banks found it easy to detach himself and deal with him as he would with any other criminal. Richmond sat in the corner taking notes.

"What did the hospital say?" he asked.

Allott shrugged and avoided looking Banks in the eye. "Not very much. They dressed the wound and sent me away with this." He held up a card which explained how to handle patients with head wounds. "I spent the rest of the night in your cells."

"Want to talk?"

Allott nodded. The first thing he did was apologize. Then he confessed to all the reported peeping incidents in addition to several more that had gone either unnoticed or unreported by the victims.

There was, however, another important matter to discuss. The timing of Allott's peeping on Carol Ellis coincided almost exactly with Alice Matlock's late evening visitor, who, if he wasn't her killer, was the last person to see her alive. Banks asked him if he had seen anyone as he ran along Cardigan Drive.

"Yes," Allott said eagerly. "I liked Alice. I've been wanting to tell you but I couldn't find a way without... It's been torturing me ever since. At first I thought he would have reported me. Then when he didn't... I'm so glad it's all over. I tried to suggest it might not have been kids, that it might have happened some other way, when you came to talk to me."

"I remember," Banks said. "But you didn't express the theory very forcefully."

"How could I? I was scared for myself."

"Who did you see?"

"It wasn't anyone I knew, but it was a man in his late thirties or early forties, I'd say. Medium height, slim. He had light brown hair combed back with a parting on the left."

"What was he wearing?"

"A beige overcoat, I think. I remember it was a chilly night. And gloves. Fawn gloves."

"Did you see where he came from?"

"No. He was by the end of Alice's house when I ran by on the other side of the street. You know, the end of the block that runs at right angles to Cardigan Drive. Gallows View."

"So he was actually on Cardigan Drive, walking by the end house of Gallows View."

"Yes. Just across the street from me."

"And you got a good look at him?"

"Good enough. There's a street-lamp only yards from the junction."

"Would you recognize him again?"

"Yes."

"Are you sure?"

"Definitely."

Jenny had asked if she could talk to Allott, and Banks had agreed, stipulating that he be present throughout the interview. When he had finished with his questions, he asked Richmond to call in at the interview room where she was waiting and send her along.

There was still something nagging at his mind. Though it often worked wonders on half-formed ideas, sleep had failed to solve the problem this time. It was like having the right word on the tip of his tongue but being unable to utter it.

Jenny seemed to be making a deliberate effort to hide her beauty by wearing some very unflattering horn-rimmed glasses and drab, baggy clothes that made her figure seem shapeless. She also wore her hair tied back in a severe bun.

Robin Allott looked up when she walked in stiffly with a file folder under her arm and a pencil behind her ear. She sat down opposite him, opened the folder, and only then, Banks noticed, did she look him in the eye.

"Would you like to tell me when you started watching women undress?" she asked first, in a business-like tone.

Now, Banks thought, it's my turn to watch the professional at work.

Allott looked away at the autumn scene on the calendar. "It was after my wife left me. I couldn't...she wasn't happy....She put up with me for a long time, but finally she couldn't stand it any longer. We hadn't had a proper life together, a real marriage. You know what I mean."

"Why was that?"

"I don't know. I didn't like to touch her. I couldn't be a man for her. I just wasn't interested. It wasn't her fault. She was a good woman, really. She put up with a great deal."

"What did she think?"

"She once told me she thought I was a latent homosexual, but I knew that was wrong. I never had any feelings like that for men. The whole idea repelled me. I never had any real feelings at all."

"What do you mean, you didn't have any real feelings?"

"You know, the things people are supposed to feel and do. Everything normal and carefree, like talking and kissing and loving. I felt like there was a big wall between me and the rest of the world, especially my wife."

"So she left you and then you started watching women get undressed. Why did you do that?"

"It was what I wanted to do. All I wanted to do, really. There was nothing else that gave me such a thrill. I know it was wrong but I couldn't...I tried to stop..."

"Can you think of any reason why you chose to do that particular thing? Why only that could satisfy you?"

Allott hesitated and bit his lip. "Yes," he said, after a few moments. "I did it before—a long time ago when I was a boy—and I couldn't get it out of my mind."

"What happened?"

He took a deep breath and his gaze turned inwards.

"We lived on a narrow street with a pub on the corner—The Barley Mow, it was called—and lots of times when I was supposed to be asleep in my room, I'd see this woman opposite walk back from the pub alone, go upstairs and undress for bed. She always left the curtains open, and I watched her.

"She was a beautiful woman and nobody in the neighbourhood really knew her. She never spoke to anyone and people tended to keep away from her, as if she was cold or above them somehow. People said she was foreign, a refugee from Eastern Europe, but nobody really knew. She was always alone. She was a mystery, but I could watch her unveil herself. At first it didn't feel like much, but I suppose it was just about that time of life when you change...and over a few weeks I had strange feelings watching her, feelings I'd never had before. They scared me, but they were exciting. I suppose I started to...to play with myself, unconsciously, and I remember thinking, 'What if she sees me, what will she do? I'll be in trouble then.' But in a way I wanted her to see me, too. I wanted her to know about me." He leaned forward on his chair and his liquid brown eyes began to shine as he talked.

"Did she ever see you?"

"No. One day she was just gone. Simple as that. I was devastated. I'd thought it would go on forever, that she was doing it just for me. When she left it felt as if my whole life had been smashed in pieces. Oh, I did all the usual things like the other boys, but it always felt like there was something missing—it was never as wonderful as the others made out it was, as I thought it should be. Even girls, real girls..."

"Why did you marry?"

"It was the normal thing to do. My mother helped me, arranged introductions, that kind of thing. It just didn't work, though. I was always thinking of this woman, even...I could only do it if I thought of her. When my wife left, something snapped in me. It was like a sort of fog came over my mind, but at the same time I felt free. I felt like I could do what I wanted, I didn't have to pretend any more. Oh, I could always be with other people easily enough—I had the Camera Club and all, but it was all inside, the mist. I felt I had to find her again, recapture what I'd lost."

"And did you?"

"No."

"What was she like?"

"Beautiful. Slender and beautiful. And she had black eyebrows and long, golden-blonde hair. That excited me, I don't know why. Maybe it was the contrast. Long, straight, blonde hair down over her shoulders. She looked like Sandra. That's why . . . I wouldn't have hurt her, never. And when it had gone so far, I just couldn't go through with it." He glanced over at Banks, who lit a cigarette and looked out of the window on the bustle of the market square.

"What did you have in mind?"

"Nothing clear. I wanted to touch her. Make love to her, I suppose. But I couldn't. Please believe me, I wouldn't have hurt her, honestly."

"But you did hurt her."

He hung his head. "I know. I'd like to tell her, say I'm sorry . . ."

"I don't think she wants to see you. You frightened her a great deal."

"I didn't mean to. It seemed like the only way."

"I'm not here to judge you," Jenny said.

"What's going to happen to me?"

"You need help. We'll try to help you."

"You?"

"Not me, but somebody qualified."

Robin gave a resigned nod. "I didn't mean to scare her. I would never have harmed a hair on her head, you've got to believe me. I thought it was the only way. I had to find out what it felt like to touch her, to have her in my power. But I couldn't do anything. I couldn't."

Jenny and Banks left him with a uniformed constable and walked out into the corridor. Jenny leaned against the institutional-green wall and took a deep breath, then she removed her glasses and loosened her hair.

"Well?" Banks asked.

"I think he's harmless," she said. "You heard him insist that he wouldn't have hurt Sandra. I believe him."

"But he did hurt her."

"I told him that, and I think he understood. He meant physically. What more can I say, Alan? He's suffering. Part of me hates him for what he did, but another part—the professional bit, I suppose—understands, in a way, that it's not his fault, that he needs help not punishment."

Banks nodded. "Coffee?"

"Oh, yes, please."

They walked across Market Street to the Golden Grill.

"You still seem a bit preoccupied, Alan," Jenny said, sipping her coffee. "Is there something else? I thought you'd caught enough criminals for one night."

"Lack of sleep, I suppose."

"That all?"

"Probably not. There's something bothering me, but I'm not quite sure what it is. You know we haven't got Alice Matlock's killer yet?"

"Yes."

"Allott gave us a description. It's definitely not the kids."

"So?"

"I feel that I ought to know who it is, and why. Like it's staring me in the face and I just can't bring it into focus."

"Is there some clue you can't think of?"

"No, it's nothing like that. It's a whole jumble of impressions. Not to worry, another night's sleep might do it. Maybe I'll even try an afternoon nap and hurry it along."

"So it's not all over?"

"Not yet."

"And our intrepid chief inspector won't rest until it is?"

Banks smiled. "Something like that. I'll tell you one thing, though. When I moved up to Yorkshire, I sure as hell expected a softer time of it than this."

II

Back at the station an excited Sergeant Hatchley came rushing to meet Banks.

"We've got him!"

"Who?"

"Lenny Webster. The fence. Mick's brother."

Banks grinned. "So London came through, then?"

"Didn't they just? Paid him a visit in the middle of the night at that address we got from the letter."

"Yes?"

"And sure enough, he was there. Babysitting an assortment of drugs—marijuana, cocaine, uppers, downers, even some heroin."

"Enough to put him away for a while?"

"Enough to put him away for a long while, sir."

"I'll bet he was intending to bring it all back up here to sell, am I right?"

"Exactly. And there's more."

"Go on."

"It seems that young Lenny's not as tough as he makes out, if you know what I mean. In fact, a little heavy leaning and he breaks down completely. First off, they've got the bloke who gave him the gun, and they found three more at his place—not duff ones, mind you. And next, Lenny sings all about his plans with Micklethwaite."

"Moxton."

"Pardon?"

"That's his real name. Moxton. Larry Moxton."

"Oh. Well, Webster knows him as Micklethwaite, and they were going to unload the stuff between them. Also, Micklethwaite put him onto the Ottershaw and Pitt jobs."

"Right, we'd better bring Larry in then, hadn't we?"

"Do you think we've got enough to nail him?"

"I think so, if we add it to what Thelma Pitt and Ottershaw have to tell us. What puzzles me is how a con-man like Larry could get mixed up with a low-life thug like Webster."

"That's explained in the telex," Hatchley said. "Apparently it's through the chap who was getting the drugs for them. He'd served time with Micklethwaite, and when he heard he was going to relocate up north he put him in touch with Lenny."

"Ah, the old-boy network. Right little den of thieves we've caught, haven't we?"

Hatchley beamed, his red balloon-face glowing with success.

"Aye, we have that, sir. Oh, I almost forgot. There's a woman waiting in your office for you."

"Not..."

"No, not that Wycombe woman. I've never seen this one before. Wouldn't say who she was. Wants to see you, though."

Curious, Banks poked his head around the office door. It was Mrs Allott, Robin's mother.

"What's all this nonsense about my son Robin?" she asked, puffing herself up.

Banks took a deep breath and sat down. It was the last thing he needed, another irate parent.

"Your son has been charged on several counts of voyeurism, Mrs Allott, and on one count of attempted rape. He threatened a woman at knife-point. That woman happened to be my wife."

Mrs Allott's tone altered not a jot. "Always look after your own, you coppers do. Well, you've got the wrong man this time. My Robin wouldn't hurt a fly."

"Perhaps not," Banks conceded, "but he's behaved very badly towards women."

"Who saw him, then? How many witnesses have you got?"

"We don't need witnesses, Mrs Allott. Your son gave us a full con- fession."

"Well, you must have sweated it out of him. You must have got the rubber hose-pipe out."

Banks got to his feet. "Mrs Allott, it's a cut and dried case. There's nothing more to be said about it. If you'll excuse me, I've got work to do."

"He was with me," she persisted. "All those times you say he was snooping on women he was with me. I've looked after him ever since that bitch of a wife ran off and left him, the no-good hussy. I warned him about her, I did. Told him she'd only bring trouble."

"Why don't you give a list of the dates and times your son was with you to the desk sergeant, then we'll see if we can match them with the incidents. I have to repeat, though, it's no use. Your son has already confessed."

"Under duress, I'm sure. He can't have done those things you say he did."

"I can assure you that he did do them."

"Then that wife of his drove him to it."

"Make up your mind, Mrs Allott. How could he be driven to do things you said he didn't do?"

"He was with me," she repeated firmly.

Banks couldn't be bothered to tell her that, in addition to her son's confession, he also had Sandra's statement. It was futile. Robin's innocence was fixed in her mind, and that was that. No amount of reason would change her opinion. She would even lie on the witness stand to save him.

"Look," Banks said in as kind a tone as he could manage, "I really do have a lot of work to do. If you'd care to give the dates to the sergeant at the front desk..."

"I'm not going to be soft-soaped like that. You're not going to fob me off with some menial. I demand my rights."

She was clinging as tight as a limpet and Banks was nearing the end of his tether. Brusquely, he picked up a clean sheet of paper and took out his pen.

"All right, then. The dates?"

"I can't remember the exact dates. What do you think I am, a computer? He's always at home. *You* know, you've seen him there. He helps me take care of his dad."

"I saw him there once, Mrs Allott. And he was expecting me. Are you telling me he's at home every night?"

"Yes."

"Including Tuesdays?"

She thought for a moment, a wary expression flickering over her pinched face. "Tuesdays. He goes to the Camera Club on Tuesdays. With his friends. Any of them will tell you what a good boy he is."

Banks could think of one who certainly wouldn't, but he said nothing. In fact, Mrs Allott's presence began to recede far into the distance as the subject of his recent brooding came slowly into focus. She had given him an idea. It still wasn't fully formed yet, and he wasn't sure what to do about it, but the lens was definitely closing in.

He forced his attention reluctantly back to the business in hand.

"So what you're telling me, Mrs Allott, is that every night of the week except Tuesdays, Robin was with you from the moment he left work till the moment he went again the next morning?"

"That's right."

"He never went out?"

"No."

"All right," Banks said, losing interest in her lies again as his idea came into sharper focus. "I'll get somebody to take your statement, Mrs Allott. You can go home now."

She got to her feet and flapped out of the office.

Almost as soon as she had slammed the door, Banks forgot her. He reached for a cigarette, asked Craig to send up some of the *special* new coffee, and slouched deep in his chair to think.

One hour, three cigarettes, and two cups of black coffee later, he knew what had been bothering him and what to do about it. He snatched up the phone and dialled the front desk.

"Put Sergeant Hatchley on," he snapped. He knew that Hatchley had a habit of chatting with Rowe.

"Sir?" Hatchley answered.

"Sergeant, I want you to go to Sharp's place and ask Graham Sharp to drop by and see me right away. Tell him it's to do with his son's statement and it's urgent. Got that?"

"Yes, sir."

"And don't take no for an answer, Sergeant. If he grumbles about locking up the shop and losing business, remind him what a difficult position young Trevor's in."

"Right," Hatchley answered, "I'm on my way, sir."

III

"Trevor Sharp's been bound over to the youth authorities," Richmond was saying. "Do you want me to get him over here?"

"No," Banks answered. "It doesn't matter. How's Webster?"

"The last I heard, sir, he's in fair shape. The surgeon managed to save that finger. Have you seen my report?"

"No, I haven't. It's been a busy morning. No time for reading. Give me a summary."

"It was just to tell you that Vic Manson got some good prints from the jewellery, sir. It seems the lads must have handled it at home after the burglaries, when they felt safe."

"And?"

"And both Sharp's and Webster's prints showed up, sir."

"We've got the buggers, then."

"Looks like it, sir. Webster's been doing a bit of talking, too. That shock to his system has shaken his ideas around no end. The doc won't let us talk to him for long yet, but he's already told us it was him and Sharp did the jobs."

"Good work," Banks said. "Could you bring in Allott for me, please?"

"The peeper, sir?"

"Yes. Robin Allott. Bring him up."

"Very well, sir. I'm afraid his mother's still downstairs on the bench. Refuses to leave until she sees the superintendent."

Banks scratched his chin. It was itchy because he hadn't shaved that morning. "I wouldn't wish her on him," he said. "Try and get rid of her. And whatever you do, make sure she doesn't see her son coming up."

"I'll do my best, sir."

A few moments later, Robin Allott was escorted into Banks's office and told to make himself comfortable. Allott still couldn't meet the inspector's eyes, and Banks almost felt like telling him to stop dwelling on it, that it was all over and done with. But he didn't. Why let the bastard off the hook after what he'd done to Sandra? If she hadn't already known Allott, Banks thought, there wouldn't have been any pity in her feelings towards him.

About fifteen minutes later, there was a knock at the door. Banks opened it to Sergeant Hatchley with an anxious Graham Sharp in tow.

"What is it, Inspector?" Sharp demanded angrily as he charged across the threshold. "Your sergeant told me it—"

And he froze. As the newcomer entered the room, Robin Allott had turned to see what the commotion was, and his jaw dropped in immediate recognition.

"That's him!" he said, pointing at Sharp. "That's the man I saw!"

Graham Sharp looked at him, then at Banks. His face drained of colour and he reached out to support himself on the edge of the flimsy desk. Banks gestured to a confused Hatchley to stay and to pull up a chair for him.

"Like to tell me about it, Mr Sharp?" he asked.

"What made you think of me?"

"Somebody else in your position."

"What do you mean?"

Banks looked at Robin, then back at Sharp. "His mother came in and swore blind he was with her when he had already admitted to being the peeper. I just got to thinking about the lengths some people would go to to protect their families. After a while, it all seemed to fit. Your son insisted that he and Webster had nothing to do with Alice Matlock's death and that was the only thing I believed from him. I'd already suspected that it was a different kind of crime. There was no senseless damage to Alice's sentimental possessions as there had been in the other cases, and she was the first victim to die.

"The problem then was who on earth would want to kill a harmless old woman, and why? Robin's mother gave me the answer. I remembered how protective you had been about Trevor, ready to perjure yourself and swear blind to false alibis. It didn't take much stretching of the imagination to figure out that you might go a lot further to protect your illusion of him. The simple fact is, Mr Sharp, that your son's a callous, vicious bastard, but to you he's a bright lad with a promising future. You would do anything to protect that future. Am I right?"

Sharp nodded.

"I don't know all the details," Banks went on, "but I think that Alice Matlock found out something about your son. Maybe she saw him leaving the scene of a break-in, saw him with some stolen goods or noticed him hiding his balaclava. She wasn't a very sociable person, but everybody knew about the other women who'd been robbed. Am I still right?"

Sharp sighed and accepted a cigarette with a trembling hand. He seemed on the verge of a nervous collapse.

"Are you all right?" Banks asked.

"Yes, Inspector. It's just the relief. You've no idea what a burden this has been for me. I don't think I could have stood it much longer, pushing it to the back of my mind, pretending it never really happened. It was an accident, you know."

"Do you mean you would have come forward eventually?"

"Possibly. I can't say. I know how far I'd go to protect my son, but not how far I'd go to save myself."

"Tell me about it."

"Yes. Alice Matlock told me that she had heard Trevor bragging about the robberies with another boy one evening when she was walking home from a friend's house. She came into my shop that Monday just before closing and told me about it. Said she was going to report him to the police the next day. She had no proof, no evidence, and at first it didn't bother me much because I thought nobody would take any notice of an old woman. But then I got to worrying about what damage it might do, what questions we might have to answer.

"I couldn't believe Trevor was guilty, even though I knew there was something wrong. Maybe I did know it, deep down. I can't say. But I wanted to protect him. Is that so unusual in a father? I thought that whatever it was it was just a phase he would pass through. I didn't want his life ruined because of a few foolish juvenile exploits."

"If you'd come forward with your suspicions a long time ago," Banks remarked, "you would have saved everybody, including your son, a lot of grief. Especially Thelma Pitt."

Sharp shook his head. "I still can't believe my Trevor did that."

"Take my word for it, Mr Sharp, he did. That's just the point."

Sharp flicked the ash off his cigarette and looked at the floor.

"What happened?" Banks asked.

"I went to talk to her that night. Just talk to her. I knocked on the door and she answered it. I'm not really sure that she recognized me. She seemed to think I was someone else. I told her what a good future Trevor had and what a crime it would be to spoil it for him. I was desperate, Inspector. I even pleaded with her, but it was no good."

"What did she say?"

"Nothing that made much sense to me. She said there was no point coming back and pretending to be him. I wasn't him. I was an evil imposter and she was going to the police. I couldn't talk any sense into her and when she started going on about calling the police I lost my temper and reached for her.

"I didn't intend to kill her, honestly. But she was so frail. I've got a terrible temper. Always have had. I couldn't help myself. She fell backwards. I tried to reach out, to stop her, but it all seemed to happen in slow motion, like one of them dreams when you can't run fast enough. I heard the sound, her skull cracking on the edge of the table. And the blood on the flags... I..." Sharp put his head in his hands and sobbed.

"What happened next?" Banks asked, after giving him a couple of minutes to pull himself together.

"I messed the place up a bit, as if I'd been a burglar, and I took some things—some money, a set of silver cutlery. You'll find it all buried on the edge of Gallows Field. I didn't touch a penny of the money, honest I didn't."

"You didn't think to call an ambulance?"

"I was scared. There would have been questions."

"We didn't find any fingerprints, Mr Sharp. Were you wearing gloves?"

"Yes."

"That would explain the muffled knocking," Hatchley interrupted, looking up from his note taking. "That Rigby woman said the knocking sounded muffled, distant, like it could have been a long way away."

Banks nodded. "Why were you wearing gloves, Mr Sharp?"

"It was a cold night. I've got bad circulation."

"But you didn't have very far to go."

"No, I suppose not."

"And you didn't take them off when you got inside."

"I never thought. Things just started happening too fast. Don't you believe me? Are you suggesting I intended to kill the woman?"

"That's for the court to decide," Banks said. "I'm just gathering the evidence. Did you see Mr Allott?"

"Yes, on my way in. He looked like he was running away from something himself. I didn't think he got a really good look at me. Still, I was a bit worried for a few days, but then I realized that, whoever he was, he hadn't come forward. Perhaps he hadn't heard of the old woman's death, or maybe he had his own secret to hide. I don't know."

"Did you have any idea why Alice Matlock didn't seem to recognize you but let you in anyway?"

Graham shrugged. "I can't say I gave it much thought. She was old. I suppose she did ramble a bit sometimes."

"Close," Banks said. "She probably couldn't even remember what day she overheard Webster and your son. You see, the irony of it is, Mr Sharp, that by the morning she would most likely have forgotten all about the incident anyway. And you were quite right to think that nobody would believe a woman who was beginning to live more in the past than the present. You killed her for nothing."

IV

There wasn't much left to do. Statements had to be written up and filed, charges laid, hearing dates fixed. But as far as Banks was concerned, the real job was finished. The rest was up to the courts and the twelve jurors "good and true."

He believed that Sharp had killed Alice Matlock by accident, that he was basically a good man driven too far. But so many criminals were good men gone wrong. It sometimes seemed a pity, or at least an inconvenience, that society seemed to have discarded the concept of evil, something which, in Banks's mind, would always separate Trevor Sharp from his father.

As he had no other pressing business, he decided to go home early and spend some time with Sandra. He would see Jenny again, too. No doubt Sandra would insist that she come over for dinner some evening. But not for a while. It was time to heal the wound and attempt to build more frail bridges between male and female; and the fewer confusing distractions, the easier that would be.

He would buy Sandra a small present, perhaps: that simple gold chain she had admired in H. Samuels' window the last time they were in Leeds; or the new lightweight camera-bag at Erricks' in Bradford. Or he could take her out for dinner and a show. Opera North were doing Gounod's *Faust* next month. But no, Sandra didn't like opera. Going to see a new film would be a better treat for her.

As he walked home in the steady drizzle, Banks began to feel some of the pleasurable release, the sense of lightness and freedom that was his usual reward at the end of a case.

Before leaving, he had slipped a cassette of highlights from *La Traviata,* usually reserved for the car, into his Walkman, and now he fumbled around in his pocket to switch it on. He walked down Market Street enjoying the cool needles of rain on his face and hummed along with the haunting prelude. Tourists heading for the car park, merchants closing up for the day, and disappointed shoppers rattling already-locked doors all seemed like actors in the opening scene of a grand opera. When the jaunty "Drinking Song" began, Banks started to sing along quietly, and his step lightened almost to a dance.

Cold Is the Grave
Peter Robinson

The daughter of Chief Constable Riddle has disappeared, and he calls upon Banks to employ his unorthodox methods to find her. Banks tracks her down, but discovers she doesn't want to be found. Drawn deeper and deeper into the young girl's life, he finds himself caught in a web of drugs and murder, police and politics, fathers and daughters.

"This is crime-fiction writing at its best."
The Globe and Mail

"A satisfyingly complex story, freshened by psychological resonance and written in Robinson's usual elegant style."
Toronto Star

Find out more about Peter Robinson mysteries at www.penguin.ca/mystery

Wednesday's Child
Peter Robinson

A seven-year-old girl is kidnapped, and there is a dreadful possibility of ritual satanic abuse. A corpse is found at an abandoned mine. When the two cases converge, Inspector Banks confronts one of the most terrifying villains he will ever meet.

"His best work yet."
The Globe and Mail

"A dark, unsettling story. Robinson has done his usual impressive job."
The New York Times

Find out more about Peter Robinson mysteries at www.penguin.ca/mystery

PENGUIN
CANADA